The Hippies
H

Julie Anne Rudd

For Carri, happy reading and best wishes! Juliette

Published by Firstlea Publishing 2018

Acknowledgments

This book is dedicated to the late Robert Bowers, Mike and Amanda Willats and Mike's late mother, Olive, without whom none of it would have been possible.

Huge thanks to Chris for affording me without complaint all the hours I have spent writing and editing this. I am equally indebted to Su Smith for advising me on spiritual matters and to my manuscript readers, Diane Clarke, Margaret Davies and Christine Fine.

My gratitude also to cartoonist Dave Anning for his brilliantly designed book cover and sincere apologises to anyone else who has helped and I have inadvertently failed to mention.

The Hippies of Haggleby Hall

CHAPTER ONE

Drunken Whim

'You wouldn't be interested in Haggleby Hall. It's terribly run-down. It will cost thousands to put right. Perhaps I can interest you in another property?'

Belinda Flowers was flabbergasted by the estate agent's tone. Having phoned to enquire about a country mansion advertised for sale in the local newspaper, she had expected Partridge and Pleasance to be eating out of her hand.

The article said: "A substantial, late Georgian/early Victorian property situated in six acres of park-like grounds in the heart of West Sussex."

The castle-like building in the photograph certainly looked impressive, with Regency-style bays, shuttered windows and tall chimneys. In its time it would have been a picture of architectural elegance, but the years had taken their toll. The white stucco walls were cracked, the castellation and chimneys weather beaten and the shutters, rotten. But its potential as a future home was huge and as Belinda's ever-optimistic husband, Tom had pointed out, there was nothing that a bit of filling and painting couldn't put right.

They had decided to join forces with close friends, Cameron and Miranda Maclaren and look for a big old house in the country. Each couple had a young son and Belinda and Tom were expecting their second child. Their homes were not big enough for growing families. Haggleby Hall sounded ideal; at £190,000 it was just affordable and whatever work was needed, they had years ahead of them. What a wonderful place it would be to bring up the children and grow old disgracefully, besides being a sound investment for the future!

Belinda had read the article so many times she practically knew it: 'A well situated, Grade 11 Listed country mansion in need of updating, offering spacious accommodation, which includes three reception rooms, outer hall, inner hall with sweeping staircase, galleried landing, eight bedrooms, two kitchens, two bathrooms, a top floor flat (originally servants' quarters) and cellars.

'The rooms are wonderfully proportioned, with plastered ceiling friezes, period fireplaces, parquet flooring, shuttered windows and Gothic doorways.

'The extensive grounds have sweeping lawns, a grass tennis court, croquet lawn and outbuildings, which include a garage, converted from the former game pantry.'

The deciding factor prompting Belinda's phone call was the small sentence footing the editorial: **"When modernised, Haggleby Hall will be a unique family home."**

But the estate agent was far from encouraging: 'I doubt very much whether it is worth you viewing Haggleby Hall. It's in need of serious modernisation and the running costs would be colossal. Partridge and Pleasance would be looking to sell to a large concern, a property developer, perhaps.'

Belinda shared the popular belief that estate agents always had their eye to the main chance and if you were not it, fobbed you off with any old story. She wished she hadn't mentioned the circumstances surrounding her inquiry; to buy Haggleby Hall they would have to sell three properties, including that of Cameron's mother, Grace. It was not the most promising set-up for a quick sale. But, determined not to let the others down, she persisted: 'I would point out that the advertisement says it is on the market so, as prospective buyers, we are just as entitled to view it as anyone else. Now, Miss Hotshot... will you please make an appointment for us this weekend?'

'It's Cockshott, Priscilla Cockshott,' the woman hissed down the phone. 'I'm afraid that's not possible. I believe there might already be somebody after Haggleby Hall. I strongly advise you to consider viewing other properties. If you would just give me more details, Mrs Towers...'

'It's Flowers, Belinda Flowers! And what do you mean there *might be* somebody already after the place? You don't sound very sure. Is it under offer or not?'

'Not as yet...'

'Well, in that case will you *kindly* make us an appointment or shall we just turn up at the property and tell the owners that Partridge and Pleasance estate agents are not doing their job?'

Belinda was put on hold and just as her patience was running out, Miss Cockshott was back on the line, grudgingly offering an appointment to view the following Sunday.

Replacing the receiver, Belinda felt triumphant, but the wait had focused her thoughts on the enormity of her actions. Just that one phone call could have a devastating effect on their lives! Had she really done the right thing? Did she really want to live in a big old pile like Haggleby Hall? She was not totally sure why they were pursuing such a place. It was all Cameron's idea, casually suggested over a few drinks too many while her and Tom were staying with him and Miranda one Christmas.

*

Boxing Day 1985 marked a huge turning point in their lives. Celebrating at the Maclaren's, recently pregnant Belinda was sipping low alcohol fix, Tom and Cameron glugging Harveys' Festive ale while Miranda was knocking back her favourite cider. Cameron had a bee in his bonnet about their new home. Belinda couldn't quite understand it. Her and Tom's cottage, "Flowerpots", in the Mid Sussex hamlet of Clatterbridge, was cramped with a pocket-size garden. But their friends' three-bedroomed, detached house at 27 Primula Drive, in sought-after Toffston, Surrey, was spacious, with all mod cons and a 70ft garden!

Belinda could still hear his words: 'I can't understand husbands round here, getting up at the crack of dawn on a Sunday morning to wash the car and cut the grass. Don't they believe in having a lie-in and spot of mating?'

'It's because *good* husbands like to get their jobs out of the way so they and their wives can enjoy the rest of the day together,' explained Miranda.

He scowled. 'If that pea-brained bloke over the road starts tinkering with his clapped out Vauxhall at seven o'clock this Sunday, I'll drive it across his manicured lawn straight into his, excuse me ladies, f...ing fish pond! If the bloody thing ever starts, that is. Every Sunday without fail, he's tinkering with the engine. I'm in the land of nod when he fires it up... on two and and-a-half cylinders it sounds like my old granny's "steam-driven" vacuum cleaner!'

Miranda, "tiddly" after copious wine, started singing the theme tune to the new Australian TV soap, "Neighbours, everybody loves good neighbours..."

Belinda, busy satisfying her latest pregnancy craving with a jar of pickled onions, was feeling holier than thou, possibly because it was Christmas, though more likely because she was stone cold sober. 'Cameron, you're supposed to love your neighbour as yourself. Why don't you loan this bloke your mechanical know-how, then your troubles will be over?'

He screwed up his nose as if confronting a bad smell. 'What? You'll have me scratching his armpits next!'

'My need for your mechanical know-how is much greater on a Sunday morning, Camay,' chipped in Miranda.

'I'll tweak your nuts and bolts anytime, Randy, but this bloke's not the only spanner in the works.'

As if waiting for the right moment, Cameron then presented his grandiose idea. 'When you think about it, we all seem pretty fed up living where we are; you two with precious little room to swing a cat and us surrounded by Mr and Mrs "Tickety-Boos". We all talk about wanting somewhere better, with a decent garden for the kids, so why don't we put all our cats into one basket, or whatever, and buy a big place in the country?'

Belinda wondered whether his suggestion was simply a drunken whim or an idea he had been contemplating since the very day the Maclaren's had moved in. She and Tom had helped, and they had barely unloaded the furniture truck when an aeroplane screaming overhead had him frothing at the mouth, insisting Miranda put the place back on the market.

By coincidence, that very minute a plane suddenly squealed its final approach to Gatwick. Christmas flights were in full swing. Nothing had changed. Cameron's ginger-whiskered face turned scarlet, as he looked heavenwards: 'Leave the bloody roof on! Bloody planes, they're enough to drive anyone to drink and the racket doesn't do much for the "nookie" either...'

'It's just something we have to live with and if *you* don't stop complaining there won't be any more,' Miranda threatened.

'What no "nookie"- I'll cut my throat now!'

His big brown eyes stared at her like an injured puppy. 'Oh Randy I've just about had enough of living here and it's not just the planes. I'm fed up with the Snobby knobs boasting about their latest egg whisk; that weird Starkey couple stripping off to do the gardening and dirty dogs crapping all over our front lawn - it's like treading through a treacle field!'

'So much for "Prim and Proper Drive", said Tom.

'More like "Sin and Improper Drive"!'

'Tell Tom and Belinda about the Lovejoys at 69,' urged Miranda.

'Ah, the swingers - if the old "rumpy-pumpy" is getting stale you can get "a bit of fresh" at their parties. Knowing my luck, I'd end up with the fattest, ugliest woman in the street.'

5

'Ever been tempted to take your car keys round?' prodded Tom.

Cameron waggled his tongue. 'I got all keyed up once, but Miranda hid them.'

He gulped his beer and looked wistful. 'Seriously chaps, the way I see it, as single couples we can't afford to buy anything much bigger than we already have. But if we pooled our little bits of worldly wealth, we could buy a decent place in the country, with only the dawn chorus and howling babies to disturb us.'

The reminder prompted Miranda to put her head round the hall door – no noise from Ollie Maclaren, 20 months, and 18-month-old Freddie Flowers, sleeping soundly upstairs.

Tom was far from convinced. 'Great idea Cam, but I don't think we could afford anything halfway decent. You must be talking at least a quarter to half a million for a big house in the country and even at that price it would need a lot of work. Our places would only fetch one hundred and twenty grand or so between them and I doubt if we could get a mortgage big enough to make up the shortfall.'

'We don't need to worry about all that,' said Cameron, casting caution to the wind in his own inimitable way. 'Mitts said she could sell Magpie Mews, buy a big place with us and live in a wing somewhere.'

Cameron's mother had been so nicknamed for boxing clever with money. A trained accountant, Grace had done the books for her late husband, managing to keep his garage business, Duncan's Motors in Blaxley, afloat through some rough seas. After his death she had leased the workshop, sold the family's Edwardian home next door and bought "Magpie Mews", a row of cottages on the other side of the village. She made one her home and lived off rent from the others. With a tidy profit she had helped Cameron finance a new venture. He always held that there was more money to be made from selling cars than repairing them and Cam's Motor Mart was proving its worth.

Grace had become like a second mother to Tom, who was concerned about her having to move again. 'We really wouldn't want to inflict more upheaval in her life.'

'But she'd love to live with us! She's not getting any younger and we worry about her being on her own, now that Alistair is up in Scotland setting up that game park.'

Alistair was Cameron's impetuous older brother, who was forever chasing pipe dreams, but Grace believed he would surprise them all one day. Tom had known the family for years. Cameron and Tom had become friends as teenagers, tinkering with motorbikes and restoring old cars. Their engineering skills were the perfect complement; Tom being a dab hand at mechanics, Cameron, red hot at welding.

Cameron had met Miranda soon after she left school, taking her for rides on his Triumph Bonneville. Many weekends were spent together at Duncan's Motors, she passing him spanners and making tea while he doctored an old Sunbeam Tiger for their first car.

With Duncan invariably at work, Grace had brought up Cameron and Alistair virtually single-handed. Belinda deduced from tales she had heard about them as boys that she must have had the staying power of a road roller! Miranda, likewise, had quickly learnt to stand her ground if her husband overstepped the mark. Tom always said that anyone married to Cameron had to be a saint and her halo was hallmarked. Eccentric and moody, at times his humour was as light and frothy as a soufflé, while others as flat as a pancake. Cameron may have been feeling deflated that night, but his proposal was perhaps not so half-baked after all.

'I suppose there's no harm in us looking to see what's on the market,' said Tom, little realising the impact of his words.

Before viewing Haggleby Hall the second Sunday in February, they met for lunch at The Nip and Tipple (saucily known as the Tit and Nipple), midway between their homes. Belinda and Tom arrived in Tom's 1928 Austin 7, "Lullabelle". Cameron and Miranda invariably travelled in Maclaren's Motor Mart's latest acquisition, but for the day's auspicious occasion they were in his personal pride and joy, a gold Rolls-Royce. He had wanted to own one for years and through wheeling and dealing the previous autumn, he had acquired a 1955 model. Appropriately christened "Goldie", she was his only permanent car in an otherwise ever-changing collection he "road tested" before selling on.

The Spirit of Ecstasy topping her radiator only normally took flight on high days and holidays. It was against his principles to exercise her in bad weather, but he wanted to look the part for visiting the "big house". Tom and Belinda were often amused by people thinking Cameron was "loaded" and if ever asked, they would simply say that he had his fingers in various pies (omitting that some might have been a trifle hot!).

Freddie had been deposited with Belinda's parents in East Grinstead, but young Ollie Maclaren was "sparked out" in his car seat. Miranda gathered his grumpy form in her arms and they went inside, choosing a table in the back room where children were allowed. Sipping soft drinks, the young speculators were soon immersed in the possibility of buying a property that the estate agent had told Belinda was "basically unfit for human habitation" - words that had made them doubly determined to go and see for themselves.

As they tucked into toasties and chips, the idea of owning a dilapidated mansion seemed insane, but increasingly appealing. Cameron lit his pipe, conjecturing: 'If this old place is as bad as Miss "Cock-and-bull" would have us believe, and it's been on the market a long time, the sellers might jump at us putting an offer on the table.'

Miranda fanned the smoke with Belinda's property paper. 'If we agree it has the potential for a comfortable family home, we must seriously consider it. With our combined capital, Tom's house bashing experience and good teamwork, we could make it our aristocratic retreat!'

Tom, affectionately patting Belinda's swelling tummy, said: 'It's a miracle the agents actually agreed to let us view it, but Bellie always was the persistent one - now look where it's got us!'

'In the club again', Cameron reminded them, 'and, who knows, we might have found a bigger place for the Flowers' little blossoms?'

Maybe it was her pregnancy, with hormones running amok, but Belinda was increasingly uneasy about uprooting their lives. Living in a run-down country mansion with vast grounds did not sound easy, especially with another Flower in bud. She wished she and Tom had not listened to Cameron. She loved Flowerpots, their "bijou residence", as Tom called it. They had spent six years restoring the 1930s end-of-terrace cottage, and now it was newly decorated, carpeted and cosy-toes warm, she wondered why they were even contemplating buying a run-down, money-eating mansion! She was scared they were being swept along by their quirky friends and fantasising about upper class life, not that class structure was supposed to exist anymore.

'Buying a place like this is mad! I know I'm always the one to get cold feet but, quite honestly, I'm really worried about being tempted. Perhaps I should phone up and cancel...'

Cameron smiled encouragingly. 'Ah, come on, Belinda. Where's your sense of adventure?'

'Don't let's be defeatist, darling! No harm in looking,' urged Tom.

9

Eternally optimistic Miranda was always up for a challenge. 'Well, I believe we *are* doing the right thing. If we don't look, we'll always regret it and we can't give those estate agents the satisfaction of us cancelling, can we? Besides, if we did decide to go for the place, just think of the fun we could have together - and never have to worry about baby-sitters again!'

Belinda's thoughts were swinging like a pendulum. She could certainly do with some company at home, particularly as Tom was commuting to London every day, working long hours at his father's commercial photography business. She had met him through her job as a PR executive and sacrificed a promising career to move to Sussex and marry him. She had managed to find a good job locally, as a sub-editor on the Horsham Weekly News and, despite her drop in income, had loved every minute. After Freddie was born life confined to home had come as a shock. Some days when he played up it was hard to cope and her brain only seemed on half power. She worried whether she would ever be back on the ball. Perhaps she needed a new challenge like Haggleby Hall to restore her bounce.

While she found motherhood tough-going, Miranda was a natural. Freddie had been wakeful and demanding, but Ollie a model baby, feeding or sleeping mostly. Her friend was a little Earth Mother, her skills cultivated as the eldest of five children and later on, as a nursery nurse. At times when Belinda came to the end of her tether with Freddie's colic or teething, she would call Miranda, whose "hands-on" experience surpassed any baby manual. If it all became too much, her friend would drive over and take him off her hands for a while. With the boys seeing each other frequently, they were already like brothers.

The prospect of living with Cameron and Miranda warmed her. She had grown very fond of them over several years she had known them. They had much in common, having married the same year and had their first babies within weeks of each other. Most weekends they either met in the pub or stayed with each other. Perhaps they would soon be sharing the same roof, she thought, quivering with anticipation.

CHAPTER TWO

"The Old Hag"

Snow had just started falling as they left The Nip and Tipple, Goldie leading Lullabelle. It was the first time in ages Tom had taken his "old girl" for a spin, though with deteriorating weather he was quietly praying she would stay on track. At least she was weatherproof; having had a new hood fitted the previous autumn. She had belonged to Tom's father, who had restored her years before for his daily commute to the family business in London. Tom had made further improvements and modifications, paying particular attention to her engine performance. Not only could Lullabelle go like the wind, she could "turn on a sixpence". Her leather passenger seats, front only, were glove tight, so it was just as well Tom and Belinda were less than 5ft 8ins.

Cautiously, they followed the Crawley to East Grinstead road and, after a series of bends, had to be ready for Haggleby Hall's drive, on the right. Goldie took it last minute, Lullabelle inches from her bumper. On the corner Belinda glimpsed an old gatekeeper's cottage, smoke spilling from its chimney. "Haggleby Lodge" was on the gate.

Before them a white carpet rolled into the distance as they slipped beneath a glistening lacework of branches, with oaks, beeches, chestnuts and silver birch skirting fields on either side. There was a strange air of expectancy, Belinda's hopes and fears whirling in the wind-teased snowflakes. Whatever lay ahead could mean a huge life change; the enormity of the moment indelible on her mind.

Goldie processed regally as a monarch while Lullabelle bounced unceremoniously behind. Not to be outdone by Cameron's salubrious transport, Tom heralded their approach with a honk of his horn. Piercing the serenity, it sounded like a sheep with a sore throat. The mile-long drive divided and they followed a field fence round to the left, passing through a gateless entrance. The secluded grounds could hardly have changed in decades. The picturesque, white satin expanse of terraced lawns dotted with snow-cloaked shrubs was breath-taking. Suddenly, through the trees an enormous castle-like building bared itself to their eager eyes. The cars stopped in their tracks, Cameron and Miranda turning to exchange looks of disbelief with their followers. Towering proudly before them, Haggleby Hall exhibited a fading grandeur that flirted immortality, like an elderly lady who had overcome life's challenges to spend her remaining days in peaceful acceptance. As a young woman she must have been a real beauty, but her pallid countenance was scarred by time. Belinda sensed she was delighted to see her visitors, beckoning them to make her acquaintance. As their wheels crunched on shingle, her haggard appearance in the cold light of day condemned the property newspaper's over-flattering photograph. The shabby grey walls were cracked and pitted, the black painted castellation was nibbled by decay and shutters fronting the Georgian, upper floor windows and ground level French bays were half hanging off, with slats missing.

Belinda felt hidden eyes scrutinising them. Perhaps it was the horse's head gazing down from the front pinnacle. The Fielding-Winters' landowning family crest resembled a chess knight and she suddenly felt uneasy, wondering whether they were pawns in the game of life. Only fate could guide their hand.

They parked near the front entrance, the mansion looming over them in an odd, lop-sided fashion. The central, three-storeyed section had two-floored wings either side, though the right one looked shorter and, worryingly, was caged in scaffolding. The rendering was fissured and the decaying castellation gave the building an uneven symmetry. Snow-capped, stone urns flanked the front door, which had lost its pillared porch years before.

They assembled apprehensively on the drive, Belinda, Tom and Miranda wearing their usual casual attire of jeans, jumpers and coats, but Cameron was dressed up to the nines. His moleskin waistcoat and trousers, brown leather boots and green, Harris Tweed sports jacket were flamboyantly contrasted with a beige check, Viyella shirt, blue dicky bow and yellow handkerchief spilling out of his top pocket.

Ollie, in Miranda's arms, peered bleary-eyed from beneath a fur-trimmed hood, clutching his favourite cuddly, Bonzo. He grumbled as she put him down, tying parcel string round his waist. 'I'm afraid we've forgotten his harness. We can't let him loose inside, so this will have to do.'

Belinda smiled to herself, embarrassment trifling with affection for her and Cameron's unconventionality. Only they could arrive in a Rolls Royce and lead their son around on string!

'This place looks fantastic!' said Miranda, keen to divert attention.

'There's certainly a lot to take in,' responded Tom cautiously.

Cameron was optimistically presumptuous. 'We've got to buy this!'

Even Belinda couldn't hide her excitement. 'It's like a castle! What do you think my fairy prince?'

Tom, nicknamed 'oracle' by his friends for his educated opinions, was unusually lost for words. 'The old hag is certainly well passed it … and it's not just plastic surgery she needs.'

Belinda sniggered at his handle for the place as they congregated on the threshold footing an unremarkable pair of white front doors. Half-glazed, the right one had a broken pane covered with cardboard, while the left, a solid-looking, octagonal-shaped doorknob, which reminded Belinda of one on the mantelpiece at home. The heavy leaden piece was a souvenir from Holloway Prison Tom had picked up while photographing rebuilding work for clients.

Cameron gasped, pointing to a little box by the doorway with the letters 'HELL' painted across it. 'Phew! For a minute I thought we'd come to the wrong place - someone's modified the B.' He pulled the bell forcibly and a distant ringing sounded deep within, followed by an eerie silence.

'Of course, Dracula sleeps in the day time,' explained Tom.

'He does but his manservant should be about.'

Belinda was irritated. 'Perhaps he's a deaf old fool.'

'Knowing your pregnancy brain fade it was probably tomorrow we were supposed to come,' her husband teased.

Further attempts by Cameron echoed emptily. But as they were returning to their cars, voicing frustration and disappointment, somewhat impolitely, a woman's voice followed them from the front door. 'Hello, I'm so sorry to keep you. You must be the people sent by the estate agents. Thank you for braving the roads on this terrible afternoon. Please come in out of the cold.'

As they did so Belinda noticed a distinct drop in temperature, despite her sheepskin coat.

Agatha Smythe was in her late 50s, thin, with a time worn face and lavender blue eyes. Her peppery-grey hair, worn in a French pleat, befitted her country-style, fawn corduroy two-piece, teamed with an olive green polo neck.

During introductions Ollie held up his teddy. 'This is Bonzo,' said Miranda. 'Please excuse the reins - not exactly Mothercare, but Ollie is into everything at the moment.'

Agatha smiled and shook the bear's hand. 'It's freezing cold, isn't it? But I have fires warming up the place downstairs.'

As they stood in the outer hall, she went on to explain that she and her brother, Roderick, were caretaking the house for their elderly Aunt Elizabeth, who was living in a nursing home.

'Unfortunately, it's been on the market for months and few people have been to view it. It's not the easiest of properties to sell. I'm sure the agents are doing their best.'

'You really think so?' Belinda cut in.

She was about to relate her experiences with the snotty Priscilla Cockshott, but a high voltage glare from Tom cut her dead.

As they entered the inner hall, she was taken aback by its colossal size, reaching up to a galleried landing with egg and rose cornices some thirty feet above. A wide, stone cantilevered staircase with mahogany rail curved round to meet them.

'Tom, we could put Flowerpots in here!'

'I suppose the place could do with a few plants,' observed Agatha.

Stifling a chuckle, Tom explained: 'My wife means we could fit Flowerpots, our cottage, in this hall! We call it *that* not just because of our name… it's filled with her triffids.'

'Oh, they'd love it here. They'd take over the place with the humidity.'

But the growing conditions of plants were the last thing on Belinda's mind as she gazed at her surroundings with awe. 'What stories this place must have to tell,' she thought, imagining an evening long ago. She could see ladies in elegant gowns, dripping diamonds, and their penguin-suited partners, clustering with cocktails below; heads turning as the belle of the ball sweeps down the staircase in her shimmering satin finery, ringlets framing her flawless face, one gloved hand gliding down the stair rail, the other clutching a fan. She saunters through the double doors, into…

'The ballroom,' said Agatha, reading Belinda's thoughts. 'I'll take you in there later.'

They followed her thick fawn stockings and brown Hush Puppies up the stairs, treading a threadbare carpet runner. The grey, distempered walls had lighter patches where family portraits once hung.

'This place hasn't been painted since the monkey shot the cat', Tom mumbled to Belinda, bringing up the rear.

'It probably explains that horrible mud colour beneath the dado rail.'

Climbing the stairs was like ascending a mountain, the temperature plummeting as cold and damp engulfed them. Belinda glimpsed the incongruity of the central light fitting which, hanging on a long chain from an elegantly plastered ceiling surround, resembled the upturned legs of an occasional table. A triple casement window spilled light across the landing. Black-threaded mould, cultured by long-term water seepage, clung in patches round it and damaged plaster littered the stairs.

Looking gingerly over the rail, her eyes panned in to the gaudy hall rug, its flaming colours a stark reminder of her parent's lounge in the Seventies. It seemed so far down she felt as if she was falling. Ollie must have been similarly fascinated by the drop for while his mother's attention was drawn to the cornices, Belinda glimpsed him feeding his beloved bear through the stair spindles. In a split second Bonzo met the cold flagstones beneath.

'Ted-dy gone!' he wailed, suddenly realising the absence of his favourite cuddly.

'Ollie that was very naughty!' chastised Miranda, ushering Cameron to retrieve the unfortunate bear before there was a tantrum. The incident was a stark warning of what could happen if Haggleby Hall was to become their home and the boys, small enough to squeeze through the spindles, got loose on the landing. Were there such things as stair gates for mansions, Belinda wondered.

Once Bonzo was back in Ollie's arms, the little boy stopped sniffling and peace was restored. As they continued around the galleried landing, its fading beauty clamoured for costly remedial work. Belinda was not sure whether even their combined pockets would be deep enough.

At the end was a corridor to the main bedroom suite, with several doors leading off.

'The master,' said Agatha, turning the brass handle on a tall, white painted door.

Belinda half expected to see the lord of the manor, clad in silken smoking jacket, flourishing a cigar, peering at them through a monocle. Preparing for a handshake and curtsey, she was instead greeted by a triple aspect room displaying much of its original Georgian styling. Incongruously set against 1950s carpets and furniture, it had been distastefully decorated in pink and white floral wallpaper, which also in-filled period wooden framing above a dado rail. Similarly carved was a white painted fireplace with green tiles, missing fender and carpeted-over grate, and a pair of half glass-fronted cupboards between the fireplace and doorway. A lime coloured carpet with pink flowers shrank from wide skirting. The room was filled with an ethereal light, the snowy ground reflecting through two double casement windows to the front and a single pane on the far side.

'What a lovely view!' Miranda exclaimed, prompting a background of verbal approval.

They were looking out on a panorama of lawns and terraces that had been their approach. The main lawn was centred by a sprawling circular shrubbery and the drive came in from the left, edged by a raised bank of trees and bushes, bordered by a wall. On the lawn perimeter below them, a birdhouse standing askew looked strangely out of place.

Cameron turned the handle on another door on the other side of the fireplace. It was locked.

'You won't get through there, the door has been walled up on the other side,' Agatha explained. 'My aunt allowed certain modifications when she rented out Haggleby Hall as a children's home back in the Sixties.'

Along the corridor they could see where part of the original bathroom had been converted to a double shower room, entered by a door from a linoleum passageway. The cream tiled showers had deep enamelled trays and aluminium showerheads. Belinda imagined 'inmates' from the children's home, huddled naked in a queue, hands strategically placed, and the stone-faced warden booming: 'Get a move on, lights out in ten minutes!'

The bathroom was pale pink with a candyfloss suite, matching tiles and grey linoleum.

'No prizes for guessing the mistress's favourite colour,' said Tom.

Belinda's eyes met a dirty enamelled bath with a graveyard of spiders and flies. Pendulums of cobwebs hung in the corners.

'Pie-ders, dadd-y!' screamed Ollie, gripping his father's legs.

'Cor, like those we have in the garden shed!' said Cameron, with dubious reassurance.

Ollie's nostrils sought Bonzo's furry, comforting aroma.

'As you can see, this bathroom is no longer used,' explained Agatha with slight embarrassment. 'There used to be a lovely roll top bath with ball and claw feet, but auntie had it taken out during alterations for the children's home and installed in the Coach House over the wall.'

'Over the wall' made the children's home sound like a prison. 'Did the inmates try to escape?' asked Tom, flippantly.

'I dare say they lost the odd one or two,' chuckled Agatha. She went on to explain that when Haggleby Hall

19

was first rented her aunt had the Coach House converted into accommodation and made it her home.

The viewing party moved on to a double aspect bedroom at the end of the corridor, overlooking the lawn to the front and drive to the left. There was a black leaded fireplace on an angled wall opposite the door. Midnight blue wallpaper was peeling off the chimney breast and flakes of plaster were scattered over the threadbare olive green carpet.

'This room would make a perfect lookout for approaching undesirables,' said Cameron, attempting to lighten the growing air of despondency.

'We could pour burning oil from the parapets!' Miranda joked.

'Our biggest fear of invasion would be water getting into that cracked chimney,' Tom responded worriedly.

Pointing to a flat roof several feet below the side window, Agatha explained: 'That's the kitchen. It was a conservatory once, with a glass roof. I have a photograph of it somewhere.'

'Sounds like there have been quite a few changes over the years,' observed Tom.

'Yes, there certainly have - some for the better, others perhaps not.'

The house would have many stories to tell and Belinda was intrigued to learn more. She was wondering how to question Agatha's obtuse comment when Miranda suddenly announced: 'Ollie's gone! The string must have slipped from my hand while we were looking out of the window. Didn't any of you notice?'

'No,' everyone chorused in alarm.

'Oh Miranda, you should have remembered his harness! We must find him quickly. We can't have him on the loose up here,' insisted Cameron.

They went off with Agatha to check rooms along the corridor, while Belinda and Tom went back along the landing. Bracing herself, she peered nervously over the

stair rail. Thank goodness Ollie had not chosen to do a
Bonzo! But where on earth could he be? Having looked
after him on several occasions, she knew what a slippery
customer he was. He loved hide and seek and seemed to
find the remotest places.

Tom headed for the opposite corridor linking the other
wing, leaving Belinda to search the rooms off the landing.
She took the bedroom door immediately behind her. The
curtains were half closed and it seemed unoccupied. But
gazing round, she sensed she was not alone. Suddenly, she
heard giggling. She couldn't discern where it came from,
but it was inside the room. It did not sound like Ollie; it
was the voice of a young woman or child. She looked
round once more, this time checking under the heavily-
covered bed, but there was nothing to explain it. She started
to feel uneasy and swiftly headed for the door, relieved to
close it behind her. Her heart was thumping and her face
flushed. Had she imagined it? Was there somebody under
the bed covers? The room had seemed empty and was too
dark to see much. The tittering resounded in her head.
Perhaps it was Ollie, hiding in the bed? She hadn't checked
the wardrobe! She should go back and search the room, but
no, she was convinced it wasn't him.

Resuming her search, she went through the next landing
door, just off the corridor where the other three were. It
opened on to a small antechamber and though dark, light
from the landing revealed a ceiling-high cupboard with
double doors to her right, with fuse boxes on the left wall
above her. Leading off the antechamber were two
bedrooms. The right one was spacious, with plain walls, a
double bed, wardrobe and dressing table cluttered with
bottles. Boxes were stacked higgledy-piggledy against a
wall. Probably Agatha's room, she thought, venturing in.
She searched high and low but there was no sign of Ollie.
Starting to regret ever viewing the place, she stared
absently through a double casement window looking across

a side lawn and rhododendron hedge to snow-laden fields and woods.

The second bedroom was long and thin, decorated with blue birds wallpaper, with a little window at the far end. She was surprised that such a small room could be so cold. Shivering in her sheepskin coat, she was relieved to see Tom appear in the doorway, saying: 'You can't be cold in that sheep!'

'I think someone's just walked over my grave.'

'Baa-ah!' a sudden voice sounded from the corner, making her jump. Ollie sprang out from the side of a wardrobe, laughing mischievously.

'There you are you little tinker!' she shouted, hugging him with relief.

'Sheep was the magic word! I'll go find mummy and daddy and tell them we've found you,' volunteered Tom, leaving the room.

'Come on Ollie,' urged Belinda.

'Play!' he insisted, trotting back to the bigger bedroom. He started running circles, giggling wildly.

'Come on young man, this is no time for playing!' she said crossly.

But as she attempted to grab his silky snowsuit, he slipped from her fingers, resuming his frenzied game and screaming: 'Wanna play wiv boy!'

'There are no boys to play with here, Ollie. We'll play later,' she insisted. Belinda could not remember Ollie being defiant with her before. He frequently tested his mother but was usually as sweet as pie with her.

Hearing all the commotion, Miranda burst in looking angry, followed by a red-faced Cameron.

'I think he's got the devil in him,' said Belinda, attempting to lighten the situation.

Cameron grabbed his son by the shoulders, lifting him to eye level. 'You're very naughty, Ollie. You shouldn't have run off like that in somebody else's house. We've been looking everywhere for you. Now stay with me and behave or else.'

'Boys will be boys,' said Agatha dismissively, blackmailing Ollie with a chocolate bar if he was a good boy.

Belinda was desperate to warm up, imagining a roaring log fire downstairs. But, as they reassembled on the landing, she soon realised the tour was far from over. Agatha explained how the two bedrooms were created from one big room when the children's home opened.

Cameron and Tom were looking down, studying a small, castellated flat roof topping the ground floor's eastern bay window. 'We could fire water pistols at poachers and tramps down there, Ollie!' Cameron joked.

The little boy whooped in agreement, tugging at his string harness, but Tom countered: 'That roof covering looks shot. Do you get water in the bay downstairs, Agatha?'

She nodded. Returning to the landing, they passed the room where Belinda had heard the giggling. 'That's my brother Roddy's room. It's a bit if a mess so I won't take you in. He would have been here but he's had to go to London on business.'

Puzzled, Belinda asked: 'Is there anyone else in the house?'

'No, only me.'

'That's strange, I went in there looking for Ollie and thought I heard someone, not that I could see anybody.'

'I don't think so. As I said, Roddy's away.'

'Perhaps it was Miranda you heard, 'suggested Cameron.

'I don't remember giggling,' she corrected him.

'You're always giggling without realising it and it's us who have to suffer.'

Their attention was quickly diverted by the sudden appearance of a fat, black tom cat with blazing green eyes, brushing its ragged coat around the corner wall, triumphantly. A minute head and tail was hanging limply from its mouth.

'Oh, Ramrod, you've caught another mouse, have you? That's the third one today. You clever boy!' praised Agatha.

Ollie wriggled, insisting Cameron put him down for a stroke, but as the little boy stretched out his hand, Ramrod growled and shot off. No-one was having this feline's catch of the day.

'That's Roddy's cat. He looks a bit scary, but he's a great mouser and certainly earns his keep.'

Probably an extension of his male ego, thought Belinda, contemplating the idea that Roderick had a woman stowed away in his room.

At the far corner of the house they came to another bedroom suite quietly overlooking the side lawn and rear garden. There were no prizes for guessing where Cameron and Miranda would sleep in the unlikely event they bought the house.

'Wouldn't our four poster look lovely in here, Cameron?' suggested Miranda mischievously as he hummed in approval.

Back in the corridor they passed a half glass panelled door with a wooden staircase. 'That goes to the old servants' quarters. I'll take you up there in a minute, if you're feeling brave,' teased Agatha.

Belinda was bemused as they went through an archway to the back stairs, which Agatha said the staff would have used to go down to the kitchen. Straight ahead was a spacious bedroom with dark stained floorboards and mismatched rugs. It could have easily accommodated six children's beds, but contained nothing more than a large Victorian oak wardrobe. Left of the door was a tall, double opening window with a safety bar across. It overlooked a stone patio, the original flooring to the demolished wing, their guide explained. The front, triple sash window looked across the drive to a grassy bank with small steps to a lawn.

Agatha, eyes twinkling, said: 'Roddy and I used to sleep in here as young children. Uncle bought us this train set and it ran right round the room.'

'Chuff! Chuff!' Ollie screamed excitedly.

'We used to load the trucks with sweets…exchange treacle toffees and sherbet lemons between our beds. We called it the Yum Yum Line.'

'The boys would just love that!' exclaimed Miranda.

'Fathers *and sons*,' observed Belinda.

'I'll be chief engineer,' volunteered Tom.

'Yes, and Cameron would be the Fat Controller, like in Thomas the Tank Engine, eating all the sweets!' said Miranda.

As they left the room chuckling, Agatha paused. 'Before we do downstairs I'd better show you the upstairs flat, though it's not very habitable.'

They returned to the glass panelled door and started climbing the steep wooden stairs; Belinda's feet so numb she could not feel the treads.

'Years ago, this is where the servants would have slept, but later on it was used as a flat.'

There was a glass door at the top. 'That goes on to the roof, though I won't take you out there today, we'd catch our deaths.'

'Is the roof sound?' asked Tom.

'I couldn't say, though old Nellie Gregory used to hang her washing out there when she and Ed lived here. They moved to the gardener's cottage up the drive some years ago now.'

It was plain to see how the exposed top floor had suffered the elements over the years. Broken plaster crunched underfoot and the air was raw with damp, vaporising their breath. Even the spiders seemed to have perished in their own cobwebs.

Rooms ran both sides of the staircase. The kitchen had a stainless steel sink unit and Sadia water heater, Belinda reckoned from the Seventies. Above the sink was a sliding glass door cupboard, like the one she remembered at home as a young girl. A daffodil yellow Formica table and pair of broken kitchen chairs stood forlornly in one corner.

In the sitting room, the angled chimney breast had lost much of its plaster, exposing a relief map of black threads and red brick.

'I see the front wall to the flat has scaffolding,' observed Tom, looking through the small front window. Is there a problem?'

'We were having remedial work done, but the weather got too bad,' Agatha answered unconvincingly. Belinda suspected it was more likely to stop the wall falling down.

On the far side of the stairs was a long bathroom with a white cracked bath, wash basin half off the wall and a funny wooden toilet cubicle.

'The views are breath-taking', said Belinda, trying to lift the general mood of dejection.

Through the bedroom window, a white blanket of fields was broken by a spinney of naked trees and small lake, reflecting like glass.

'That land was all part of the old Haggleby Estate, with hundreds of acres stretching down to the road and beyond,' explained Agatha.

The air of neglect hung heavily, as if the old woman Belinda had pictured on first seeing the house was being left to perish with time. 'Poor old hag', she thought, coining Tom's label for Haggleby Hall that was to stick with the strongest adhesive.

CHAPTER THREE

Uncle Milton

Belinda desperately wanted to get back to her snug little home and young Freddie, most likely driving Tom's parents mad by now. But a few more minutes had to be endured as Agatha began the ground floor viewing. They were led into a stunning mahogany panelled room with matching double doors adjoining what she called 'the ballroom'. The neutral painted walls, yellowed with time, were crowned with cornices of intertwined leaves. The matching, circular light rose boasted a brass chandelier, blackened for want of a polish.

A large window overlooked the side lawn and two smaller ones a rear area of grass and outbuildings. The tour party, chilled to the bone after the rooftops, was heartened to see a blazing log fire and quickly gathered round.

'We're in the billiards room,' said Agatha, peeling back the green carpet to reveal a sunken floor with brass trim. 'This is where the table would have stood.'

'I'm game for this room,' enthused Cameron, whose love for snooker had in his younger days frequently landed him in hot water for arriving home late from the pub to a dried-up Sunday roast. Belinda smiled, remembering the story about him doing it once too often and his angry mother plonking his dinner on the bar.

The fireside worshippers were reluctant to leave their positions, but Agatha's promise of tea after the viewing sparked them into action. They returned to the outer hall, where they had entered the house and went through a tall, white painted door to the right, opening into a long kitchen that formed part of the west wing. Dominating the front wall and overlooking the drive where their cars were parked, were two huge windows, their frames curving elegantly to the ceiling. There was a parquet floor and

27

cream units with white, tea-ringed work surfaces. A white melamine table and two plastic turquoise benches with white ironmongery stood under one window and a long, open-fronted chiller, probably from the same 1960s coffee bar, were beneath the other.

Another sizeable door, again white glossed but attractively carved, opened into a large sitting room. Robbed of its former glory, its decorative, gold-painted 'egg and rose' cornices protested against magnolia woodchip walls. But its saving grace was a triple, French bay window giving a panoramic view of the sweeping drive and snow-brushed lawns. The central area was broken by an island of shrubbery.

'Come Spring that tangle of rhododendrons and azaleas bursts into flower,' said Agatha.

'You could really go to town with the gardening here, Tom,' enthused Belinda.

'Who'd ever want to go to town with such beautiful grounds?'

'We're in what used to be the ladies' withdrawing room,' explained Agatha. 'After dinner the women would congregate here for conversation, music and embroidery.'

'Where did the men go?' asked Miranda, predictably.

'Oh, we chaps would have been in the billiards room, sipping whisky and potting balls,' retorted Cameron with a superior air.

'That sounds much more fun. You'd have allowed me in for a game, wouldn't you, Camay?'

'Absolutely not, the billiards room was totally out of bounds for the ladies, but you and I could have enjoyed a quick pot later.'

'Just give me the cue', responded Miranda, suggestively.

Agatha gave a nervous cough.

The room was filled with dark, wooden antique furniture; dressers, a dining suite and Chinese screen. They feasted their eyes on a long, solid oak sideboard, curiously carved with game birds, dog head drawer handles and gargoyles.

'Looks like Bavarian MFI,' exclaimed Tom, interested to hear that it had been designed for a hunting lodge.

At the far end of the room was a white painted, wooden fireplace, attractively marked, with mantle and gold lacquered mirror above. Yellow flames struggled half-heartedly in the grate.

Cameron pulled a knob on a panel fronting the French window shutters and Agatha demonstrated how the concertina arrangement unfolded.

'Me 'ide!' shouted Ollie, jumping into the shutter box.

Miranda started playing peep-o with the shutter door as the little voice inside tittered with glee.

'This place, it's a playground paradise!' exclaimed Belinda.

'Yes, for children and the grown-ups. I bet Camay would find plenty of places to hide from the chores.'

'The light fitting is *interesting*,' he announced, eager to divert their attention to a small table adaptation similar to the one in the hall.

Without comment Agatha led them through another door into the family drawing room; the most spectacular of all. It was at least 40ft long, with French windows in the north and west-facing bays and, at the opposite end, the mahogany double doors to the former billiards room. A large, disappointedly-plain stone fireplace with smouldering logs was surrounded by a chunky, comfortable-looking, Sanderson fabric sofa and armchairs.

The polished parquet floor, broken by faded, time-worn rugs, was perfect for dancing. It was easy to picture a party in full swing.

'With such a beautiful floor you can see why this is also known as 'the ballroom'. We've had some good dos in here,' said Agatha, echoing Belinda's thoughts.

Like the rest of the house, the room desperately needed decorating, but the visitors found its grandeur awesome.

'It's as big as our parish hall!' remarked Tom.

'Yes, and we could play badminton in here!' agreed Belinda, both of them players in their village club.

Unlike the former billiards room, the cornices of intertwined leaves had been sprayed gold and were brassy looking in the snowy light. A grand piano, which Agatha referred to as Aunt Elizabeth's, occupied most of one bay. In the other was a large globe. She lifted the top, revealing several bottles. 'You can plan your dream cruise as you sink cocktails. Roddy keeps it well stocked and after a few gins I'm going round the world.'

'War-ta,' announced Ollie.

'No, son, this stuff's much stronger, not for little boys!' answered Cameron, failing to notice a large puddle at the child's feet.

'You haven't done a wee have you?' chided Miranda, having earlier mentioned that the potty training needed work.

'That's not Ollie. I was right - the roof over the bay windows is leaking,' observed Tom.

Cameron's attention was drawn to the gold-sprayed ceiling rose radiating large leaves. 'Either I'm going cuckoo or those are owls.'

'What are you on?' mocked Miranda.

'Just look up there. What a hoot!'

There was a series of chuckles as one by one the party observed the leaves neatly rounded off with little owls.

Agatha's cheeks flushed. 'Roddy and I were aghast when we spotted the, uh hum, modification. We only noticed them after a sculptor had rented the place to do a commission for London Zoo... Now, I'm sure we could all do with a nice cup of tea.'

Relieved to hear the warming suggestion, they followed her back through the hall and through a door to the other wing. A stone floor passage led to a dog-clawed door scrawled in black felt tip with misspelt words:

'NUCLEER FALL-OUT SHELTAR ! Come in here at your peril. Radiashun wouldn't dare!'

Belinda wondered if it was done by the same hand that modified the bell sign.

Noticing everyone's reluctance to enter, Agatha said: 'That was my nephew's boy - his spelling is atrocious - of course, he denies it.'

The large square room had a low ceiling with a window overlooking the drive. A small calor gas fire struggled to keep a comfortable temperature. Agatha busied herself rinsing mugs under the tap. 'This is where I spend most of my time. It's the warmest place in the house.'

Looking round, Belinda's craving for a steaming cup of tea waned. The kitchen was grubby and untidy. A sink unit stood in the middle of the green quarry-tiled floor like a hostile island, harbouring a blackened, water-filled saucepan. Surrounding work surfaces were littered with newspapers and paraphernalia. There was an old Baby Belling cooker like the one she had used at school, but unlike this one coated in grease, that had had to be kept pristine. A plastic lidless bin spilled over with packets and tins and beside it, a wooden crate piled with beer and wine bottles told of a good party.

Belinda observed Agatha using one tea bag for every two mugs, gabbling on about the appalling weather and how summertime transformed Haggleby Hall. Her back turned, Cameron jokingly whispered: 'I wonder if the radiation's got to her yet?'

'It certainly hasn't helped the parrot,' muttered Tom, gazing at a straggly-looking African Grey, peering dolefully from its cage by the window. 'This place must be hell for the poor thing.'

As if in confirmation the creature sprang to life, squawking: 'Hell's bells ... Hell's bells.' A bird able to talk was a new experience for Ollie. Alarmed, he burst into tears.

'Don't be frightened, this parrot won't hurt you - he's nailed to the perch!' Tom comforted, quoting his favourite sketch with John Cleese and Michael Palin, from BBC TV's "Monty Python's Flying Circus". Ollie howled the louder and Agatha, appeasing him with Kit-Kat, said: 'Funny you should say that, Mr Flowers, but the parrot was actually named after Field Marshall Montgomery, who uncle served under during the Second World War.

The parrot cocked its head, repeating: 'Hello Milt… Hello Milt…'

'Monty called uncle 'Milt',' explained Agatha, her voice tinged with sadness. 'The parrot was his… it has given us endless amusement.'

Belinda would have liked to have heard more about Milton's war-time service, but didn't press Agatha, suddenly looking sorrowful, as if reminiscing. After a brief pause she continued: 'Uncle Milton and Aunt Elizabeth brought me and my brother up, you know?'

'Really - so Haggleby Hall was your home for some while?' deduced Tom.

Her eyes glistened. 'That's right. Sadly, our parents were killed in a train crash. I was 11 and Roddy, nine. It was a terrible time, but uncle - father's brother - and auntie adopted us. Our years growing up in this house with our cousin, James, I'll never forget.'

'It must have been an amazing place to live with all these rooms and the grounds,' said Belinda, attempting to lighten the mood.

'Oh yes, happy days! Before we went to boarding school we had a governess called Miss Benson. When the lessons got too much we used to sneak off and make camps. We always picked the most hidden away places. She would spend hours looking for us. She could never find us and, of course, didn't dare tell uncle and auntie for fear of losing her job.'

'Does the lake we saw from upstairs belong to Haggleby Hall?' quizzed Tom.

'It does, though it's now rented by the local fishing club. Uncle was a keen fisherman and used to keep it stocked with trout.' She paused, fighting the back tears. 'Uncle was such a lovely man. He taught us so much; how to fish, ride, play croquet... not that I ever got the hang of it!'

'What about your aunt?' asked Belinda, curiosity getting the better of her.

Agatha's face lightened. 'Aunt Elizabeth was a wonderful lady, like a mother to Rod and me. She taught me to embroider and play the piano. She was a real socialite, while uncle was more into country pursuits. Auntie loved holding weekend parties and while the women amused themselves, he would take the male guests shooting and fishing. Sadly, when war broke out and he became an army officer all that stopped.'

Suddenly, Ramrod leapt on to a worktop near Monty's cage. The parrot's hackles stiffened and with an alarming squawk it thudded on to the cage floor. Cursing, Agatha grabbed the hissing cat by the scruff of its neck and dumped it outside the door, muttering: 'Uncle would never have tolerated that mangy animal.'

As she returned to her chair, Cameron asked: 'Forgive me for asking, but I assume your uncle is no longer with us?'

'Cameron, don't be so nosey!' scolded Miranda, aware of upsetting Agatha again.

'Please don't worry,' she assured them. 'It is right to assume that. I suppose I had better explain, else you will hear it from somebody else.' She sipped her tea, tears filling her eyes again, but dabbing them with a handkerchief, continued: 'Twelve years ago, September the 26th, 1973 it was, Uncle Milton went out to buy something

33

and never came back. He disappeared into thin air and was never heard of again.'

'September 26, 1973, that date's familiar. Wasn't it when Concorde broke the world record crossing the Atlantic?' Cameron chipped in.

'Not now!' hushed Miranda.

Ignoring the comments, Agatha continued: 'The place was crawling with police for weeks and a wide search was made of the area, but he'd vanished without trace. Aunt Elizabeth was beside herself and Rod and I tried to support her as much as we could, although we had our own families to look after.'

She sighed, the frustration of not knowing what became of her uncle etched on her face.

'We still don't have a clue what happened. Following the war uncle used to go abroad a lot on business. One theory is he had somebody else and ran off with her. He was in his early 60s. Poor auntie became a recluse…never went out and had little to do with anyone.'

Curiosity mounting, Belinda asked: 'What became of your cousin, James?'

'Oh, he'd married a girl from Adelaide years before, much to uncle and auntie's disapproval, and went to live out there. The family lost touch…With uncle gone, Aunt Elizabeth couldn't afford to keep the estate going, so she sold or leased most of the land and, as Haggleby Hall was so big, she rented it out.'

'Where did your auntie go?' asked Miranda.

'She lived in the coach house, over the wall here, which she had had converted into a separate property, as with the stable block. That was sold.'

Cameron rose to his feet, looking restless, but Agatha was focused on finishing her story. 'She was never the same after uncle disappeared and became too ill to live alone, so we decided it best to put her in a nursing home. She's 80 now and, sadly, has senile dementia.'

'That's a really sad story,' empathised Belinda. 'I can understand your need to sell Haggleby Hall as soon as possible.'

Although sympathetic, Tom had burning questions to ask about the property, enquiring why the east wing appeared to look shorter than the west wing.

'I was hoping you wouldn't ask that,' answered Agatha, uncomfortably. 'It was rather an embarrassment for the family. In the early 60s Uncle Milton and Aunt Elizabeth went travelling and the place was rented out to a London borough as a children's home. The roof in the east wing started leaking, so the agents had the builders in. When uncle and auntie returned, they were horrified to find the wing leaking like a sieve. The builders had stripped the lead off the roof and scarpered. The damage was so bad part of the wing had to be pulled down.

'As you can see, in the last few years Haggleby Hall has deteriorated further. It's in desperate need of a buyer with plenty of money. It needs to go to someone who will love and care for it, restore it and live in it as a family home again... someone like you, perhaps?'

'Hells bells!' screeched Monty - Belinda's thoughts exactly.

CHAPTER FOUR

Coup de Grace

Belinda and Tom returned home, having had no exchange of thoughts with Cameron and Miranda because Ollie had become impossibly fractious. As Tom opened the front door the telephone started ringing. Freddie, excited to see them, rushed into Belinda's arms. Nuzzling her nose in his blonde curls, she listened with baited breath to Tom's conversation with Cameron. 'It sure needs a hell of a lot of work, Cam, but it can be done. I'll have to talk to the memsahib' (herself, of course).

His animated words contradicted the misgivings he had expressed in the car. Had their friends taken a shine to Haggleby Hall when she thought Tom and her had agreed it would all be too much work? Freddie wriggled to be put down and she followed him into the lounge to thank her parents for babysitting. It was some minutes before Tom appeared and after a hasty greeting, announced enthusiastically: 'Cameron and Miranda really love the place. They think we should go for it.'

Belinda was dumbfounded. What could she say in front of her parents? Cameron must have talked Tom round. Her poker-faced father did not mince his words: 'I think you two are bonkers to even contemplate it. And where are you or the Maclaren's going to get that sort of money? You don't want a hefty mortgage round your necks, especially now Belinda's not working.'

'We've been reading the estate agents' details, dear. With another baby on the way do you really want all that work?' chipped in her mother, frowning.

Belinda was angry with Tom and her parents for their negativity, but managed to bite her tongue. 'Don't worry; we'll have a really good think about it. No rash decisions.'

That night the self-inflicted dilemma gnawed at her sleep. Viewing Haggleby Hall with Cameron and Miranda as potential neighbours was hugely exciting, but seriously contemplating buying it was another matter. Her parents were probably right to question them, but she wasn't a little girl any more. Her immediate loyalties were to Tom and in the face of her friends she hated being a stick in the mud. She was loath to dampen their enthusiasm. Besides, she and Tom had only just turned 30. They had plenty of time to be adventurous, take risks here and there. As for doing up the place, Tom was completely dependable. He could do practically anything DIY and having worked for a small property developer before joining the family business, had 'hands-on' experience of renovation. There was also a second baby to consider. Freddie and new arrival could not share the same room for too long. And the garden at Flowerpots was too small. But thinking about the six acres at Haggleby Hall, it was perfect for growing children!

Next morning at breakfast Tom broached the obvious question: 'Had any more thoughts on the old Hag?'

'The old Hag', she loved the sound of it. 'Are you kidding? I've hardly slept. Despite our initial misgivings I keep thinking how fantastic it would be living there. The kids would be in their element with all that space, and being with Cameron and Miranda would be such fun, wouldn't it?'

'Yes, Bellie, with them around life would be anything but dull! And just think, no longer having to drive 20-odd miles to stay with them, or carting all the baby paraphernalia.'

She rubbed her growing bump, her smile widening. 'And babysitters right under our roof. Living there, we could have our friends round all in one go, throw parties, get slaughtered on the terrace and drown our hang-overs in the swimming pool!'

'Sounds great, but we'll have to think hard about all the work that needs doing?' cautioned Tom, suddenly looking serious. 'It's going to take years without much money coming in, though between us all we should be able to raise some extra cash.'

'Darling, we have years. What else would we be doing?'

'I take that as a green light, then?'

'I suppose it is.'

After a split second's hesitation he picked up the wall phone and dialled the Maclaren's. 'Now you two, what do you say about going back to Haggleby Hall for another look; see exactly what we would be letting ourselves in for?'

The following Saturday, despite a predictable battle with the agents for another appointment, they returned for another viewing. This time Grace accompanied them, together with Tom's architect cousin, Philip Wendover, who had offered to cast a discerning eye over the place if they were going to make the quantum leap.

Once again Roderick was away, but Agatha was amenable to them wandering round unaccompanied. Grace quickly warmed to the place and, despite the state of the flat, loved its space and countryside views. Cameron and Tom assured her that if they did decide to buy, the flat would be restored first and in the meantime there would be ample alternative accommodation.

Afterwards, Philip accepted Belinda's invitation to meet everyone at Flowerpots next day to 'talk turkey' over a roast and his feedback proved positive. 'Structurally, there's nothing seriously wrong with the building, though you'd have to be careful about any changes or improvements because it's Grade Two Listed. We would need to have a closer look at the roof timbers to see if there's any woodworm or decay, and the valley gutters, which I suspect are clogged up. There's some wet rot in the front wall of the flat but, surprisingly, no dry rot that I can see. It looks like your main expenditure would be on re-rendering the external walls and painting the place.'

Tom reflected his point. 'Obviously, our priority would have to be making the place warm and dry. We would need to install a new central heating system before next winter, but re-wiring and re-plumbing could wait, as could re-decorating.'

Cameron, exercising his serious side, reminded them: 'What we have to realise is that even with Mitts' income, we couldn't do it all in one go. It would be a project for life.'

'Not a life sentence, I hope,' said Belinda, tongue-in-cheek.

'I could do life in a place like that,' chipped in Miranda flippantly, 'though I'm not great on porridge.'

'But, Randy, you know how you love your oats!' retorted her husband, waggling his tongue suggestively.

Grace, who in her advancing years loved the idea of living in the flat with its countryside views and being so close to her son and family, emphasised the house' investment potential. 'You know my motto; putting your money in bricks and mortar is the best you can do for your children's future. If we can buy it at rock bottom price, we can do the improvements as and when we can afford them, then sell when the time is right. Yes, we could certainly make a killing.'

'It could certainly be the making of us', said Belinda, swept along.

'Or break us!' cautioned Cameron, 'but nothing ventured, nothing gained.'

Without further ado Tom raised his glass. 'Ladies and gentlemen, let's drink to uniting in what must be the most hair-brained scheme of our lives!'

Tom and Cameron went in person to Partridge and Pleasance to offer £170,000 for Haggleby Hall - £20,000 below the asking price. All the time Tom was gone Belinda's tummy wrestled with excitement and apprehension weighing up the pros and cons for the umpteenth time. When he finally returned, he was po-faced and reluctant to talk.

'Come on, Tom, tell me what happened?' she chided.

'Not much; they weren't interested in our offer and, well… we owe the estate agents for a new door.'

'What on earth do you mean? What have you two been up to?'

She had visions of an infuriated Cameron driving the latest acquisition of his sales cars through the front door - but he wouldn't do that, would he? Tom drew breath as if about to dive into water and went "twice round the houses". 'How can I put this? Umh, Cameron explained our situation admirably, using his best patter, stressing our confidence in the marketability of our properties and our determination to restore Haggleby Hall - or, as he put it, 'to make it a desirable residence again'. He sweet-talked Miss Cockshott, promising that if we bought the place she would be the first to sip champagne and eat caviar on the terrace'.

'A bit over the top - trust Cameron!' she despaired.

'Yes, she certainly deserves to be thrown over the balustrades!'

'Oh dear - so, come on, what then?'

'Well, she sounded game for the "champus" and black stuff, but refused to accept it because we haven't any buyers lined up for our properties.'

'But we're not even on the market yet.'

'She said we should be on the market by now, if we're looking to buy.'

'We can put our places on tomorrow.'

'But we would have to sell all three before she'd accept an offer.'

'That's impossible!'

'Her words exactly; she was adamant that Haggleby Hall would remain on the market because somebody could suddenly turn up with cash.'

'But it's been on the market so long what chance is there?'

'That's what Cameron said, but she didn't want to listen and we were dismissed like naughty schoolboys.'

'She's weighed you two up well. What did she say about Agatha and Roderick?'

'That they were keen to sell as soon as possible *to the right buyers*. That's obviously not us'.

'Agatha seemed to think we were.'

'Perhaps, but we have no idea what her brother was thinking and I dare say he has the whip hand.'

'So, how have you left it?'

Tom looked sheepish. 'Badly, I'm afraid.'

'What do you mean?'

'Well, let's just say that Cameron made the "feathers fly" at Partridge and *Pheasants.*'

'This is no time for Tom-foolery. What has he done?'

'That's almost funny, Bellie. But this isn't; Cameron stormed out hurling abuse and told Miss Cockshott to stick our offer up her… well, you know…

'Oh God, trust Cameron! That's definitely done it for us!'

'Then he slammed Miss Snotty Nose's office door so hard the glass shattered.'

'Oh that's just brilliant! So what are we going to do now, you idiots?'

'Don't blame me. You know how Cameron hates being beaten…but all is not lost.'

'Meaning…?'

Tom smiled teasingly. 'There is a Plan B - Grace's, actually.'

41

Belinda shuddered, reluctant to hear, but as it was Grace's…

'We called round to Grace's to tell her what had happened and she was so cross that after giving Cameron a piece of her mind, she rang Agatha. Apparently, the agents had already phoned Roderick, telling him we no longer wished to pursue the property.'

'What liars!'

'Grace explained everything. Apparently, Agatha and Roderick have been dis-enamoured with the agents for some time and have invited us round as soon as possible to discuss it all   further.'

*

Arriving on the dot at Haggleby Hall, they were greeted by Agatha, who took them into the ballroom, announcing her brother would be with them shortly. Belinda sat beneath the chandelier and eyed the owls embellishing the ceiling rose. She wondered whether she and her friends were like owls, supposedly wise, or more like lemmings, foolishly following each other over the cliff. But this was not the time to consider U-turns. They were on a mission and had to see it through. Belinda was feeling nervous and sorry Miranda wasn't with them for moral support. Their friendship had been cemented with Freddie's arrival, Miranda always being there for her when she couldn't cope. But today her friend had volunteered to stay home, minding the boys. Cameron had expressed relief, having labelled Roderick a ladies' man after hearing Belinda's story about the giggling she had heard in his bedroom the first time they toured the house. Possessive at the best of times, Cameron didn't want the fellow eyeing up his wife on such a critical occasion. Tom, on the other hand, argued that her shapely attributes would have been a distinct asset.

Belinda's thoughts retraced the last few days when she and Freddie had visited Haggleby to look round the village.

She had learnt from the postmistress of two other buyers interested in   the Hall; the Treetops Hotels chain and a gentleman's club in Haywards Heath. Both had lodged planning applications to convert the building, though permission had previously been refused on the grounds of dangerous access.

When she told Tom he was furious and said Partridge and Pleasance had obviously been waiting for planning permission to be granted and was playing one off against the other. There was bound to be a backhander involved.

Belinda's feedback seemed to unite the four of them in a purpose; the more challenging buying "The old Hag" became, the harder they would fight to buy it. She strongly believed in fighting for their rights, but staring at the owls, she feared fall-out from their vendors' feathered friends.

Suddenly, the double mahogany doors opened and in walked a smartly dressed gentleman.

'Good afternoon. I'm Wod-wick Fielding-Winters, but do call me Wod. I am so sorry not to have made your acquaintance before. I am vewy pleased to meet you all.'

Belinda was amused by Roderick's lisp, which did nothing to flatter this otherwise ruggedly handsome, impeccably dressed man. He must have been in his early 50s, with a care-worn face, deep set brown eyes, thin moustache and dark hair, sleek with Brylcream, greying at the temples. He stood a proud 6ft 2ins and used his tall slim figure to good advantage, wearing a pair of good fitting, perfectly creased black trousers, starched white shirt, a green and white tie, embroidered with a crest Belinda guessed was his golf club, and navy blazer with brass buttons. Agatha had mentioned he was a divorcee.

After the round of handshakes, he asked: 'Would anyone care for a Madeirwa?'
He peeled back the globe cocktail cabinet and responded to Grace and Belinda's preference for a small sherry and Agatha a "G and T."

'Have you got a beer, sir?' asked Cameron, who Belinda deduced was addressing his host formally to turn the situation to his advantage, rather than out of respect.

'I'll get some from the fridge,' Agatha volunteered, quickly leaving the room. She was gone for some minutes and awaiting her return, Cameron expressed his liking for Roderick's XJS Jaguar parked on the drive.

'Yes, I'm vewy happy with it, but I'm not weally a car man. Actually, I'm thinking of learning to fly. I've always wanted to and it could prove vewy useful wiv the amount of twavelling I do.'

'You mean buy your own plane?'

'I would love to, if I could get one at the right price.'

'It's a pity Cameron is not an aeroplane salesman,' remarked Tom.

Cameron accepted a cigar from Roderick. 'Mum's got her, what is it, Mitts, your PLP?'

Roderick looked down his nose: 'A member of the Parliamentary Labour Party?'

'Now let's not labour under any illusions, Mr Fielding-Winters,' said Grace quick-firing. 'It's PPL - my Private Pilot's Licence.'

'Weally, how clever of you! Could you teach me?'

Agatha returned with two beer cans. She took glasses from the sideboard, sniffling.

'My dear Aggie, what on earth is the matter?' her brother asked.

She looked pale, fighting back tears: 'Monty's cage has fallen over - he's gone! I left the kitchen window open. There are feathers everywhere.

'I bet W-Wamrod was after him again. H-How many times have I told you to keep that w-wetched animal out of the kitchen?'

Roderick must have been referring to his cat, Ramrod. The room fell silent. Belinda guiltily remembered Tom mimicking the Monty Python sketch on their previous visit;

almost as if he had willed it to happen! Cameron, commiserating, emptily suggested a search party. Quickly composing herself, Agatha passed Cameron and Tom a beer and headed for the door.

'Never mind that d-damned bird, this is far more important. As you left the window open the chances are he's in T-Timbuckto by now!' stormed Roderick.

She stopped and turned, red-faced. 'He's escaped before and I found him then. I really should go.'

'But you d-didn't leave the window open last time! Now, let's get the b-business over with. I'll help you look for Monty, later.'

Belinda was fascinated watching Roderick close the cocktail cabinet at the equator. As he and Agatha sat down, Cameron turned on his "sales patter", which this time worked in reverse. 'We are aware, sir, that the property has been on the market some time and you have had a succession of people looking round without any offer being made. We understand there are certain parties on the side-lines interested in buying the place with a view to convert it into a leisure concern, but only if they can get the planning authorities to play ball - and that is proving a sticking point. In the meantime, you have to worry about keeping the place up to scratch. It must be very stressful for you both.'

He paused to puff on his cigar. 'From what we have been told, the district planners would never give permission for any leisure use anyway, because of the dangerous access. Philip Wendover, the architect we brought with us last time, reckoned a better access would be required to satisfy the planners, but there is nowhere else because Haggleby Hall no longer owns the land fronting the road.'

Cutting to the chase, he quoted the architect's report warning that without any serious remedial work, the house would not survive another winter.

The air was highly charged as Cameron wound up the tone. 'Your agents seem to be working from their own agenda, which certainly excludes us, and they are not doing you any favours. You're struggling to keep the place standing and how much longer will you have to wait before anyone puts in an actual offer?'

Cameron stood up, commanding the floor. 'We will make you an offer here and now for £170,000 -OK, it is £20,000 below the asking price, but as you well aware, there is a huge amount of work to do. Will you accept it here and now?'

Belinda shuddered at Cameron's directness, known in the car sales trade. Tom would have towed a softer line. Unsurprisingly, Roderick took umbrage. 'You obviously don't believe in bargaining, Mr Maclaren, and I am not in the habit of wunning head first into any business deal. We have allowed you here tonight against the agents' wishes, knowing they are working hard to get the best possible price for us. Aggie and I need to exercise extweem caution. We are not p-wpared to take the first offer that comes along.'

Cameron persisted: 'And how much longer can you wait for the agents to tie up a deal when, as we have learnt, planning permission has already been refused to turn the place into a leisure concern? Haggleby Hall has already been on the market two years, hasn't it?'

Roderick nodded, expressionless. Agatha broke an awkward pause: 'Let's have a serious think about it, Roddy. We have to sell this place soon with Aunt Elizabeth in that nursing home.'

'Yes, but £20,000 below the asking price! We need every penny for her care.'

Cameron interrupted: 'Look, we'll offer you the full asking price tonight - £190,000. We can't do any better than that. Do we have a deal?'

Roderick, taken aback, poured himself another whisky. 'Mr Maclaren, Agatha tells me you have three properties to sell to raise the capital... that's a bit optimistic, isn't it?

And do you serwiously expect to sell them all quickly and at the same time?'

His speech impediment would have been amusing but for the seriousness of the situation.

'Agweed, Haggleby Hall needs a substantial amount of westowashun, but you need to prove you have both the cash and the commitment to put the place to wights.'

Tom stepped in: 'Wod-wick, um, Roderick, we wouldn't be here if there was any shadow of doubt. We have all known each other many years and we're almost like family. I trust Cameron implicitly, as he does me. We wouldn't dream of embarking on such a venture if we didn't believe we could do it.'

Agatha was desperate to help her visitors. 'Roddy, from the conversations I have had with these good people I can tell how much they want Haggleby Hall. They plan to restore it sympathetically and turn it into a comfortable family home, like it used to be. That's what Aunt Elizabeth would want and Haggleby Hall deserves.'

Roderick pinched his ear undecidedly. 'I am not disputing what you say, Aggie. It's just that I am extwemely weluctant to sell the house to the wong people after all poor Aunt Elizabeth has been through.'

Perhaps Roderick was sticking out for more money, thought Belinda. There was no chance! Grace put her glass down, determinedly. It was time to put her feminine wiles to work. Returning to her seat next to Roderick, she eyed him coyly: 'Mr Fielding-Winters, it is very nice to have met you at last and to be here with you in this lovely house. It has so much potential and it would be a privilege for us to buy it and return it to a loving family home.'

His face softened. 'Oh, do call me Wodwick. It's vewy nice to make your acquaintance, my dear ...er, Gwace, and I am sure that a lovely lady such as yourself can appweciate the pwedicament Agatha and I are in, twying to find the wight buyers.'

47

She nodded. 'Agatha has told me of your success as an hotelier in the West Country. I would expect a man of your business experience and with such loyalty towards your aunt to surely give the whole matter a great deal of thought; the question of whether to sell the treasured family home to complete strangers is a huge one. And, of course, we appreciate the predicament you are in with other potential buyers seeking to convert Haggleby Hall into, perhaps, a hotel or country club. But I am sure you are most concerned about the local planning authorities' reluctance to grant planning permission for such a venture and the situation dragging on interminably, while all the time the house is devaluing through deterioration. Of course, you want to wait for the best possible price. But as my son said, the house desperately needs attention and if it doesn't get it soon, with the weather getting in the fate of Haggleby Hall doesn't bear thinking about!'

Grace paused, allowing her words to sink in. 'You wouldn't want it demolished, would you? Or maybe that's what other interested parties are waiting for.'

Roderick looked alarmed. 'No, heaven forbid! They couldn't. It's Grade Two Listed.'

'If they failed to get planning permission and went away, what would happen then? Do you have the wherewithal to restore it, or would *you* have to leave it to fall down?'

'No! That's last thing we would want,' asserted Agatha.

'So, you are asking £190,000 for the property and we are offering it, with complete reassurance that Haggleby Hall would remain a family home. And we would do our best to retain as much of its original features as possible.'

Grace's persuasiveness was felt around the room, but was it sufficient to sway Roderick?

'Well, Roddy?' asked Agatha after some minutes.

'I need time to think about it,' he hesitated.

An aeroplane sounded in the distance. A clock ticked on the sideboard. Belinda could hardly stand the tension. She wished she was back at home, reading Freddie a bedtime story. She felt she had been swept along. She so wanted Haggleby Hall to be her home, but was terrified of her and Tom making the wrong decision. For better or worse, her marriage vows were never as hard as this.

Grace broke the silence, asking Roderick if they could have a few minutes alone. Agatha showed the others into the hall and excused herself, saying she was going to look for Monty. She declined Cameron and Tom's offer to assist her, inviting them to wait on an old church pew.

Belinda's posterior was starting to go numb. She was just contemplating what they would do if Monty suddenly swooped down, when the ballroom door opened. Grace appeared beaming with satisfaction, followed by Roderick, looking hugely relieved.

'We've got a deal - £190,000', announced Grace.

'Delighted to sell the place to such agreeable people,' said Roderick, shaking everyone's hand.

Belinda could hardly believe his sudden change of mind and there were loud cheers. Agatha, coming downstairs, her expression transformed on hearing the good news, chortled: 'Blast the parrot! I'll go and find that champagne.'

After a toast they finally left, Roderick kissing Grace's hand. In the car Cameron said to her: 'You certainly won him over, Mitts, how on earth did you do it?'

'Oh, I have my ways. Roderick and I have come to an understanding. He's asked me out to dinner next Friday.'

Cameron looked shocked. 'What have you got yourself into, Mitts? You'll have to watch him. Belinda reckons he's a real ladies' man.'

'I never said that, you did,' corrected Belinda.

'I think I'm old enough to look after myself,' his mother assured him.

'What, with that hot Rod around?'

'Trust you to think of Roderick in terms of wheels, Cameron.'

'He's a bit fast with the ladies, that's for sure - but thanks for clinching the deal, Mum.'

CHAPTER FIVE

Narrow Squeak

The baby was starting to kick and maternal thoughts were taking precedence over Haggleby Hall. Belinda had decided to breast feed again. With Freddie it was initially a struggle, but she had persevered and he eventually got the hang of it. She remembered being like an eating and drinking machine to make enough milk, but enjoyed the feeling of complete fulfilment. She decided to continue her membership of the Mid Sussex National Childbirth Trust. Through its classes she had not only learnt about natural childbirth (and proudly achieved it with Freddie) she had also made several new friends. She had discovered that she was not the only woman in the world to cast a good career aside to start a family and then have to spend months afterwards learning to accept it. The NCT coffee mornings and tea afternoons in members' homes had given her the opportunity to indulge in baby talk and exchange notes on motherhood. Being housebound much of the time, she had found it liberating to strap Freddie in his car seat, drive off and be able to plonk him on someone else's floor for him to learn the basics of social behaviour while she nattered with other mums. If he screamed or threw up, it was all part of the fun!

Having always enjoyed writing, she had also joined the trust's group of "Potty Poets". She was amused by the double-entendre in the word 'Potty'; apart from the obvious baby meaning, she certainly found some members outside the usual parameters of normal. It was hardly surprising; babies did that to you, she told herself, trying not to question her own sanity too closely. The group's leader set topics for waxing lyrical and Belinda kept a notebook handy to jot down odd lines, usually in the middle of some humdrum household chore, such as:

HORMONAL WASHDAY

Yesterday I was happy,
Today I'm in the dumps.
How does a woman handle
Her hormonal grumps?
I'll stick mine in the washing,
Like they are pairs of socks,
And each day wear a fresh lot,
To keep me off the rocks.

Despite such musings Belinda considered herself fairly conventional woman, as she did Miranda, but Grace was far less so. She loved fast cars, understood 'things mechanical', was good at DIY and as for flying, thought nothing of winging her way up to Scotland or across the Channel for days out. Her promise to take Tom and her up in the Piper she flew as part of a syndicate was an exciting prospect. Having never flown before, Belinda couldn't wait, but in her present condition that was out of the question. Day dreaming, she imagined soaring through the sky, the countryside flitting beneath her like a giant patchwork quilt.

Suddenly the phone rang, bringing her back to earth with a bump. It was Priscilla Cockshott. Belinda squirmed, expecting some strong language after Cameron's outburst.

'Mrs Flowers, setting aside Mr Maclaren's appalling behaviour in the office for one moment, I have to say it was most improper of him and your husband to make an offer directly to the vendors when they had already made one to us!'

Belinda was momentarily lost for words, but kept her cool: 'Perhaps, but you did not take their offer seriously? We could have waited until kingdom come for any co-operation from Partridge and Pleasance. Our architect's view is that if Haggleby Hall were to remain on the market much longer without restoration, it would be best knocked down - though demolition might suit certain parties we know are waiting in the wings.'

'How we conduct our business is nothing to do with you, Mrs Towers. As with any property we market, we strive to achieve the highest price for our client, but it seems these clients have taken the sale completely out of our hands.'

Priscilla slammed the phone down. 'She still gets my name wrong,' Belinda winced, but slowly her smile broadened. She and the others had, effectively, gazumped the estate agents! Now all they had to do was sell three properties and complete on the same day to make Haggleby Hall theirs! But her elation was fleeting. Supposing it didn't all come together and they couldn't raise the full asking price? They would have to take out a bridging loan, wiping out any spare capital for essential repairs. The realisation suddenly filled her with dread - she, Tom and their expanding family could end up with no home at all! Her tummy muscles tightened, her racing thoughts prompting a wave of 'practice contractions'. She breathed through, determined to keep calm.

*

The waiting game to find the right buyers became more knuckle-gnawing by the day. Fortunately, the property market was buoyant and within a few weeks Grace's home, Magpie Mews, went under offer. A fortnight later Flowerpots did and ten days after, Primula Drive! Everything was miraculously falling into place and a completion date was fixed for Friday, June 13.

The friends were quick to dismiss any superstition about the date, but it was a bad omen because sure enough, just as everything was looking ready to go, Grace's buyer suddenly pulled out. What a disaster! With final completion just a month away the chances of finding another in time were practically impossible.

53

Struggling to stay positive, there was little they could do but hope for the best and continue with the packing. Doubts continued to invade Belinda's thoughts. Perhaps Haggleby Hall was not meant to be? Even if, by some miracle, everything went ahead, would it be the home of their dreams - or nightmares?

That Saturday, to ease the mounting tension, she and Tom decided to go to Haggleby's church fete, which Belinda had seen advertised on one of their visits to the house. It was a still cloudless day and they temporarily forgot their troubles as they helped Freddie fish for a duck, play hoopla, winning a teddy, and ride a donkey. It was lovely to share in his joy but deep down, Belinda was feeling guilty about dismantling the family home. If they didn't pull it off, what then? Whether her insecurity was making her feel worse she wasn't sure, but her Braxton Hicks contractions sorely tried her that day. Several times she had to stop and use the breathing technique she had learnt at National Childbirth Trust classes.

During the donkey ride, as Belinda trotted alongside Tom holding Freddie's reign, she felt a band tighten round her tummy worse than ever before. She could barely manage the pain. The baby was more active than usual and instead of little heels and fists prodding her, its whole body seemed to be moving. Beads of sweat trickled down her face and scared of giving birth on the church field, she instructed Tom to take her to hospital. Freddie, oblivious to the emergency, was handed over to Haggleby vicar, the Reverend Makepeace, and his wife, Matilda, with whom they had become acquainted in the tea tent earlier. Little did they realise that one day the couple would make quite an impact on their lives, though not necessarily in the religious sense! Freddie happily trotted off with the promise of ice cream.

Tom drove faster than he should to Cuckfield Hospital, Belinda cursing every bump in the road. They were speedily checked in and rushed to the maternity suite. Helping her undress, he said: 'the excitement of the church fete was just too much for you, wasn't it, Bellie? We'll have to stick to bungee jumping in future!'

She appreciated Tom's efforts to make her laugh. He was always her rock in a crisis, but there was no hiding their fears that she was only 32 weeks pregnant - far too soon for the baby to be born. Trying to relax, she silently prayed that 'He-she' would quieten down and remain cocooned a few weeks longer. Reading her thoughts, Tom rubbed her bump: 'Now, stay where you are, little Miss. You're supposed to wait till we've moved!'

'How do you know it's 'a little Miss?'

'Because I think she's going to be just like you, Bellie, impetuous at times!'

Had Belinda not felt so vulnerable she would have hit back, but He-she did as Daddy instructed and the contractions stopped.

*

The following week Tom and Belinda reconciled themselves with the thought that if Grace didn't find a new buyer by the weekend, they would reluctantly withdraw Flowerpots from sale. Tom felt that with the baby being so close, the stress was becoming too much. He was sure their friends would understand, but the next few days were like walking a tightrope, with no further progress and a cloud of despondency hanging over them.

The morning they were getting ready to meet Cameron and Miranda for lunch and announce their decision, the phone rang. Belinda picked it up to hear Grace's excited voice: 'I've just met up with Margie, an old friend, recently back from the States, and would you believe it, she wants to buy Magpie Mews? She's always loved my little house and when I told her my buyers had pulled out, she jumped in…and she is a cash buyer!'

Belinda burst into tears and Tom gave her the biggest squeeze her bump would permit. Instead of commiserations at The Nip and Tipple there were celebrations - even He-she enjoyed a swig of champagne. Suddenly the wheels were in motion again - only this time revolving twice as fast. As Margie did not have a property to sell and much of the legal work had been done already, the transaction was expected to go through quickly. Frantic phone calls between estate agents, solicitors, vendors and buyers ensued and everyone agreed to put back the completion date by three weeks, thankfully moving it from Friday June 13th to Friday 4th July – Independence Day, an admirable choice and a real tribute to Margie's return from the USA. Belinda was over the moon. It had been touch and go, but Grace's friend had saved the day!

*

Moving day should have been plain sailing, but it was far from a breeze. In fact, at Flowerpots there was something very strange in the air.

As the purchase of Haggleby Hall was combined, the friends had to complete by mid-day and pay £190,000 to Roderick and Agatha's solicitors. With Freddie deposited with grandparents, Belinda started packing final kitchen items, uninterrupted. The last few weeks had been such a rollercoaster she was feeling very mixed; elated at moving to a country mansion with their closest friends, relieved that it was all finally happening, yet sad at having to leave their cherished little home after six years.

Tom spent the morning supervising four muscle men from Smooth Movers. They were certainly living up to their name, performing superhuman skills shoehorning furniture, carpets, boxes and other of the Flowers' prized possessions into the van. Belinda kept them fuelled on coffee, leaving each brew on the hearth. But every time she went into the living room she noticed a funny smell, which seemed to be getting worse. It was rather unpleasant, like rotten stew. She sniffed around the diminishing pile of items, but couldn't trace it. The lounge carpet was half rolled and looking at the bare floorboards, she wondered if there was a decaying mouse beneath. She watched while Bill and Hugh rolled the rest of the carpet and carried it out. Upstairs, she was impressed to see how much Joe and Eddie had packed. The Smooth Movers were sweeping through the place like human vacuum cleaners sucking up everything in their path! Their banter jollied along the great exodus and Belinda was upbeat. Back in the kitchen she told Tom about the bad smell. He followed her into the lounge and taking several deep breaths, grimaced. 'You're right. It's probably a mouse. That's all we need to greet the buyers. There's air freshener in that box, you'd better spray round.'

Doubting its efficacy, she stepped outside for some fresh air and watched Hugh testing the bendy qualities of her six-foot rubber plant, squeezing it into the van. She heard the phone ring and knowing Tom was in the shed showing Bill which garden implements to pack, she rushed into the hall and picked it up nervously, expecting to hear the estate agents or solicitors.

Grace gabbled away: 'Would you believe it? At this stage of the game there's some hold-up over the money going through on Magpie Mews; something to do with the American end, where Margie's cash is invested.' She must have heard Belinda gasp, as she quickly reassured her: 'The solicitors are doing everything possible. I'm sure it will be OK.'

Mortified, Belinda ran out and told Tom, who suggested she made tea while he rang the agents? She retreated to her inner sanctuary, the kitchen, which now almost empty failed to provide its usual solace. Waiting for the kettle to boil, she perched on the Raeburn rail, disappointed it could not offer its usual warming comfort. She shuddered, trying not to contemplate what would happen if the sale of Magpie Mews did not go through. Her watch said 11 30am - just 30 minutes to completion! Perhaps Partridge and Pleasance were right. The agents had warned from the beginning that selling three properties together was Mission Impossible.

A nail-biting ten minutes later Tom came in: 'The good news is Flowerpots is ready to go through. The bad news is we are advised to stay put and on no account let the buyers in until Magpie Mews completes. I suppose they'll be telling us next to barricade the front door!'

She was on tenterhooks as he then phoned Cameron and Miranda to check on their progress. Surprisingly, everything was going along swimmingly. The sale had gone through on Primula Drive and as their buyers were not moving in until the following week, there was no immediate pressure to leave.

Tom's attempts to reassure Belinda that they would be moving before the day was out were thwarted as two faces appeared at the doorway. It was the Flowerpots' buyers, Peter and Paula Piggott.

With a cheery "Good morning", Mr Piggott said: 'Sorry we're a few minutes early, but everything's gone without a hitch. We managed to load up quickly and, of course, we only had a few miles to travel. How are you doing?'

'Progressing, but not quite done yet', answered Tom vaguely, quickly changing the subject with an offer of coffee.

Belinda, determined to keep them away from the house, volunteered to take it out to their Volkswagen parked opposite. Pre-empting more questions, she insisted: 'Got to get back... still tons to do!' chastising herself for saying the wrong thing.

At 1.30pm Flowerpots was all packed save the kettle. Another half hour ticked by and there was still no news about Grace's completion. Tom went out and a few minutes later reported that the Piggott's had driven off. 'They've probably gone for lunch. The removal blokes said if something didn't happen soon, would we mind if they popped down the pub for a pie and a pint.'

'They can't do that, surely?' she groaned.

'Well, there's not much happening here. Think we'll join them.'

Tears filled her eyes. Hugging her he suggested she went round to her parents to see if Freddie was behaving and have lunch there. The thought was appealing, but their son would find her visit too unsettling. Tom left to buy something to eat from the local shop and she collapsed on a stool, the only item of furniture remaining. Fortunately, the baby was being unusually quiet.

Ten minutes later he re-appeared with sandwiches, yogurts and drinks and fetched a blanket from the car. He spread it on the lounge floor. 'This is the weirdest picnic you'll ever have and not much to recommend it, sitting next to the gas works.'

'You're as romantic as ever,' she said, struggling with her bump to sit next to him. They chuckled, trying to ignore the pong that had defied the air freshener. There was still no word about Grace's completion, so while Belinda cleared up, Tom rang the solicitors once more, who advised them to sit tight till the money came through.

Even normally unflappable Tom was reaching boiling point. Belinda started pacing the floor, for the umpteenth time going into the lounge to sniff the pungent air. Peering through the window, she was relieved to see the Piggott's car had not returned and, thankfully, the removal men had wisely decided to stay put. Bill and Joe were in the cab eating sandwiches, Eddie stood on the pavement swigging coke as he chatted to them, while Hugh sat alone on the garden wall, smoking.

To relieve the tension Belinda decided to do another spray of air freshener. Curses! The box containing the aerosol had been packed. She looked in her handbag for her perfume and filled the air with its provocative smell.

When Tom walked in, his nose did a double-take. 'That beats Spring Meadows any day. In fact, it really turns me on.'

'It should do, it's that Wild Passion you bought me for Christmas.'

'Umh, what are you doing, later darling, though I'm not sure where we will be sleeping?'

Uptight and heavily pregnant, passion was the last thing on her mind, especially if they had to spend the night in a local hotel.

At 3.30pm the telephone sounded for the umpteenth time. Her heart skipped a beat as Tom grabbed the receiver. It was Cameron to say that if Grace's money wasn't through soon, they would have no choice but to find a bridging loan double quick! More tea was urgently required and as Belinda made it, discussed with Tom whether they should let their buyers in, store their furniture and find a hotel for the night.

The doorbell rang. 'Not the Piggott's again – that's the third time in an hour,' he said, exasperated. Seeing her face crumple, he kissed her comfortingly and gingerly answered the door. She half expected to see Mr Piggott bursting through on his charger. He certainly looked in fighting mode.

'We can't sit out here all day. What the hell's happening? Our solicitors haven't heard a …'

The phone erupted, cutting him short and she grabbed it. …

'It's our solicitors - everything's gone through, thank heavens! We'll be out of here in a jiffy, Mr Piggott.'

*

Belinda could scarcely believe they had finally made it to Haggleby Hall! Toasting their success, she and Tom,

Cameron and Miranda were sitting in her new run-down kitchen that was to become Mansion HQ. It was 8 30pm and as the boys were staying with friends overnight, they could all relax for the first time in what seemed months. Grace, exhausted after the day's emotional rollercoaster, was having an early night, having promised to join in celebrations the following lunchtime.

'What a day! I don't want to go through all that again for at least 60 years,' moaned Cameron wearily.

'And some,' sighed Tom, exhausted.

Miranda was elated: 'Hooray, we're here – put the flags out!'

'Now, there's an idea,' beamed Cameron, twiddling his whiskers.

'I suppose the Piggott's were quite patient, really,' said Belinda.

'Yes, I've only got one black eye,' responded Tom.

Sidling up to him, Miranda examined the swelling. 'That Mr Piggott must have clocked you one! It looks nasty, Tom – I have some witch hazel somewhere…'

'He stepped on a rake clearing out the shed,' Belinda corrected, too weary to offer any more sympathy. 'I wonder what the Piggott's are making of that awful smell. I wouldn't wish that on anyone.'

'What smell?' asked Miranda.

'We think it was a dead mouse under the floorboards. I couldn't get rid of it, so I let rip with Wild Passion.'

'Do bad smells turn you on, Belinda?' she giggled.

'You bet!' answered Tom. 'She loves it when I'm all sweaty - but that Wild Passion cost me a fortune!'

'I thought it came free!' exclaimed Miranda, as Cameron snorted into his beer.

Tom suddenly put two and two together. 'Oh Bellie, that smell wasn't a dead mouse…didn't you notice the removal men calling Hugh, 'Pooh'?'

'I thought they were just taking the Mickey.'

'I did, too, till I realised that every time they stopped for a break, three of them sat one end of the room and Hugh the other.'

'Of course - when they were waiting outside, he sat *alone* on the garden wall! The others wouldn't go near him...come to think of it, he was rather niffy.'

'That would explain the strange smell in the hall when your furniture came in,' said Cameron. 'I thought Roderick's cat had left us an unwelcome present.'

Tom leaned back on his chair, eyeing the stained kitchen ceiling. 'With all this damp around we'll have to get used to unpleasant smells.'

'Perhaps we need some de-humanisers,' suggested Miranda, trying to sound knowledgeable.

'I think you mean dehumidifiers,' corrected Cameron.

'After today I think I've been de-humanised,' groaned Belinda.

Miranda fiddled nervously with her hair. Belinda knew there was something on her mind and it was nothing to do with her wrong use of words. 'Is everything all right, Miranda? You look dead worried about something. We are going to be fine you know.'

'Yes, I'm sure we are, but there is something I must tell you. We seem to have inherited some Haggleby Hall inmates...umh, live ones...'

'You don't mean the woodworm. They come with the fixtures and fittings,' joked Tom.

'No, it's nothing like that.'

'Spit it out, Randy, it's time for another beer!' urged Cameron.

'I - I've offered to have Ramrod and Monty, well, for the time being, anyway. I saw Agatha briefly as we arrived and, out of desperation, she was about to deposit them with the RSPCA. She can't take them back to her home in Wales and Roderick can't accommodate them at his hotel.

Cameron looked incredulous. 'Randy, what is it about children and small animals - you can't resist them, can you?'

Miranda turned on her most provocative look. 'Camay, yes I love children and small animals, but *you* are the only one on this planet that I can't resist!'

'Hang on,' said Tom. 'I thought Monty had met his demise that night we were tying up the deal over Haggleby Hall?'

'No, didn't we tell you? With everything going on we must have forgotten,' said Cameron, a degree calmer. 'Agatha heard him making a racket in one of those big cupboards in the kitchen. He must have gone in there to get away from that damned cat.'

'As he survived we simply have to keep him - and Ramrod, he's a good mouser. I don't want smelly mice decaying under our floorboards!' insisted Miranda.

CHAPTER SIX

Flower Power

Belinda luxuriated under the sheets, fantasising she was lady of the manor as she awaited the butler with tea. She couldn't focus without that first cup of the day and every morning Tom brought it up before leaving for work. Since they had moved to Haggleby Hall it was only lukewarm after its long journey from the kitchen, but the privilege of waking up in the spacious master bedroom more than compensated. With Freddie still asleep, she spent her few minutes of cherished solitude counting her blessings. She could hardly believe that she, Tom and their son had eventually made it to this palatial home of their dreams together with their 'extended family'. She was so lucky to have this 'go-getting' husband. They had met in their mid-20s (when she hired him to take photographs for PR clients), quickly fell in love and tied the knot within a year.

Now, after nine wonderful years of marriage, she seemed to love him more each day. She wanted to show him at that moment, entwine limbs and entice him to her silky inner depths - but her bump was like a boulder between them! Anyway, such thoughts had to be pushed aside, with so many other demands on their energies, trying to make their new home serviceable by the time the baby was born.

Tom worked for the family business, an industrial and commercial photographer's. Frederick Flowers & Sons was started in the 1920s by his grandfather, taking pictures for the early aviation and motor industries. As time passed, the West London-based company's portfolio of manufacturing clients rapidly grew and Tom became a partner alongside his father, Harold, and Uncle Henry. A talented all-rounder, Tom was a dab hand at black and white printing and his technical photography was masterful. Work invariably had to come first and there was little opportunity for time off, but having moved to Haggleby Hall he was allowed an entire fortnight to get the place up and running and find a builder for the renovation work. In those two weeks Tom and Cameron were going flat out, toolboxes flying in all directions. Two or three times a day they exchanged progress reports over brews at Mansion HQ.

On a friend's recommendation, they hired a local firm, Barry Allsop Builders, to do the major renovation work. Cameron agreed to oversee building operations, expected to take a few months, as he could be more flexible with his car sales work. The Flowers' side of the house had not been occupied for years and nothing worked properly. Tom's first task was to sort out the hot water, which flowed into the bath like melted chocolate.

With only a month before the birth, Belinda was bounding with energy, but the housework had become a struggle, so Tom had to put his back into sanitising the floors, which hadn't seen a vacuum cleaner or mop in years.

Grace, whose upstairs flat was uninhabitable until it was rewired and re-plastered, had moved into the twin bedroom suite intended for Freddie and the baby. Temporarily, the little boy was put in a bedroom at the front (after Tom had sponged black mould off the walls, removed loose plaster and stuck back peeling wallpaper). Freddie missed his colourfully decorated bedroom at Flowerpots, but for his new one Belinda won him over with a prize catch of animal posters. The baby, who would eventually have the smaller of the two rooms, would be sleeping in with Belinda and Tom.

Over the landing, Miranda had insisted that Cameron installed a new bathroom suite as a priority. But plumbing was not his strongest point and when she complained that the toilet was flushing hot water, he asked why she was moaning about having a new bidet 'just like the big houses!'

It was a hot summer and throughout the house everything felt damp, even the bedding and cushions. Cameron's suggestion to hire dehumidifiers was taken up and they were used in various rooms, humming day and night extracting bucketful's of water. In the lounge, a gauge Tom bought to measure the humidity remained on Maximum for weeks, despite increasingly warm weather. Eventually the little needle slowly started returning to Normal.

Haggleby Hall was yearning to be loved and as the Flowers and Maclaren's consolidated their efforts, putting their hearts and souls into their new home, they bonded like glue. Captivated by their fancies of living like lords and ladies, they buzzed with energy and enthusiasm as they became immersed in an exciting adventure. Certain friends were curiously envious of their incongruous, upper-class lifestyle, while others admired their vision of the mansion restored. Both Tom and Belinda's parents thought they were downright foolhardy, while Miranda's mother was reservedly supportive. Meanwhile, in the village word was spreading about "the Hippies of Haggleby Hall" and it took the Flowers and Maclaren's some time to convince people otherwise.

That morning in the bedroom Belinda's reverie was shattered as Tom blew out his electric shaver in the wastepaper basket and reminded her: 'Don't forget we've got the scaffolders coming today to do the front, ready for the re-rendering work.'

Her tummy felt in need of scaffolding as she climbed out of bed and struggled into her maternity jeans. She desperately wanted her body back, particularly with so much work to do around the house, not to mention the garden. Nearing her time, she longed for the birth; then they would not only have Freddie and their new 'orphan', Haggleby Hall, to consider, but another child, who was not so likely to receive the attention Freddie had as a new born.

She could hardly believe that any day now there would be a new bloom among the Flowers and she prayed it would be pink and pretty. She and Tom were still undecided about a name - as long as it wasn't Iris, Petunia or Rose! Her daily attire was the Haggleby Hall 'uniform' – jeans, T-shirt and sweatshirt, which she and the others had to wear most of the time to deal with the endless dirty chores. She went into the bathroom and picked up the bucket of Freddie's nappies Tom had rinsed out ready for the washing machine. It was a job he could do without, but she could no longer kneel over the bath to do it. Miranda had persevered with Ollie's potty training and he was dry during the day, but Freddie refused to co-operate, instead enjoying the attention of being sat on the potty as many times as Belinda chose. He rarely performed, instead leaving a puddle on the floor a few minutes later, which she believed was his way of seeking attention. She was frustrated at having so little time to give him, but there always seemed to be so much else to do.

Going along the landing she felt a strange inner glow. Perhaps the novelty of its expanse had not yet worn off, or today He-she would come into the world. Poor child, about to be born of madcap parents living a chaotic, unconventional lifestyle! The sound of Freddie playing downstairs with Ollie surprised her, as she thought he was still asleep. They were on their "ride-on's", competing in their first race of the day. Squeals echoed round the hall to the tune of plastic wheels thundering on the flagstone floor and honking red-nosed hooters.

Tom followed her from the bedroom as Miranda simultaneously appeared from the Maclaren's corridor. She looked fresh and bright, wearing tight denims and an orange T-shirt with slinky black felines on each breast and 'A Purr-fect Pair!' emblazoned beneath.

'Good morning and how are you both today?' she chirruped.

67

'We hope as well as your pair,' Tom replied suggestively.

Belinda thrust the nappy bucket into his hand to take down to the washing machine: 'I envy you, Miranda, having done with nappies. I can't wait to get Freddie potty trained - and to think we'll have this all over again.'

'Everything will be fine. Perhaps for the next baby you should think about disposable nappies?'

'Great idea,' chipped in Tom, 'but we need disposable income for such luxuries and bricks and mortar come first.'

'Talking of income, we need to discuss the bills,' answered Miranda, volunteering to be the Old Hag's treasurer. She might have been naive in some directions, but having come from a large family with little cash, she was adept at handling money. Cameron always left domestic finances to her, frequently using the excuse for his empty pockets.

'Perhaps we can have a get-together later. I'd better be off, I'm late for work,' said Tom, quickly kissing Belinda.

'Before you go, is the septic tank still being emptied today?'

'Meant to tell you, Cam and I thought better of it, with the scaffolding going up, so I've changed it to next week.'

As he rushed downstairs to negotiate the Haggleby Hall Grand Prix, she continued her grumblings with Miranda. 'This baby had better come soon. God knows why we make the same mistake twice.'

'Guess it was fun at the time... by the way, I meant to beg Tom's services this weekend.' Belinda glowered.

'What I mean is his plumbing is much better than Cameron's and our...umh, bidet...toilet, it's too hot.'

'Oh, you mean your hot flushes!'

She nodded, wincing. 'Ollie pulled the handle while I was on it and I can hardly sit down this morning.'

'I'll have an urgent word. Now I'd better get on - another day at the fun factory!'

Loud screams from the boy racers challenged her eardrums and with more than one life to safeguard, she dashed across the circuit as fast as the other would let her. Competing with the din, she ordered Freddie to breakfast.

The Flowers' long kitchen was originally a conservatory. Historic photographs discovered in an old box in Ollie's wardrobe showed its slanting glass roof and a huge window in the far wall, which, now filled in, was just visible in outline. It had been one of three, the remaining two, with elegant frames curving up to the ceiling, overlooking the drive. They already had existing curtains, which were difficult to pull on their old brass runners, but Tom said unless he won the football pools they would have to do for the time being.

Years before, the conservatory's pinnacle-shaped glass roof had been replaced with felt, which was now giving out. Rainwater seeping through over time had formed cloudy patterns on the plasterboard ceiling, which in some places had bellied. The Flowers had yet to find out just how waterproof the kitchen was because it hadn't rained since before they moved in. The pastry white walls had flaked in many places, but were much improved since Tom had brushed them down, aided by an excited Freddie wearing his anorak to play in the 'snow showers.'

At least Belinda had got the kitchen into some working order. Before moving in, Agatha had invited her to spend an afternoon cleaning it, at the risk of catching botulism! She had thrown out rusty food tins, years-out-of-date cereal boxes and strange clumps of dehydrated culture. The stainless steel sink took bags of elbow grease, as did the totally impractical, white melamine work surfaces ringed with tea. Though dated and in dire need of refitting and re-decorating, the room at least now looked sanitary.

Belinda and Tom had decided to keep the white table and plastic turquoise chairs for the time being as they couldn't afford anything else, but they had ditched the glass-fronted chiller to make way for their own, more modest chest freezer. She was delighted to learn that there was a 'pick your own' farm up the road and romantically determined to stack it with their favourite fruits and vegetables.

How she missed the Raeburn at Flowerpots! At least she and Tom no longer had to go to the coke shed, fill the scuttle, open the dampers, stoke the fire and wait a good half hour before there was enough heat to cook. Now, she had to make do with an old Baby Belling, which worked perfectly apart from two broken rings. Tom had promised to replace them at the earliest opportunity, but they were way down his list. At least he had "de-scaberised" the oven - another of Tom's made-up words that should have been in the dictionary! Among his many endearing qualities was his unique turn of phrase, much of which had been coined from his father during his early life. Tom's cleverly contrived words and obscure quotations carried them through many trying moments.

Despite advancing pregnancy, Belinda was able to tackle some tasks, such as the parquet floor mottled by rain from the leaking roof. She found their latest toy, an electric polisher that Tom had rescued from the local dump, a breeze. It required little effort, gliding round the kitchen like an ice skater on speed. The fun machine reminded her of the one used by the caretaker back in her schooldays and the smell of polish of the beginning of each new term. The kitchen lights, two long fluorescent tubes suspended by chains, similarly prompted thoughts of her early classrooms.

There were two doors; one with decorative carvings echoing the curved window frames, which opened on to the lounge, the other, taller and thinner, with a shiny brass knob, to the outer hall. Here there were double doors into the inner hall and a long thin cupboard with small windows, perfect for accommodating the boys' "ride-on's" and household paraphernalia. The huge double front doors were fortress-style with substantial bolts fastening to the floor. Normally, the right hand door was used for coming and going, the left one only being opened for large deliveries. The doorbell, sounded by a knob, was so feeble it could hardly be heard more than a few feet away, so Tom devised a "Heath Robinson" type contraption with an old school bell, wire and rope. Resounding in the hall, it proved highly effective and could be heard from all over the house.

Every morning Belinda would pop out to collect the milk from a crate on the doorstep. If she put a note in an empty bottle the milkman would leave other groceries and usually she was impressed by the standard of delivery. But one day her expectations plummeted as she went to pick up the wholemeal loaf she had ordered. She was horrified to see the plastic bag had been spiked! Opening it, a large hole ran through several slices. An air bubble couldn't have caused that, surely? So what the dickens had?

Freddie and Ollie, who often played with sticks, were immediately summoned from their "ride-on's", smiling mischievously.

'Do either of you know how this bread came to have a hole in it?'

They shook their heads, grinning blankly. Cameron, coming from his car, took a look. 'I'd say it was a very big blue-tit.'

Unconvinced, Belinda eyed the boys suspiciously. 'I've never known blue-tits peck bread. They usually go for cream on the milk - but that's in the depths of winter, not July.'

Eyeing Freddie, she threatened: 'No more sweeties if you go anywhere near the milk crate, understand?'

He nodded solemnly as Cameron repeated her threat to Ollie. As they were going inside, there was the sound of a heavy vehicle rattling along the drive. Belinda looked round to see in the approaching dust cloud a lorry laden with poles and boards.

'Ah, just the people I've been waiting for,' enthused Cameron, asking Belinda to look after Ollie as Miranda had gone shopping, so he could set the scaffolders to work.

Back inside, Belinda put Ollie with Freddie at the kitchen table. After wiping it she took three balls of play dough from the fridge, which Miranda had made the day before. 'Right, you two, can you make me some circus animals - lions, tigers, horses, that sort of thing?'

They busied themselves, cutting the blue, green and pink balls with plastic knives and noisily smacking the pieces into shapes with their palms. Belinda managed to spend an hour clearing up the kitchen and rewarded their good behaviour with a beaker of squash and little box of raisins. While they were chomping away she went into the lounge to hear the sound of metal resonating. The scaffolders were hard at work, the view from the French window already obscured by poles and planks.

When she returned to the kitchen the strange play dough shapes had been given raisin eyes, ears and other body parts. The boys introduced her to their 'animals' using loud farmyard noises. She praised them with gusto, her ears ringing, and was wondering what to suggest next when Freddie pleaded: 'Mummy, wanna see wot men doing.'

'Well, if I take you out there, you must stay with me and promise to be good!'

Nodding, they jumped from their booster seats and scampered off through the front door. She was relieved to see Cameron on the lawn, checking progress, and they joined him a healthy distance from the activity. Sitting on the grass in the sunshine, the boys were entranced watching the steel frame grow. A cacophony of clanging filled her ears as four muscular males worked effortlessly extracting poles from the lorry and bolting them into place before laying planks along. They swung through the bars with monkey-like precision, balancing precariously as they secured the rising assembly.

Belinda shared the boys' fascination. 'It's amazing to watch. I would hate my man having to risk life and limb doing that every day. All Tom has to worry about is a sticky shutter or fogging the film.'

'Let's think ourselves lucky we can at least afford somebody else to get it done,' said Cameron.

Later, when Tom returned from work, Belinda and Freddie joined him to view the finished result. Belinda thought the scaffolding mounted on three levels made The Old Hag look like a caged animal desperate to be freed. But within a few weeks it would be at liberty again to show off its smooth new coat, its aesthetic appeal restored after many years of neglect; the prospect made her feel like a child eagerly awaiting Christmas.

When Belinda took Freddie inside to put him to bed, the hour seemed later because the scaffolding darkened the inside of the house. As she watched him splashing in the bath, she felt claustrophobic. The evening sun usually brightened Freddie's room, but the reduced light made it dismal. Even his animal posters seemed to pale into the dark blue wallpaper. For a moment she wished they were back in his cosy little bedroom at Flowerpots, but she quickly re-focused on his request for a Noddy story.

After the day's excitement Freddie was soon asleep. Weary herself, Belinda joined Tom and Cameron on the terrace for a welcome drink. Miranda, having performed mirror rituals putting Ollie to bed, appeared with Grace a few seconds later, still looking fresh as a daisy.

They talked about everything from the scaffolding and the holey wholemeal, to Tom's day at the studio and whether they would have enough money to build a swimming pool.

Grace, who sought them out to beg an onion, stayed for a gin and gave a brief run-down on the latest developments in her life. 'I enjoyed dinner with Roderick. We never stopped talking and he's invited me down to his hotel in Dorset. I think I shall take up his invitation.'

'Oooh, lucky you!' piped up Miranda.

'You'd better behave yourself, Mitts. I wouldn't trust that man as far as I could see him,' cautioned Cameron, addressing his mother like a teenager.

Tom, concerned what Grace had said about sleeping badly since moving in, urged her to go. 'The sea air will do you good and we'll press on with sorting out the flat.'

'Ok, I might fly down if I can get the Piper for a few days.'

'Does Amy Johnson fancy coming to The Mucky Duck for another gin?' asked Cameron, hoping for an opportunity to give her a word of advice about her new male friend.

Knowing what she was in for, Grace declined, saying she needed an early night. When Miranda turned down his invitation for a pint in preference for her TV soap, followed by Tom, with phone calls to make, he sweet-talked Belinda to join him.

'Go on, we can eat later, you've got a casserole in the oven,' encouraged Tom. 'Besides, once the baby is born you won't get the opportunity for a while.'

The previous night, while Cameron was on his way back from a car delivery in Devon, Tom had taken Miranda to the pub while Belinda had stayed behind babysitting - so no further encouragement was needed.

Besides, Belinda enjoyed Cameron's company. Like most people he could be moody at times, but was usually amiable and fun, especially after a pint or two. She smiled as she recalled Tom's story about Cameron working at his village pub one evening some years before. He and a friend were minding the pub in the landlord's absence and Cameron's friend bet him a fiver to do a half-hour's 'bare-tending'. Always game for a dare, Cameron took off his trousers and managed to keep his male attributes quietly to himself until just before the time was up, when the barmaid pulled the wrong 'pump handle'. It was a dare he had never lived down.

The Mucky Duck, an eighteenth century inn next to Haggleby village pond, looked inviting with its colourful hanging baskets and people clustered around tables in the neatly kept garden. Belinda had visited once before with Tom before moving in, and loved its beamed ceilings, inglenook fireplace and polished brasses.

As she followed Cameron through the door, the landlord, a tall burly man with cherry blossom cheeks, greeted them. 'Are you two new round here? What can I get you?'

'We've just moved into Haggleby Hall a couple of weeks back,' said Cameron.

The landlord looked bemused. 'Oh, so you live at the same place as that couple in here last night?'

'Ah yes, you mean Tom and my wife, Miranda. I'm Cameron by the way and this is Belinda, Tom's wife. Pleasure to meet you, uhm…?'

'Nigel.'

He ordered a pint of Harvey's, a St Clement's for Belinda and offered Nigel a drink. The landlord took Cameron's five-pound note, handing over the change. 'So, there are **two** couples living at the old place, then?'

'That's right,' said Belinda, repeating Cameron's words: 'Me and my husband, Tom, Cameron and his wife, Miranda, our sons and Cameron's mother, Granny Grace.'

Confused, Nigel eyed Belinda's bump. Sensing his next question, she confirmed: 'Tom's and my baby is due any day now.'

'So, you *all* live in that big house?'

Cameron, in wind-up mode, reaffirmed: 'Yep, we're all under one roof. Great place to bring up the kids, lots of rooms, acres of garden, no nosey neighbours to worry about…so if we fancy, we can all sunbathe in our birthday suits.'

Nigel took the next order, his eyes popping almost ahead of the wine cork. Two women being served tittered. 'Sunbathe in your what?' he asked, incredulously.

'Our *bathing* suits,' Belinda quickly corrected. 'We're thinking of building a swimming pool.'

Nigel rang the till, handed the women change and asked: 'so, who is Granny what's-her-name?'

'That's my mum, Grace. She's everyone's granny, really. We're just one big family.'

Nigel's eyebrows rose. 'That old place needs a hell of a lot of work from what I've heard. It was on the market ages. The owner disappeared, you know? Funny business. His wife let the house go... I wondered about her... she rented it out and that pop group moved in. All they ever did was shake the woodworm about with their racket. Just as well the place is out in the sticks.'

Belinda wanted to press Nigel further about the Fielding-Winters family, but his questions kept rolling. 'How many bedrooms did you say it had?'

'I didn't...lots,' said Cameron.

'Eight, to be precise,' volunteered Belinda.

'There's plenty of room for Hippies, then?'

'Oh yes, Hippies,' said Cameron, playing the game. 'We're all for Love and Peace, aren't we Belinda? And love our "Flowers"!' He pecked her cheek.

Nigel rang the bell above the bar, well before "time", sparking loud protests. 'Now listen, everybody, I have a toast - to the Hippies of Haggleby Hall!'

Some locals responded amiably, others looked aghast. Mortified, Belinda went beetroot. She would have crawled under the table if she had fit. 'I'll get you later, Cameron!'

He waggled his tongue. 'I can't wait, darling!'

CHAPTER SEVEN

Express Delivery

Standing in a queue at the village butcher's, Belinda overheard two middle-aged women talking: 'Them Hippies down at Haggleby Hall, they're having the 'ouse done up by Barry Basher. My Frank saw 'im in the pub and 'e says there's enough work to keep 'im going for months.'

'That old place - I bet 'e's got 'is work cut out with that lot!'

Barry, whom Cameron had christened 'the medallion man', had grown up in the village and was known by everybody. Signed up to do the restoration work at Haggleby Hall, he was now part of the local gossip.

Back at home Belinda told the others what she had heard. It seemed their 'Hippies' label was here to stay. She wondered how long it would take people to accept there was no 'funny business' going on at the Hall.

Later that week, Belinda had to throw away more bread delivered by the milkman because something had got at it again. Freddie and Ollie heard her fulminating on the doorstep and hastily retreated to the Maclaren's. She couldn't believe it was the boys when the prospect of losing their sweeties was at stake, so she decided to ring the dairy to complain:

'The bread your milkman delivered this morning has a large hole in it. Can you explain that? It looks like something with big teeth has bored into it. I've had to throw half away and I'm not sure we fancy eating the rest. I am very cross; this is the second time this has happened in a few days.'

The man on the line, speaking in what Belinda could only think was the old Sussex dialect, was far from reassuring. 'Well, madam, all milk and growceries from Gubbins

Dairy are in perfeck condition when delivered. Sounds like you got rats! I'd git on to the cansel if I was yoh.'

He suggested she left a secure box on the doorstep for deliveries. Belinda would ask Tom to find a sturdy one from the cellar. But as for rats, well, that was highly unlikely with Ramrod prowling around. Agatha had probably asked Miranda to keep Roderick's cat because he knew there were rats. As if Belinda was psychic, there was a knock at the kitchen door and her friend appeared. She had offered to take Freddie off her hands for the day, as she and Ollie were meeting a friend at Tiggles Farm, where children could stroke the animals and play in the adventure playground. She handed her Freddie's picnic box.

When she told Miranda about the bread, she volunteered to get another loaf while they were out, adding: 'I'll throw Ramrod out before the milkman comes.'

'What did the milkman do to deserve that?' teased Belinda.

'You have more important things to worry about. While we're out you put your feet up and have a rest - that baby can't be far off now.'

The boys scampered off excitedly. Belinda watched as Miranda transferred Freddie's special seat from her car, a canary yellow Ford Fiesta, into her Fiat Panda, a fluorescent pea green, parked alongside. Waving them off, she was relieved to have the day all to herself. Along the drive 'the medallion man' was filling the cement mixer. A gold eagle nestled in his dark chest hair, adorning a beefy set of pectoral muscles. His shoulders were bulbous and his tanned, shorts-clad body was taut with years of labouring on building sites. He was middle-aged, with greying temples, gold fillings and a beer belly, but Belinda and Miranda agreed he had a certain sex appeal. A likeable rogue, he knew when to turn on the charm.

'Hello, Mrs Flowers, you're looking radiant this morning. How's the bump coming along? It's more of a mountain than a mole hill now, aint it?'

'Morning, Barry, I am fine, thank you. Not long to go now. How are you?'

'Well, if it weren't for this terrible toothache everything would be hunky-dory. I'm off to the dentist later to get it sorted. It's driving me to distraction.'

'Let's hope it's not extraction,' she said, tongue in cheek.

Barry was a one-man band apart from an eighteen-year-old apprentice builder, who spent most of his time mixing the pug to fill the fissures his boss made banging out the decayed rendering. Watching Barry at work reminded Belinda of a dentist filling a tooth. His hammer pounded the crumbling walls rhythmically; thump… thump… thump reverberating in her head. The walls seemed to vibrate with every blow. There was no escaping the noise. Despite her disquiet, she was physically blooming. Her cheeks glowed, more likely from the hot weather, and, as Barry indelicately put it, her molehill had grown into a mountain! She was enjoying some respite from He-she's poking and prodding. Perhaps her large bundle was saving energy for the big day.

With a day to herself Belinda would have likely gone upstairs to see Grace for a cup of tea, but she had gone to stay at Roderick's hotel. Cameron had left for work, so she was alone in the house. Unable to stomach coffee since her pregnancy, she made herself tea and decided to read - a rare treat! She retreated to the Maclaren's lounge, furthest away from the noise, knowing they wouldn't mind under the circumstances. She chose the comfiest armchair, opened her book, but just couldn't relax. She kept reading over the same words. There was too much on her mind. Finishing her drink, she decided to have a walk to the lake, which she had yet to visit.

79

She opened the mahogany doors to the ballroom and left through the French doors. The hammering noise rose an octave, though was more bearable without the walls resonating. She crossed the front lawn that Cameron and Tom had rough cut for the first time the previous weekend. The mowers from their previous homes had proved woefully inadequate. It had taken a whole day just to do the main lawn; it was so long it had to be scythed first. Watching the others raking up the vast mounds of cut grass had reminded her of a photograph of her great-grandfather with his threshing machine and his workers posing with pitch forks during haymaking. He would have been comfortably off, but her mother said he was a drinker and had to sell his thresher to pay off his debts. Belinda wasn't proud of her ancestry, recalling the story of how he used to arrive home from the pub and her great-grandmother would wait until he was comatose before going through his pockets for pennies to feed their nine children. Harvesting all those years ago must have been magical; the sweet, rich smell of freshly cut grass, men swinging scythes, women raking up, excited children rolling in the hay and, highlight of the day, the family picnic lunch.

The Old Hag's grass looked chewed rather than cut, but at least the generous sprinkling of buttercups had disappeared. Tom assured everyone that once it was mown it would soon start to look like a lawn. He was keeping an eye open in the small ads for a second-hand tractor, which would take a fraction of the time of their petrol mowers.

Belinda walked round the back of the house, where a long rhododendron hedge separated a narrow strip of lawn from an abandoned area. It had once been the site of a swimming pool, with patches of blue peeping through the weedy undergrowth. She and the others had talked about resurrecting it, but with far more important work to be done, she wondered whether they ever would. Passing through a half-open wooden field gate, she could feel the sun tantalising her neck and arms. Fortunately, she had automatically picked up her straw hat sitting on the Maclaren's piano in the ballroom.

Thistles and brambles pronounced themselves as she picked her way through tangled grass. Passing through a small group of sycamores halfway across the field, she could see the lake coming into view. It was much larger than she had imagined. Agatha had said that after Uncle Milton disappeared, Aunt Elizabeth had rented it to a local fishing club.

She joined a path circling the lake, occasionally broken by a wooden boardwalk and fishing stage. It passed beneath a thick canopy of trees, barely penetrated by sunshine. The coolness was welcoming, but her inhospitable surroundings made her uneasy. Perhaps it was the contrast of her passing from bright light into deep shade, or remembering the faded 'Trespassers Will Be Prosecuted' sign on the gate, pointing out that she should not have been there at all. If she were caught, she wondered as an owner of Haggleby Hall whether justice would be done, but the lake looked deserted and the rotting boardwalk rarely visited. She had to pick her way carefully through undergrowth invading her path. The further she went the more uncomfortable she felt. It was strangely silent, with no sign of life other than a few ducks bobbing on the water. A few unhappy moments along the boardwalk she encountered a missing section of planks and decided to go back.

Returning to the head of the lake, she paused to take a closer look at the boathouse. Trees were threatening to obscure the sadly neglected, decaying structure. Although some cladding was missing, it was basically in-tact, its rotting wood clawed by ivy.

Belinda recalled Agatha's story in the kitchen the day they viewed the house, about her and Roderick going fishing with Uncle Milton as children. Looking across the murky brown expanse of water, she pictured them in a rowing boat packed with fishing tackle, a lunchbox and flask of tea, their rods cast out as they eyed the water earnestly. Agatha had described their catches as 'mainly tiddlers'. She said that if it rained, Uncle Milton rowed into the boathouse and they would climb the ladder to a little room above and enjoy their picnic in the dry. It all must have been such an adventure!

Now, as Belinda peered inside, the ladder was missing most of its rungs, the mooring area, what was left of it, illuminated by sunlight spilling through missing roof slats on to the water. Gazing into the depths, she wondered what dark secrets they held. Had Uncle Milton become bait for the fish that he had so loved to catch? She shivered at the thought of how poor Agatha, Roderick and Aunt Elizabeth must have felt after he vanished. And never knowing what happened to him - it must have been unbearable!

Once more her eyes wandered across the deserted lake, rippling in a sudden breeze and she had a sudden urge to return home. Hurrying out of the shadows, she left her wild imaginings behind and was relieved to feel the sun on her back again. A sudden contraction returned her to the moment, forcing her to stop for a couple of minutes to breathe through. 'Ooh, that was a bad one!' She had been aware of her tummy tightening several times that morning, but contractions had almost become a way of life. When the pain had passed she quickly crossed the field, but approaching the broken gate, she felt strangely wet. Warm liquid was running down her legs. Her waters had broken - and in the middle of nowhere! At least she was wearing a loose patterned dress that wouldn't show the stains. Her heart was racing. She forced herself to breathe deeply, trying not to panic. 'OK, this is for real this time… this is not a false alarm.' Then it dawned on her - there was nobody home! Only Barry Basher was there with his young worker. He would have to take her to hospital.

Moving as quickly as she could, she was on auto-pilot, as if watching someone else. She managed to reach the gate without another contraction. But as she rounded the rhododendron hedge and saw the house, there was no sign of activity. The scaffolding looked deserted, triggering alarm bells. Of course, Barry had gone to the dentist! He must have given his young worker the afternoon off. She had to get to the phone!

Crossing the side lawn she felt desperately alone and never in greater need of help. She despaired at the thought of stories of women in Third World countries giving birth by the roadside, then carrying on their daily round. But this was England and she should be on her way to the maternity hospital! Suddenly, she thought she heard whistling. It was hard to place, but was definitely human! 'Hello? Hello-ooo?' she called.

A lithesome figure appeared from shadows on the scaffolding near her and Tom's bedroom window. Thank God, it was Barry's worker! She felt a lump in her throat, asking a question to which she already knew the answer: 'Is Barry around?'

'No, he's gone to the dentist.' The youth must have noticed her distress: 'Are you OK?'

She struggled to hide the wobble in her voice, praying he would keep calm at what she was about to say: 'My baby is on the way. I need you to call an ambulance, but don't worry, when I had my son, Freddie, I was in labour 12 hours before he was born.'

Why was she telling a stranger this; because it might reassure him not to panic? It had been such a life-changing moment. She had been two weeks late and adamant about not being induced. She had decided to follow her NCT teacher's advice to make love, supposedly a way of starting the baby off. After some weeks' abstinence Tom had been all for it, and sure enough, her labour had started later that

83

afternoon. She had been so laid back. With contractions still an hour apart, she had cajoled him into meeting friends for a curry, also meant to stimulate birth. That evening she had been ravenous and enjoyed the meal more than Tom and their friends, who had stiffened in their seats every time she had labour pains. After, she and Tom had gone back to their house for coffee, before going home to bed. It was not until two o'clock next morning that she had finally succumbed to having to go hospital. Poor Tom! It had been quite a scramble getting there and with hours to spare! What she would have done without him at Freddie's birth she could not imagine. How she needed him now, to comfort her and hold her hand, but he was miles away and it would be a miracle if he made it back from London in time.

The youth put down his tools and hastily clambered down the ladder, two rungs at a time. When he reached her she was slightly surprised by his composure, considering what must be, to a young man, a daunting situation. 'Don't worry, Mrs Flowers. I'll go and call an ambulance.'

'There's a phone on our kitchen wall and a pad on the unit with numbers for Cuckfield Hospital and Tom's work.

'Now please don't worry. I'll just go and wash my hands, then make the calls. You sit on the bench there and try to relax. I'll be back in two ticks.'

Belinda's apprehension eased as the youth - she didn't even know his name - took control. Her mind in a whirl, she flopped with relief on the garden seat. His absence was interminable. With the contraction over and her waters broken, she was surprised how normal she was feeling. Her mind began to wander and, suddenly, her eyes were drawn to a stone slab in the grass a few feet away. She had never seen it before. It must have been exposed after Tom had cut down brambles. Curiosity fired, she struggled to her feet to examine it. She could make out some sort of inscription:

84

BILLIE…   June 5, 1957, to Octob…
Flying with God's Angels. Rest in pea…

Being unable to read the dates in full was frustrating. The stone had to be a memorial to a cherished pet; a dog or cat, perhaps, or a bird? Yet she felt somehow that 'Billie' could have been a person, of what age she couldn't read. But there was no time for further conjecture as her abdomen started tightening again, the pain becoming so intense she had to cling to the bench as she breathed through. The youth stepped out of the French doors and, seeing her contorted face, dashed over, taking her hand. She squeezed it until the pain relented. His voice was gentle and reassuring. 'You're gonna be OK, Mrs Flowers. I've rung the hospital and an ambulance is on its way. I've also spoken to your husband. He's coming straight back and will meet you there. Now, when you feel ready, I'll help you inside.'

Belinda had no time to be amazed by his calmness and obediently let him assist. In all her wild imaginings she would never have believed that an 18-year-old builder's apprentice was the only person who could help at such a critical time. The idea of giving birth now was as scary to contemplate as it was that day at the church fete a few weeks before. Perhaps the present situation was fractionally less so - at least she wouldn't have half the village looking on. But, unlike previously, this was for real!

According to her calculations, she was two days overdue and her contractions were stronger and closer together. Not daring to leave the bench, she insisted: 'I think I'd better wait here for the ambulance. Would you mind going inside and fetching a blanket from the airing cupboard? Please hurry!' She hated being alone with the 'bearing down' feeling she remembered from Freddie's birth, warning her that the baby would be born soon. She prayed for the ambulance to arrive.

As the youth shot out of the French door carrying a blanket, she was struck by another contraction. He coaxed her to her feet and she gripped his strong shoulders. 'Now do your panting,' he instructed gently. Belinda was impressed by his know-how and obeyed, drawing short sharp breaths. Thanks to NCT classes, she wanted to give birth naturally, as she had with Freddie. But this time there was not the luxury of a maternity hospital delivery suite with "gas and air"! She remembered the weird sensation of inhaling copious amounts; her mind detached, the extreme pain hers but not hers, as if it was being borne by somebody else on the bed. She thought of Tom spending what seemed like hours standing over her, holding her hand, his words, soft and encouraging as he trickled water into her mouth from a sponge. She remembered the bright lights above and a sea of faces … only now the lights were sunshine rays splintering the lime tree leaves and the faces, two paramedics. A mask covered her nose and gripping it, she pushed with all her might, her mind floating in blue-sky obscurity.

In the ambulance, Belinda caressed her daughter, soft and warm. The satin form was suckling her and although she felt exhausted, she was high on adrenaline. Giving birth was the ultimate bittersweet experience and she acknowledged the same feeling of *arrival* she had witnessed with Freddie. She so wanted to share her ecstasy with Tom, who would be on his way to the hospital.

When she had been put to bed in a little room, the youth knocked the door and came in, his freckly face smiling delightedly.

'You were amazing!' she said. 'I cannot thank you enough…sorry, I don't even know your name?'

'Carl. Carl Edwards.'

'Then we shall call our daughter Carla, Carla Flowers,' she said triumphantly.

The ambulance man appeared and asked if he could peep at the baby, now she was all cleaned up.

'You came in the nick of time,' she thanked him.

'I could see you were already in good hands, Mrs Flowers. This young man here certainly had the situation well under control.'

'My mum had six children and I helped when the last two were born. Our home was like a maternity hospital - she popped out babies like shelling peas!' said Carl, joyfully.

Belinda was feeling rather shell-shocked; having Carla had been a bit of a battle! Then who better to aid her recovery than her other knight in shining armour, Tom, breezing in with a huge bunch of flowers and broad smile.

CHAPTER EIGHT

Flights of Fancy

Armed with a clothes basket, Belinda paused outside the front door to examine Tom and Cameron's progress on a trench for Calor gas. It was to link the house with a huge tank being installed round the back. The spouses had been drilling a few days (the noise was excruciating) as a central heating engineer was due to begin work inside shortly. Upstairs, heavy cast iron radiators were being replaced with modern slim-line ones and downstairs, wall convectors installed. For the hall, an ingenious system had been devised for a fan to be fixed to the ceiling to blow warm air back down to the hall. Both the Flowers and Maclaren's were to have separate 'combi' boilers, as was Grace. It was quite exciting and reassuring to know the place would be properly heated for the winter, but Belinda dreaded the ensuing chaos.

Turning towards the clothes line, she glimpsed a small, white feathery form vanishing through the front door. Was it a fox, a cat, a rodent? It wouldn't survive long if Ramrod was on the prowl. Slightly apprehensive, she gingerly followed it into the hall, praying that the door to the lounge, where Carla was sleeping in her carrycot, was closed.

A hen was circling the stone floor. Belinda hated to coin the phrase 'like a headless chicken', but the poor thing looked totally disorientated. She instinctively grabbed her mac from the coat stand, fondly imagining she might catch it. Startled, it launched itself clumsily on to the sideboard and plonked straight in the middle of her vase of dried flowers. They must have been rather prickly, for there was an almighty 'Beeurk!'

Fearing the noise might wake Carla, Belinda closed the lounge door. Typically, everyone was out. Tom and Freddie had gone to the ironmongers, Cameron was working and Miranda and Ollie were food shopping. As usual, Ramrod was not in sight; that darned cat was never around when there was a job to be done. She sidled over to open Maclaren's door; perhaps he would smell the intruder and chase it out?

Despite her village upbringing, Belinda had no experience of handling hens and fearing its pecking abilities, approached it in bull-fight fashion. The creature, comfortably ensconced in its new nest, glared defiantly with cross-eyes, puffing its feathers to announce a long term stay. Belinda had visions of eggs tumbling into her dried flowers - probably not a bad thing!

Suddenly, the kitchen wall phone rang and she was relieved to go and answer it.

'Hello.' Her voice was shaky.

'Good morning. Are you one of the new people at Haggleby Hall?'

'Yes. Belinda Flowers speaking.'

'You don't know me, but I'm your neighbour Nellie Gregory. Me and my 'usband Ed live in the gardener's cottage up the drive.'

'Oh, hello there, it's lovely to speak to you. We've been meaning to come and ...'

'Sorry to bother you,' Mrs Gregory interrupted, 'but you wouldn't 'ave seen an 'en wandering about there, would you?'

'You mean the one sitting in my dried flowers on the sideboard?'

'If it's white with funny eyes that would be our Chloe; she does daft things like that. We've bin looking for 'er everywhere. She keeps getting out of the 'en run. We must get her wings clipped! If it's OK with you, I'll be over to collect 'er directly.'

Trying to hide the urgency in her voice, Belinda asked that she came sooner rather than later.

'Right-o, be there in a few ticks. Oh, and if Chloe Clutterbuck is a bother you could put some bits of brown bread down. She loves that.'

'Don't I know,' said Belinda, suddenly realising the identity of the phantom loaf-pecker!

As she replaced the receiver, there was a knock at the kitchen door and Pru Payne appeared. That's all she needed; her health visitor, arriving as usual unannounced, as if she were trying to catch Belinda doing something unimaginable to Carla! Pru, well into her 40s, was an 'old-school' health visitor. She looked very prim and proper in her navy and white uniform, her hair wound in a perfect bun and angular face framed with large-rimmed black spectacles. She had visited daily since Carla was born ten days before, each time lecturing Belinda on what she termed "baby craft". Her lectures on cleanliness and ordered living (which at Haggleby Hall were tall orders) drove Belinda witless. Undoubtedly, livestock in the house would be a black mark on Pru's report. But before Belinda could tell her about Chloe Clutterbuck, the hen struggled out of the dried flowers and fluttered off the sideboard, clucking. Rounding on it, Belinda clapped her hands: 'Get out! Get out!' It only made the errant bird even more frightened, and ducking and diving, it took to the stairs. Then, to Belinda's complete surprise, Pru put her black wallet on the pew and gave chase. A bizarre game of "follow my leader" had Belinda bringing up the rear. On the landing, Chloe paused and Pru tiptoed stealthily forward. When she was nearly upon it, the hen took off with a whoosh, narrowly clearing the banister, and descended awkwardly to the floor.

Downstairs, Belinda tried cornering the slippery customer, but it was not up for grabs! It rang rings round her and suddenly took off, causing a strong breeze, and flew - straight into the arms of a grey-haired women! Knowing her mistress, Chloe was immediately calm and seemed relieved when Nellie Gregory tucked her into a basket she had brought with her.

'Perfect timing, thank you!' said Belinda, hugely relieved, and invited them into the kitchen for tea.

They sat at the table, Pru bouncing Carla on her knee with intermittent coos from Nellie, sounding not unlike a contented hen. Belinda seized the opportunity to apologise to the old woman for the drilling noise, explaining about the new central heating. 'It's going to be a real mess, with floorboards coming up, walls being drilled and no hot water for a few days. I don't know how I'm going to cope...' she suddenly regretted sounding like a drama queen, especially within Pru's earshot.

'You'll 'ave your 'ands full with two young uns to look after - and I thought keeping hens was an 'eadache!' Nellie commiserated.

'It'll be good when it's done. I'll just have to be organised.

Now Pru had heard her challenges, Belinda prayed she wouldn't bang on about them, which of course she did: 'Humh, that all sounds a bit much for a new mum. You know what hormones are like. It can be a very emotional time, and exhausting, as if you haven't got enough on your plate with a new baby and young son to look after. I would strongly advise you to make other arrangements for the children!'

Sensing Belinda's uneasiness, Nellie chipped in: 'You could always bring 'em up to us for a bath.'

Belinda's face flushed. 'I couldn't possibly impose on you like that.' She was desperate to reassure Pru that everything would be ok, but Chloe clucking wildly outside the kitchen door stopped her short. Nellie rushed out, followed by Belinda and Pru, to see the basket lying on its side and Ramrod clawing the wicker demonically.

'Shoo, you blasted cat!' yelled Belinda as Nellie clapped her hands.

91

Ramrod glared with steely eyes and darted out.

'Goodness me, I hope all this doesn't upset Chloe's layin'!' said Nellie, taken aback. 'I'd better get her 'ome.'

As Belinda waved her off, Pru unlocked her car to leave, but not before she had the final say: 'Mrs Flowers, I'm not at all happy about Chloe and Freddie's care when there is so much work going on in the house. I strongly urge you to take them away until the worst is over, for your sanity.'

That could be years, Belinda thought hopelessly. 'I could take them to my parents for a while.'

'Good idea, the sooner the better!'

'I'll try to get away at the weekend. And thank you for trying to help round up Chloe. I would never have thought that you ...'

'Me of all people would be chasing chickens,' said Pru, finishing her sentence. 'I am a farmer's daughter, you know.'

Belinda hated clichés, but you could have knocked her over with a feather!

*

A week at her parents was as long as Belinda could bear, with all their fussing. She had told Pru she would be staying a fortnight and decided not to announce her early return. At least the trench was finished and the new hot water system up and running, but life was no easier. With Grace occupying the children's rooms until the flat was re-plastered, Carla, unsettled after being away, was sleeping in Belinda and Tom's bedroom and continued to wake regularly. She would feed little at night and then was ravenous during the day. Various workmen about the place grew used to seeing her shoved up Belinda's sweatshirt.

With the house still upside down as the central heating work progressed, the days were very demanding. If Belinda wasn't cleaning up brick dust, she was making hot drinks for builders and heating engineers. Come evenings, she was so whacked Tom invariably had to cook supper. Even Freddie was being a pain with his toilet training and had her at his beck and call with the potty. He seemed to delight in refusing to perform and leaving little pools around it. He was fascinated by his new baby sister and when she was good, loved to stroke her head, hold hands and kiss her. When Carla whimpered he would alert Belinda, but when she reached full pitch he would be off – straight round the Maclaren's.

One afternoon Belinda busied herself cleaning the stainless steel kitchen sink to bathe her daughter. It was far easier than using the baby bath, with the draining board and kitchen table for drying and dressing her. Carla's little pink body was lowered into the warm bubbles and she gurgled contentedly. The quietness was blissful with just the two of them. Tom, Freddie and Ollie had left after lunch to spectate the septic tank being emptied, a surprising choice of entertainment. Belinda expected them to be gone for some while and was dismayed to suddenly hear the big lorry returning.

Excited voices sounded in the hall and Tom, Freddie and Ollie appeared, followed by a tall, grimy figure in overalls emanating a pungent cloud. A foul smell wafted across the kitchen and Belinda glowered at two white rings staring from a dirty face.

'Bellie, this is Bill. He's finished cleaning out the septic tank and I asked him back for tea,' announced Tom breezily.

Silently cursing, she forced a smile: 'Oh, h-hello... Sorry I can't shake your hand; I have mine rather full right now.'

'Probably best you don't,' said Bill, wiping his hand on his overalls. Much to Belinda's disdain, he went over, the nasty aroma intensifying: 'What a beautiful baby. She's gonna be a looker.'

'You bet!' agreed Tom.

'She'll have to be tough, growing up round here.'

Belinda couldn't agree more. She quickly dried Carla, threading her tiny fingers through a baby-grow sleeves while Tom made tea. Bill sat with the boys at the kitchen table and Belinda reluctantly joined them. Pru Payne was due any time and she prayed it would not be yet. Her health visitor would certainly not approve of bathing Carla in the kitchen sink with a beast from the black slime standing over. Her daughter would likely be whisked off into care! As if the baby knew her thoughts, she started grizzling. The door opened and Belinda's heart missed a beat.

'How's it all going, chaps?' asked Cameron.

'It's all squeaky clean!' announced Tom.

'Yes, just like Carla after her bath, but wouldn't it be better if you all went round to Cameron's kitchen for tea?' Belinda suggested forcefully. Much to her relief Cameron was happy to take Bill off her hands, the boys trotting off with them. But she was cross with Tom, who was about to leave with the tea tray: 'What were you thinking, inviting that walking stink bomb in? This is our kitchen, not the sewage works canteen! You knew I was going to bath Carla.'

'Sorry Bellie. I'd have thought after that last day at Flowerpots a pong wouldn't bother you, though Bill is a bit ripe. You know, outside I didn't notice - perhaps we were standing upwind.'

To feed Carla she took sanctuary in the lounge and after winding her, put her in the pram on the lawn. The baby nodded off almost instantly, but within a few minutes was screaming her head off as Bill's lorry exploded into life and departed, trailing dust clouds in its wake. Perhaps Pru Payne was right all along; this was no place for a young baby.

*

Carla refused to settle so Belinda decided to take her for a walk, releasing the pram brake she headed across the grass in a huff. Leaving Haggleby Hall confines she was quickly uplifted by the sweet summer scents. From the drive, she followed the gentle incline towards the gardener's cottage. It was another hot day, the sky a cloudless azure and she was relieved to reach the dappled shade of the lane.

Approaching Nellie and Ed's cottage, she recalled Agatha telling her that Nellie had been housekeeper at the Hall and Ed, the head gardener. Agatha and Roderick's Aunt Elizabeth still owned the cottage, allowing the retired couple to stay on for a peppercorn rent and see out their days.

The early Victorian, Sussex tile-hung property was full of character, with variegated ivy and Virginia creeper snaking up and pink roses cascading in profusion over the porch. Belinda left the pram on paving by the washing line. Ed's green fingers were evident in the charming English country garden. Wild colours splashed its plant-packed borders, broken by azalea shrubs and heathers, and in the bottom right hand corner a weeping willow was bowing over a lily pond.

Belinda approached the elderly man, who was breathing heavily, his brow rolling with sweat as he chopped weeds with a hoe. He reminded Belinda of her grandfather when she was a child. His baggy grey flannels were supported by a leather belt around his generous girth, his green- striped cotton shirt with rolled-up sleeves was ragged and soiled, his Wellington boots incongruous on such a hot day.

He puffed a greeting with red cheeks: 'Aft'noon young lady, you must be Mrs Flowers from the big 'ouse. I'm Edwin Gregory, but everyone calls me Ed. Nellie said you'd be popping round with the babby. She'll be so pleased to see you.'

'Good afternoon Ed, call me Belinda. It's a pleasure to meet you and get away from the house for a while. It's all very busy. I hope the drilling hasn't disturbed you too much.'

'Oh, no bother. I don't hear much with my ears. The clinic gave me a hearing aid but I don't get on with it, so you'll have to speak up.'

Belinda attempted to explain the latest building activities, but he stared blankly at her. Taking off his hat, he wiped his face with his neck-kerchief and bid her to follow him back up the garden. Carla was sleeping peacefully beneath the floral sunshade clipped to her pram and he asked Belinda's permission to take a peep.

'What a bootiful baby, ma'am. Nell will be tickled pink to see her. Leave the pram by the back door and come in for some refreshment.'

A heavenly fragrance filled the kitchen from a vase of multi-coloured sweet peas on an old pine table. Tidied beneath were two ladder back chairs and rush mats were spread across the green quarry-tiled floor. Under the window was an enamel sink and there was a mismatch of wooden cupboards, including a wall one with glass sliding doors like ones Belinda had seen in her childhood. Despite the open window and door, the room was unbearably hot, with a black kitchen range, like one she remembered at her grandparents, simmering a kettle. Her grandmother would toast slices of bread on a fork by the glowing bars and spread them thickly with dripping. Washed down with a strong cup of tea, they were a special winter treat in Belinda's school holidays.

'Nell!' Ed 's voice boomed up the stairs. 'We 'ave a visitor, two in fact, come on down!'

The old woman quickly appeared, looking delighted. 'Well, Mrs Flowers, 'ow lovely to see you. Welcome to Frogs' Leap Cottage.'

She offered tea or home-made lemonade and Belinda, accepting the latter, followed Ed to the pond to sit on cane chairs beneath the weeping willow. Nellie came down a few minutes later holding a tea tray and a freshly baked fruit cake.

'It's as well you've stopped Ed working, he does overdo it. He felt so queer the other day we 'ad to have the doctor out.'

'Sorry to hear that, Ed. Are you feeling better?' asked Belinda, concerned.

'Better than I was. I thought I was having one of them cardigan arrests…'

'Cardiac arrests,' corrected Nellie, 'but it wasn't that bad else they would have carted you orf to 'ospital.'

Belinda tried again to explain the work at Haggleby Hall, but despite Nellie prompting Ed to turn up his hearing aid, it was hard work. She encouraged the conversation to digress to the elderly couple's working days at "the big house".

'We worked for Milton and Elizabeth Fielding-Winters,' explained Nellie. 'I was in charge of the cleaning, with three other girls, and Ed was 'ead gardener. He and his men used to grow fruit and vegetables for the family. I expect you've met the niece and nephew they 'elped bring up, though they were away most the time at boarding school.'

Realising she meant Roderick and Agatha, Belinda nodded attentively.

'We 'ad nine acres to look after then,' Ed continued. 'Cutting that grass with them 'eavy mowers, that was 'ard work. We grew everything imag'nable; the walled kitchen garden's still there, you know, and the greenhouses - though they're fallin' to bits. I used to grow bootiful cucumbers, marrows, pumpkins - you name it…'

'Ed used to win prizes galore in the village show,' interrupted Nellie, her blue eyes twinkling. 'We've got an old picture of him with 'is prize-winnin' marrow; it was the biggest 'aggleby Agricultural Society had ever had.'

'We used to work six, sometimes seven days a week when the Fielding-Winters had people to stay,' cut in Nellie.

97

Ed elaborated: 'The master was a real country gent, loved his fishin' and shootin'. He used to catch whoppers in the lake, and 'e was good with the gun. The old game pantry is still out the back, where 'e used to 'ang the rabbits and pheasants. But all that came to an end during the war. The army commissioned the hall and the master and mistress had to leave. A load of Canadian soldiers came and I was kept on to turn a lot of the garden over for food.'

Nellie explained: 'Ed couldn't go to war on account of his hearing. We stayed here and I carried on running the domestic side. It was 'ard work with all them soldiers.'

'What happened to Milton and Elizabeth?' asked Belinda.

'They went to live in 'aggleby'.

'Leaving Haggleby Hall must have been a wrench for them.'

'It was, but they were OK about it. The master did have an eye for the ladies, mind. There was one from the village who did his secretarial work, a Rosie somebody. After the war, when they returned, she carried on with him for years.'

Belinda, puzzled by her cryptic words, asked: 'Did you know her?

'Not very well; she used to drive down from the village a couple of times a week. The funny thing was, she moved away about the time Mr Fielding-Winters went missing.'

'September 26, 1973 to be precise,' volunteered Belinda.

Nellie's face flickered surprise. 'That's right. He vanished just like that', she clicked her fingers. 'The police looked everywhere for 'im. Ed took 'em round the grounds and helped search the fields.'

'They was 'ere for weeks,' he interrupted. 'They even 'ad divers in the lake, but nothing came of it. They found 'is boat floating in the middle, a bit odd, but no sign of 'im.'

'According to Roderick, he hadn't gone fishing,' Belinda interjected. 'His rod and tackle were still in the boathouse.'

'P'raps he just rowed out for a bit o' peace and quiet, felt ill and fell overboard. That lake's full of weeds,' Ed suggested.

'Or jumped in, or was pushed - we'll never know,' conjectured Nellie darkly. 'It was so strange with him gone. Madam was beside herself...they say his spirit never left the place.'

'You don't want to go worryin' this young lady with your stories, Nel', prompted Ed.

Belinda was totally absorbed in the strange story when Carla started whimpering for attention. The elderly couple watched enchanted as she was lifted from the pram and given a drink of water. It wouldn't appease her for long.

'I'm afraid I'll have to go. Her next feed is due.'

'Hang on a couple of ticks. I'll get you some eggs. It's the least Chloe can do to make up for her bad behaviour last week,' said Nellie, rushing off.

*

That evening the Flowers and Maclaren's were having a drink on the terrace when Grace joined them. She had just returned from visiting Roderick's hotel. Clutching a gin and tonic, she explained: 'It's in this remote Dorset seaside village called Kittywink, with this lovely little bay and beautiful countryside. It's not touristy - a perfect place for getting away from it all.'

'So you feel better for your break?' asked Belinda.

'Completely refreshed, thank you; I just needed to be out of here for a few days. I'll be even happier once I've moved into the flat.'

'Won't we all!' she had to agree. Grace was still occupying two of her and Tom's bedrooms, but Cameron had assured her: 'Next on the works schedule is replacing the ceilings in the flat, then once the plaster boarding's done the plumbers can work on your central heating.'

'You make it all sound so easy, dear.'

'How's Roderick?' enquired Miranda.

'Quite chipper now he is able to sort out Aunt Elizabeth's affairs. You know, when you get him on his own he doesn't stutter half as much.'

'So, you get him on his own, Mitts?' teased Cameron, raising an eyebrow. 'You'll have to watch it, though; spend too much time with that man and you'll be into mischief!'

'Camay, leave your mother alone. She's a big girl now,' chastised Miranda.

'Roderick and I are just good friends,' quickly retorted Grace, an old hand at playing her son's games. Looking out of the window, she said: 'Well done for finishing the trench, by the way - and we have hot water!'

'Thanks Mitts, though that drilling nearly killed me. I'm all shook up,' said Cameron, twitching in demonstration.

'Wasn't that Elvis?' asked Belinda.

'Yeah, I was wiggling my hips just like him, trying to keep that damned drill under control.'

'Bit before my time,' said Miranda. 'What you need, Camay is calming therapy.'

'I need something. You've heard of trench foot, like the soldiers used to get? Well I think I've got trench brain. My head's still vibrating.'

Belinda updated Grace on the Gregory's hen. 'You missed all the drama and then I had to take the children to my parents for a few days on Pru's orders.'

'At least your health visitor tried to catch it,' chipped in Miranda. 'She doesn't sound the type to make a mountain out of an ant hill.'

'A mole hill,' corrected Tom.

'Talking of moles, I've been doing a bit of digging round at the Gregory's, announced Belinda. 'I asked them what they thought about Uncle Milton's disappearance.'

'Roderick is convinced he ran off with this woman who took down his letters,' said Grace.

'Rosie, I believe,' cut in Belinda.

'I bet letters weren't the only things she took down!' Cameron winked.

Grace continued: 'This woman, Rosie, moved from Haggleby the same day Milton disappeared. A lot of people should remember it; the day Concorde broke the record crossing the Atlantic.

'September 26th, 1973', Cameron, Tom and Belinda chorused.

'That's very good, that you all know the date!'

'It has come up once or twice before,' Belinda reminded her.

'The Concorde was carrying passengers, wasn't it?' asked Tom.

'A small number, I believe.'

'I bet Uncle M and his fancy woman had one-way tickets,' teased Cameron.

'They wouldn't have been on that flight - it was from Washington to Paris. It did it in three and a-half hours, cutting the previous record of a transatlantic airliner in half.'

'Just because you have your wings, why do you have to be such a know-it-all, Mitts?'

'According to Roderick, Rosie told everyone she was off to Derbyshire to live with her cousin, but whether she did? The police never managed to trace her.'

'Funny, isn't it? You'd never think of people running off together at such a time of life. Milton was in his early 60s,' remarked Belinda.

'We can only assume that they went away together. It could have been sheer coincidence that Rosie left the village the same day. I doubt we'll ever know what became of them,' said Grace.

'If they're still alive I bet they're living on some exotic island in the Pacific,' conjectured Cameron.

'Why the Pacific?' queried Belinda.

'All those lovely women doing the hula and the big coconuts…!'

Miranda cosied up to Cameron: 'Shall we fly away to our little haven, darling?'

'I'm ready for take-off but don't expect any record breakers tonight.'

CHAPTER NINE

Supporting Act

Despite her home undergoing major surgery, Belinda's boredom as a full-time mum was becoming too much. Since having Carla she was suffering from brain fade, sometimes struggling to string words together. Broken nights and stressful days hindered by workmen did not help.

She had always been creative with words, enjoying writing since a child, when she spent hours penning stories and rhymes. In her early 20s she worked as a PR account executive and loved playing word games to give sparkle to her advertising copy. Waxing lyrical about furniture polish and breakfast cereals was not always easy. But it was not her cup of tea, so she trained as a journalist on a London provincial. Eventually, she became a sub-editor and relished headline writing and glossing dull stories. But now, bogged down with motherhood, she needed impetus to drag her creativity from the mire.

Becoming an author was Belinda's ultimate ambition, though with such a pressured life writing a book was light years away. For the last couple of years she had been capturing flashes of inspiration in a notebook kept in the kitchen drawer. One day she would publish her rhymes as a collection - she fancied calling it "Female Facets" as most were about women. Her flair for poetry was triggered when she joined Mid Sussex NCT's "Potty Poetry Group" (for young mums, of course). Freddie was a young baby then.

The day she had to host the group was a first for Haggleby Hall and was a good dry run for future social events (though with all the lactating mothers it was far from dry!). Belinda held it in the ballroom, leaving Miranda and her friend, Marietta, supervising toddlers in the lounge, Freddie and Ollie among them.

103

Guest speaker was a published poet called Penny Lines, a chirpy, plump, middle-aged woman with red tousled curls and pink-framed glasses. She was wearing a flamboyant gypsy-style skirt and with her shimmering blue eyelids, rouged cheeks and bright red lips, she gave a colourful talk, called "Expressing Oneself". Belinda, with Carla 'plugged in' beneath her baggy Mickey Mouse sweatshirt, smiled at associated thoughts of the breast pump! Penny recited poems from her book, Lipstick and Toilet Water, accompanied by gurgles, burps and slurps and titters.

At the previous meeting Penny had set some homework entitled "Getting it off Your Chest" and asked for a volunteer to read hers. Belinda had just started to drift off, but the words, 'Let's hear our hostess's poem!' brought her to with a start. She had never been asked to read out her efforts before and tired after a difficult night with Carla, was not in the mood. But there was no escaping it. Passing her daughter over, she fumbled in her jeans for her folded A4. All eyes were on her as she continued nervously:

BOSOM BUDDIES
Over shoulder boulder holders,
Bras both lacy and silky smooth,
Stretch elastic for easy move,
Cups for small and larger measure,
Just the job for work and pleasure,
Underwire lifts and separates,
Ensures your pair remains firm mates.
Removable pads, support for sags,
Ranging in colours, styles and tags,
Clips and fastenings front or back,
Adjustable straps for balancing pack.
Cross my heart this is my size,
But looks all wrong, the label lies.
Finding the perfect fit for tits
Can simply drive you out of your wits!

Laughter erupted, but did Belinda's fellow poets find it funny or were they just being polite? Crimson-faced, she quickly retrieved Carla and excused herself. To her complete surprise, everyone clapped as she left the room and compliments followed during the break.

In the kitchen she helped Miranda and Mariettta make drinks. Among the general hubbub one member was extolling the joys of breast-feeding. 'I have so much milk I get through umpteen T-shirts. Boots think I've got shares in breast pads.'

'Have you tried those plastic cups inside your bra?' asked another. 'They're very good as long as you remember to empty them.'

Belinda, brewing tea, was keeping abreast with the conversation: 'Why don't you decant them into a bottle to keep in the fridge for when your milk runs low?'

Patty, winding her baby, said: 'If he doesn't take enough I become solid as a rock and I'm like a fountain in the bath.'

'Have you tried a breast pump?' enquired Suzanne.

'Yes, it helps, though it makes me feel like a cow.'

Pamela, nursing her infant beneath a loose cotton top, winced. 'Arnie's such a frenzied feeder, I'm sure he's got fangs coming through!'

There was sympathy all round. Belinda was surprised to hear Miranda, normally pro-breast feeding, suggest putting him on the bottle: 'Nothing's worth a woman having to go through all that.'

Belinda recounted the time the two of them were feeding the boys under the apple tree at Flowerpots. 'Do you remember that apple landing on Ollie's head? He didn't half have a bump?'

'It's probably why he won't touch apples now.'

'Or why he's the apple of your eye!'

Maggie was making no secret of her sizeable "feeders": 'Timmy is so tiny it's a miracle he doesn't suffocate.'

'That's why babies have good lungs!' suggested Belinda.

Maureen, with little Simon peering over her shoulder like a parrot, complained: 'He has trouble locking on and gets drenched.'

'Milk's very good for cradle cap,' Miranda reassured her, offering a custard cream.

Sally despaired: 'I don't know why we commit ourselves to months of being sucked, bitten and chewed and end up looking diminished.'

'Because you can't beat the real thing!' replied Belinda, pouring milk.

Patty mentioned having to feed her friend's baby a few days before because she'd forgotten the bottle.

'Ever thought of wet nursing for a living?' asked Miranda. 'You would have been paid for it years ago and likely have free accommodation.'

The second half of the afternoon had more readings and a rhyming couplets workshop, which was curtailed by fractious toddlers. Belinda was relieved to close the door on the last of her visitors. She carried Carla over to the Maclaren's for a combined supper. Freddie and Ollie were already strapped into their booster seats, chewing bread sticks.

'Why don't you have a bash at writing poetry?' Belinda asked Miranda, serving cocktail sausages and cheese cubes.

'I'm rubbish at things like that. I'll stick to minding the little horrors. By the way, I must tell you about this mum I was chatting to this afternoon. I think her name was Sarah. She should have been in the poetry class, but her little boy was being a pain.'

'Yes, I know who you mean, though I don't know her very well.'

'As you can imagine, with screaming kids our conversation was a bit fragmented, but from what I gathered she has an aunt who used to work for Uncle Milton. Sarah was a girl then, but remembers her Aunt Rosie typing his letters.'

Belinda was flabbergasted. 'The very same Rosie we were all talking about that night on the terrace?'

Miranda nodded. 'Apparently, she went missing the same time as him. Everyone thought they'd run away together.'

'I already told everyone that, Miranda, but at least it corroborates the story.'

'Did you? I was probably away with the fairies. Anyway, Sarah's family didn't hear a word from Rosie in 13 years and then, the other day, she turned up on the doorstep - she's been living in Scotland.'

Belinda gasped. 'What? She's come back! She either had nothing to do with Milton disappearing, or if she did, she's very stupid. The police will be after her. I wonder if they know she's back.'

'I would have thought so. Perhaps we should tell Roderick? I'll get Grace to ring him and try and find out where this Sarah lives.'

*

The Flowers were expecting Haggleby Church vicar, the Reverend Makepeace, and wife Matilda for tea. He had been first to make contact, reminding Belinda they were already acquainted through the church fete. The couple had minded Freddie while Tom had taken her to hospital with labour pains. How could she not invite them round? She was feeling guilty that Tom and she had had no time to attend church, but the reverend's visit would be opportune to ask about Carla's christening.

As back then, the afternoon was glorious, the Indian summer sunshine reflecting a myriad of autumnal hues. Belinda had laid the table on the terrace. As her visitors arrived, Tom and Freddie were washing their hands after gardening, so she went out to greet them. After a polite exchange about the weather, she seated them on the terrace and went in to make tea. Tom carried out a plateful of jam and cream scones, Freddie trotted behind with a box of chocolate fingers and Belinda followed with the tea tray.

'I must say you're working wonders here,' said Rev Makepeace, gazing round. 'Last time I came to Haggleby Hall, a few years ago now, a pop group was renting it. They used to make a devil of a noise, drumming day and night. It was fortunate there were only a few people living in the neighbourhood, but I kept having my ear bent at church and the police weren't doing anything, so I came to have a gentle word. There were four of them. They seemed very polite, but I did take a dim view of being offered hash cake? When I joked that *such food* was against my religion, they got very silly, so I left sharpish.'

'Someone told me the group was called "Pot Luck" - an appropriate name by the sound of things,' observed Belinda. 'I was a fan of theirs, though they went to America and haven't been heard of since.'

'Roderick, whose aunt used to live here, mentioned them,' said Tom, 'but don't worry, vicar, there are no *special* ingredients in these scones.'

Belinda kicked him under the table. Matilda raised her eyebrows. 'We had heard that some Hippies had moved in, but we didn't know what to believe.'

'There's nobody like that here. Hippies, you say? Doesn't ring any bells with me,' joked Tom.

'Oh, really?' she sounded incredulous.

'I hear grannie flies,' the vicar went on.

'Only when there's a full moon!' retorted Tom.

The reverend laughed and Belinda glared. 'Tom likes to joke. You're quite right, vicar, Granny Grace is a pilot. She has her PPL.'

'A PPL, what's that?'

'It means she's a high flyer,' said Tom casually.

108

Belinda quickly explained, 'It's a Private Pilot's Licence.'

'Grace sounds an *interesting* woman,' responded Matilda.

The reverend redirected the conversation: 'Now, about Carla's christening. That shouldn't be a problem. You do come to church, umh, regularly?'

'Well, we did when we lived in Clatterbridge, though here our hands are rather full just now,' said Belinda.

'Yes, of course, there must be a lot of work. And your children - having had three children ourselves we know how it is, don't we, dear?'

'Oh, yes, it was not the easiest of times. You're a photographer, aren't you, Tom?'

'That's right. I work for the family business.'

'That's useful. We need some up to date pictures of the church,' the reverend cut in.

Matilda asked: 'What do your, umh, *house friends*, do?'

'The Maclaren's - Miranda's also a busy mum and Cameron runs a car business.'

'Not *the* racing cars?' queried the vicar excitedly, getting the wrong end of the gearstick.

'No, that's McLaren,' Tom spelled it out. 'Nothing to do with baby buggies either.'

Sensing the vicar's embarrassment, Belinda offered him a flapjack she had made with honey. She was desperate to keep him sweet. Tom had warned her not to pass on too much information about each other. He feared anything they said would be round the village in no time, twisting the local grapevine even tighter.

Rev Makepeace asked for more tea and Belinda poured another round. The christening pushed aside, he started prodding them for a donation for the Bell Tower Fund. 'The PCC is very concerned about the crumbling stonework. If urgent work is not carried out soon, the damp will rot the internal woodwork and that would be disastrous.'

109

'Sounds like Haggleby Hall,' responded Tom, unsympathetically.

Belinda, realising the vicar's veiled request for money, asked how much he needed to raise.

'At least £20,000; we have set up a fund, though repair costs are rising more quickly than any money we collect. As I am sure you can appreciate, it's a slow process. We are organising various fund-raising events and, of course, any contributions are gratefully received.'

Tom, not wanting to give any false impression, was direct: 'we have a fund here we call The Haggleby Hall Sinking Fund and we have to sink every spare penny into that.'

Belinda felt awkward. How could anyone believe that they could live in a mansion (depleted as it was!) and be as poor as church mice? Sponging Freddie's chocolatey face, she suggested their visitors might like a tour round the garden.

Matilda, delighted at the diversion, jumped up: 'We love big gardens. We're lifelong members of the National Trust and visit different ones whenever Maurice can extract himself from his ministry.'

The Rev *Maurice* Makepeace…sounds like a name in Happy Families, thought Belinda, recalling her favourite card game as a child. She followed them out, heading to Carla's pram.

'What a lovely baby!' cried Matilda.

'A beautiful child,' agreed the reverend.

Carla started whining as they strolled to the tennis court, he and Belinda chatting as they followed Matilda and Tom, holding Freddie's hand. With the baby's feed due, Belinda was on borrowed time: 'When would suit you for the christening, vicar? We were wondering about some time after Christmas?'

'I'll have to check the church calendar and get back to you … now about the Bell Tower Fund; do you think you could find it in your hearts to show support?'

He obviously wanted to strike a bargain first. Belinda baulked: 'I'm s-sure we can find something…' she struggled to find words as a strange noise came out of the blue. It was like a squeaky wheelbarrow. Puzzled stares were exchanged at barely discernible words: 'Not on your life…not on your life…'

The reverend crossed his chest as if the Almighty was speaking. For a split second Belinda thought Tom was somehow projecting his voice in response to the vicar's request. 'Was that you, Tom? Your lips didn't move!'

'Not me - but you know who! It's Monty! He must have got out again. I bet it was that damned cat …sorry vicar …knocking his cage over again. It happened that day we came to see Roderick and Agatha about buying the house, remember?'

Sure enough, Monty, the African Grey parrot Cameron and Miranda had taken on with the house, swooped down and settled on the, now levelled, bird table. As if rejuvenated, its grey feathers and bright red tail glistened in the sun. Obviously delighted to see them, its solid black beak gabbled: 'Not on your life… Hell's bells…'

'God bless us!' exclaimed the Reverend Makepeace.

Belinda handed Carla to Tom and crept up to Monty, saying his name and offering her finger, fondly imagining he would hop on. The parrot cocked his head inquisitively. A finger away from his chest feathers was close enough. He flapped and took off. So near but so far! Disappointment filled her throat as she instinctively followed Monty's rapidly diminishing form vanishing behind the chimney pots.

*

That evening everyone was subdued, though there was an interesting development. In the ballroom Tom's home brew was working hard to lighten the mood, but shortly later Grace and Roderick arrived back from a flying trip to the Isle of Wight. They couldn't have come at a worst time.

'I nearly knocked Monty's cage over. What's it doing on the front drive?' asked Grace worriedly. He hasn't gone to the big birdcage in the sky?'

'Oh no, n -ot Monty! He's been with us years, m-more than I care to remember,' gasped Roderick, his old stutter reignited.

'I'm afraid so, old friend,' Cameron commiserated. 'But he's not gone in the true sense of the word. He's happily flying about out there with his feathered friends.'

'You m-mean, he got out again?'

'I'm sorry to say so and you can guess who is to blame.'

'Not that bloody Ramrod - I'll skin him alive!'

'Now calm down. You need a drink.'

Tom handed Roderick a large whisky. 'Monty will come back, Roderick, wait and see. We've filled his cage with his favourite goodies, so just let's be patient.'

Miranda attempted reassurance. 'We've seen him on the parapet a couple of times. He'll be OK, the weather's warm and there is plenty of fruit and seeds for him in Ripe n' Ready's fields.'

'He'll be lapping up his new found freedom, Roderick,' comforted Grace.

'But he's not used to living out there with wild birds.'

'No, but African Greys are a flock bird. He'll be OK.'

Thinking of the beloved pet originally Uncle Milton's, Belinda said: 'Somehow, I think Monty's not too far away, as if he is out there looking for his real owner.'

Roderick smiled weakly. 'Oh, that reminds me. There's something I must tell you. I went to Horley police station yesterday.'

112

'Don't tell me, Rods, they've finally traced your uncle, alive and well and living in Outer Mongolia!' chirruped Cameron.

'Oh do shut up and be serious for once!' stormed Grace.

Roderick continued: 'After Grace's phone call about that Sarah who was at Belinda's do, and her Aunt Rosie's sudden reappearance, I called into the station and spoke to someone in CID. An officer had already interviewed Aunt Rosie and it seems she's off the hook regarding uncle's disappearance.'

'So, nothing to do with her then!' reiterated Miranda.

'It would appear not. Rosie was in Scotland the day uncle vanished. She must have travelled up there a day or two before. The police have evidence she was admitted to hospital in Edinburgh. I shouldn't be telling you this, but apparently she had a miscarriage.'

'How sad, she wasn't married, was she?' asked Belinda.

'No, not at the time, though she did marry later. I think it would be best not to conjecture who the father was,' advised Roderick, 'at least we know she had nothing to do with uncle vanishing.'

*

Once Belinda and Tom were alone he lit their first fire of autumn. It was a speedy exercise as Tom had already filled the log basket. Recognising her subdued mood, he offered to treat her to a Chinese take-away and she took little persuasion. She listened to his wheels crunching along the drive as the blaze crackled and hissed like an awakening monster. It had been a strange afternoon. She contemplated their lack of progress with organising Carla's christening, though the question mark hanging over Uncle Milton's so-called "fancy woman" had at least been ruled out. But where one question had been answered, others were mounting over his fate. Then, there was poor Monty, assumedly roosting somewhere outside in the darkness, and the fear of him struggling to survive the winter. Poor Ollie was so distraught Cameron had agreed to keep watch until bedtime in case the parrot flew back into his cage. But perhaps his new found freedom was too much to relinquish after all his years behind bars? As Belinda sat fire-gazing, fairies sparkled and dragons writhed, weaving red trails around a castle wonderland.

Oriental cooking smells announced Tom's appearance with two steaming plates of prawn balls, sweet and sour chicken, crispy pancakes and fried rice. The tasty fare, washed down with a bottle of Sauvignon Rouge, had the desired effect as they sank into their matured, brown leather sofa that had once graced a lounge at London's Carlton Hotel. Tom's late grandfather had acquired it (probably as part payment for taking photographs) and was in his imposing 1930s home for years. The old man had been a pipe lover and despite Tom's arduous efforts with saddle soap and leather feed, the tobacco aroma still lingered.

'Oh Tom, this is the life,' Belinda slurred, ever so slightly. 'Who'd ever have thought we'd be wining and dining in such decadence?'

'If you call a Chinese take-away, a bottle of plonk and a smelly old settee 'decadence', Bellie, you're an easy woman to please.'

The fireside warmth wrapped blissfully around her like crimson velvet. She watched the flickering shadows creating scenarios on the ceiling. In Tom's arms she blanked the day's unhappy events, but as his Hoi-Sin-seasoned lips sought hers, the kitchen phone rang. Thankfully, it was taken by their "newly employed", bumbling old butler, Fred Crum! Tom's message for the Flowers' new answerphone was so entertaining people kept calling back to hear it over again. When the phone rang a second time Tom turned up the stereo playing her favourite Genesis album, "Selling England by the Pound". He nuzzled into the open neck of her crisp cotton shirt, his hand creeping inside and gently cupping her breast. His finger circled her nipple, ripples of excitement radiating through her. Their bodies submitted to the hearth rug, the fire's radiance licking her bare cheeks erotically. Mellifluous rhythms of her favourite track, "The Cinema Show", were mounting to a crescendo...

'Let's go upstairs,' he whispered.

She took his hand, her legs like jelly, unable to climb the stairs quickly enough. She had often counted them with Freddie and they seemed to be taking forever. How much longer could she wait? The need pulsing inside her was nearing impossible to bear! At last, sinking into bed, they locked embrace, two as one. Later, she wrote:

LOVESICK BLUES
Saturday is "nookie" night.
Supper served nice 'n early,
Offspring safely tucked up,
Dishwasher loaded sharpish.
Wine is working wonders,
Cuddles by fireside heating
To caresses under covers.

Earth is moving darling,
Soaring to the heavens,
Going into orbit,
Nearing point of no return.
Banging getting louder,
'Mummy, gonna be sick!'
Rocket turning turtle,
Diving rapidly downwards,
Astronaut, anti-climaxed,
Crashed in bath plughole!

CHAPTER TEN

High Jinx

Belinda was chopping onions for the evening meal when someone knocked the kitchen door and a watery figure of Miranda appeared, sounding irritable. 'Have you seen Cameron? He promised to bath Ollie. I've got the horticultural society's meeting at seven thirty.'

The society, in its hundredth and something year, was desperate for members and Miranda, in a weaker moment standing at The Mucky Duck bar one evening, had volunteered to join the committee. She never grew anything other than prize cobwebs, but fancied entering in the show her best jams and pickles, made with Ripe and Ready's pick your own produce. Like her, Belinda and the children spent hours gathering soft fruits and vegetables in the fields around Haggleby Hall and making numerous pots of jam that were all too quickly consumed.

'I did see Cameron drive off a while ago. I thought he'd sneaked out for a quick one.'

Suddenly the sound of scrunching gravel announced the imminent arrival of a heavy vehicle. 'We're not expecting a lorry at this time of day, surely?'

'Not to my knowledge.'

A big, dusty yellow lorry with a wobbly hydraulic platform, spewing clouds of black fumes grated to a halt outside. They were surprised to see Cameron jump out of the cab.

'That monstrous thing can't be from the car mart, or has he started dealing in lorries as well?' asked Belinda incredulously.

'Well, if he has he hasn't told me!'

Belinda had to feel sorry for her. She never knew from one day to the next what her man was doing. At least life with Cameron was anything but boring. And there was usually a good reason behind anything he did. He appeared at the door like a dog with two tails. 'Oh, hello ladies, is the governor about?'

Tom burst through the lounge door, right on cue: 'Cameron, what *have* you got there?'

'Ah, dear boy, this is my new toy - you know the one I was telling you about a while back. Patrick I drink with at the Mucky Duck is loaning it to us for a few weeks to paint the house.'

'Oh Camay, you've found a lorry that can paint houses, how clever,' Miranda said innocently. 'But why didn't you tell me?'

Cameron had volunteered to paint the exterior once the re-rendering was finished. 'Uhmh, didn't I? Well, I've found this "old dog" to help me reach the bits other things cannot reach.'

'Sounds like the lager advert,' said Tom.

'She might need a bit of fine tuning; she stopped three times driving over - but she'll help do the job without costing us an arm and a leg.'

'So, what is this 'old dog' costing us?'

'Oh, Patrick only wants a few beers.'

Although Tom had acquired exterior paint in a deal with a client, the Haggleby Hall Sinking Fund couldn't run to hiring painters, so Cameron, with the most time on his hands, had jumped into the breach. He had already started painting the lower level of the house and aimed to progress upwards before the scaffolding was taken down in three weeks' time. 'This miracle machine can get me to the awkward bits and speed things up no end. I can take my coffee and "bickis" up with me. It'll be a picnic!'

'We'd better toast this wonder dog', suggested Tom, divvying out halves of his 'secret recipe' homebrew. There was invariably a barrel on in the Flowers' kitchen. Belinda always dreaded brewing day, when his painstakingly measured malt, hops and water would bubble away for hours on the cooker. Its pungent, sticky-sweet smell reached the remotest corners of the house, hanging about for days; though she had to admit that brewing in her preserving pan did give her jam a special edge! Following Chloe Clutterbuck's visit, Tom had named his homebrew "Old Haggleby Hen". Real ale lovers would always jump at the chance of a pint, which slipped down the gullet so easily they invariably ended up in the spare room for the night!

'A toast to your brilliant acquisition!' said Tom, raising his tankard.

'Of course, the old girl needs a good going-over.'

Miranda, feigning offence, joked: 'But you did **that** this morning, Camay - and I'm not *old!'*

Tom appeased her with a pint. 'Perhaps this might help the *young lady* feel better.'

Miranda never refused a beer and Belinda was astounded how well she could keep up drinking with the men. One evening she had downed a pint in eight seconds to win a bet!

'Randy, I wasn't referring to you as the old girl. I meant the cherry picker,' Cameron assured her.

Perhaps Tom's homebrew was kicking in too quickly: 'Old dog, old girl, cherry picker? We don't have any cherries, do we?'

'Oh, I wouldn't say that,' said Tom suggestively, 'but what you probably don't know is that vehicles with hydraulic platforms are called "cherry pickers".'

'Whatever it is, it's a disgrace! It looks like it has come straight from the breaker's yard.'

Tom stood firmly with Cameron. 'You've certainly cherry-picked the cheapest option for getting the house done.'

'Buttercup is an amazing feat of engineering. She is going to help me transform this place,' said Cameron enthusiastically.

'Buttercup?' everyone chorused.

'That's her name.'

Miranda laughed. 'So where's Buttercup's brush?'

'I have the brush and by simply pushing her buttons, I can make her go up and down to paint at different levels.'

'I didn't know I'd got competition! Is this contraption called Buttercup because it's yellow?'

'You never cease to astound me, Randy, but Patrick calls her that because she moos when she's in motion.'

'As long as she doesn't leave cow pats all over the lawn,' Tom joked. 'Seriously, Cam, what's "the deal"?'

'I told you, a few pints at The Mucky Duck.

'Buttercup's not "half-inched" is she, or she's going straight back!'

Cameron tapped his nose: 'Trust me, dear boy, she's Kosher!'

*

Buttercup's mechanical overhaul took the husbands an entire Saturday morning and she was duly put to work. For maiden lift-off everyone gathered on the front lawn, where she had been parked for starting the painting. Cameron, clad in navy overalls and back-to-front sun cap, mounted the platform where he had placed a roller, several brushes and two large paint cans. But his initial bravado quickly expired at the prospect of leaving terra-firma. He started prevaricating; re-positioning his materials on the platform, double-checking switches and picking up the flask Miranda had made him, pouring coffee.

'Hey, that's for when you've started painting!' she yelled.

Glugging it back, he screwed up the cup and nervously addressed his patiently waiting well-wishers. 'Before I go, I would just like to say I hope you lot realise that this thing is so clapped out, if the engine stops when I'm mid-air, I will be completely stuck.'

'Don't worry old chap - we'll be here to rescue you,' Tom reassured him, heading for the cab.

Cameron, like a captain on the bridge of a stricken vessel, looked resigned as Tom turned the key. The engine coughed and spluttered. The second time it chugged away for a few seconds then died. "Captain Maclaren" appeared relieved that he would not be leaving port after all. But Tom persevered and several attempts later HMS Buttercup reluctantly fired up, raising cheers all round.

'Bon Voyage! Send us a postcard,' shouted Grace.

The lorry's engine was deafening and clouds of exhaust smoke made everyone splutter. Cameron looked terrified, as if being made to climb the crow's nest on his maiden voyage. Tom climbed out of the cabin and joined the others to watch his old friend operate the platform to ascend Haggleby Hall. It squeaked in protest, swayed hesitantly and started inching upwards. Interminable seconds later, all they could see was the platform bottom and the whites of Cameron's eyes, peering over nervously. Amid the din Belinda thought she heard him scream, 'Get me down!' but no one was taking any notice. Committed, he had no choice but to get on with it. Belinda held her breath as the platform crept towards the wall, quivered and stopped with a lurch. Seconds later an arm could be seen flourishing a paintbrush.

*

Belinda had to admit that Barry Basher and Carl had done a wonderful job with the re-rendering. Over the previous weeks she had observed the cracked, dingy white walls slowly transforming from the proverbial ugly duckling into a beautiful swan, her new coat glistening in the autumn sunshine.

One evening over a drink, Grace praised her son's painting efforts and as a reward promised to take him up in the Piper. 'Now that you have conquered your fear of heights, we can fly over to France for the day.'

Cameron, who had made every excuse under the sun to avoid going up, retorted: 'Oh no, Mitts, the parapet is as high as I am going. Flying with Buttercup is enough for me.'

For the next two weeks his brushwork continued without a hitch. Then the inevitable happened, while he was parked above the front door of all places, painting the landing window wall. Desperate to answer the call of nature, he was swinging his little metal box across ready to descend when the engine stopped dead. Despite several attempts to restart it, all he got was a cough and splutter. Without the engine to manoeuvre him he was stuck mid-air! Inevitably, there was no-one around.

Cameron described his experience later that evening in the Flowers' kitchen, everyone agog listening to his story over a beer. 'As you can imagine, after all that coffee I was bursting... the bloody thing wouldn't budge... you lot weren't coming back for hours...' Typically, he piled on the drama and suddenly stopped mid-air, as it were.

'So what did you do, put a cork in it?' asked Tom impatiently.

'I was hanging up there another hour - a cork wouldn't have stopped me. I was bursting. I had to go ...'

'I'm glad it wasn't me in that predicament. I can't even go behind trees,' said Miranda.

Cameron glared lecherously: 'Don't undervalue yourself darling!'

'So tell us how you managed to get down?' urged Belinda.

'Easier than you think, though I might have upset the postman.'

'What have you done, Camay?' pressed Miranda.

'I didn't know he was underneath,' he squirmed. 'You know how he always parks his van at the Coach House and

121

comes through the door in the wall? Well, he must have been putting the post through our letter box, when…'

'You didn't!' exclaimed Tom, the penny dropping with a clunk. 'We'll be lucky to get any post from now on.'

'No, actually, the poor chap was all right about it - brilliant, in fact. He hopped into the cab, soggy jacket and all, and managed to fire up Buttercup and run her long enough for me to get down. I hope you don't mind, Tom, I lent him that jacket of yours that was hanging in the hall.'

*

The mansion was only painted halfway round and despite Tom replacing Buttercup's plugs, Cameron was reluctant to "rise to the occasion" again. For a few days he lay low at the car mart with excuses about mountains of paper work. Miranda suggested he might be encouraged back into action if Tom were to brave the heights and 'take over' the painting temporarily. This he reluctantly agreed, provided she did some lawn mowing. She knew her husband well! Cameron, too proud to have his job snatched away, resumed his role, insisting somebody be at the ready to rescue him should Buttercup go on strike.

Belinda would never forget the first day Miranda cut the grass, but not only because she took to the tractor like a farmer's daughter. After an excusable amount of gear crunching, she settled into chugging backwards and forwards rhythmically. The job was time-consuming and interminably boring. It required patience and concentration to keep the machine in perfect line, the best result achieved at snail's pace. Being a sun-worshipper, Miranda basked at the wheel in her bikini, prompting wolf whistles from the spouses painting above. After the hot summer she was already brown and was taking on a chocolate coating. She only had to look at a light bulb to tan whereas Belinda struggled to get any colour at all. So Belinda determined to start doing the ironing on the lawn in her bikini!

122

One afternoon, while Carla was sparked out in her cot, she set up her "work station", complete with Tom's extra-long extension. Freddie and Ollie were happily engaged filling their dumper trucks with sand left over from the renovation work. As Belinda worked her way down a mountain of laundry, her thoughts were soon racing away with ideas for her next exercise for Mid Sussex Potty Poets; write a poem on the theme, 'Your Favourite Holiday Destination'. She had a little notebook tucked in her clothes basket and intermittently scribbled down her mental meanderings.

PRESSING ENGAGEMENT
My ironing board's a plane, a boat,
A train; I'm going globe-trotting,
Travelling to places of great note,
Really I'm experience plotting.
Buttons, collars and cuffs
Around them I am riding,
How can I get the huff
When I'm out astral gliding?

To America I'll fly Concorde,
Sail the world in 80 days,
The Orient Express I'll board,
Touring in oh, so many ways!
Now my excursions have ended,
Ironing done and energy spent,
Travel is temporarily suspended,
Till my next pressing engagement!

Belinda's pile of clothes had not reduced as much as she had hoped, but at least her poem was written. Thirsty after her combined efforts, she decided to make tea. Miranda had progressed to mowing the side lawn, Ollie, in cowboy hat, riding shotgun. The tractor lines had become distinctly wobbly and Belinda hoped Tom, a stickler for symmetry, would turn a blind eye. She headed down the side of the house to offer the boys squash, but Freddie was not to be seen. Where the dickens was he? She started walking round the front of the house, breaking into a run. Thinking he might have gone inside, she dashed through the French doors, calling. Panicking, she hastily searched room by room every corner of the house. A lump in her throat, she was completely baffled, desperately trying to reassure herself he would not be far away. Surely, Freddie wouldn't have gone to see Grace? He was forbidden to go up to the flat on his own.

She hurried outside to call up to Tom. Shielding the sun from her eyes, she surveyed the scaffolding where he was working. Her heart skipped a beat. Halfway up the ladder, she could see a small pair of red Wellingtons. Fear flooded her. 'Oh my God, Freddie's too young to climb ladders. He's going to fall!'

Her heart was thumping in her chest. The plucky little boy was halfway up, with several more feet to reach the scaffolding. Tom was busy painting with his back turned, completely unaware. Belinda hesitated to call in case she startled Freddie. Trying to keep calm, she instinctively shot back into the house and rushed upstairs to Carla's room, the nearest to where Tom was working.

She tiptoed in, hardly daring to breathe lest she disturbed her daughter's afternoon nap. She went to the window and pushed it open. Outside, Tom was in his own little world painting, oblivious to the danger his son was in just below him. When he saw Belinda waving, he shouted: 'Hey, you up there, I could kill a cup of tea!'

Shaking, she held her finger to her mouth, shushing him. He could see the panic in her eyes. 'Tom, Freddie's coming up the ladder to see you. Do something!'

Aghast, Tom dropped his brush and sprang along the scaffolding, kneeling down where the ladder came up. She

124

could hear his voice gently coaxing: 'Now, Freddie, very slowly, take one step at a time…hold on tight now… that's it, climb up to Daddy'. Belinda's heart was in her mouth. She ignored Carla, starting to grizzle in her cot. She hardly dared watch. Suddenly, a little blonde head popped up and Freddie was soon in the safety of his father's arms.

Returning to the lawn with Carla in her arms, she noticed the tractor unoccupied nearby. Miranda, completely unaware of the drama, had gone to make tea and appeared on the lawn seconds after her, carrying a tray. Belinda, after the most frightening experience of her life, settled her daughter on the grass with a biscuit and drinking cup, and sat beside her, embracing Freddie between her legs. Breathing in the warmth of his silky curls, she kissed his hair. Tom passed the biscuit tin, urging him to take the last chocolate one: 'You deserve it, little man, for climbing all the way up.'

Belinda thought Tom was being too lenient, no doubt through sheer relief! As Freddie nibbled his digestive, she said: 'I suppose you thought you were being clever, but no more climbing ladders until you are a big boy, understand? Ladders are **very dangerous** and you could have fallen down, dead!'

He whined: 'Billie wanted me to play up d'ere.'

'Who's Billy?'

'I think he's an imaginary friend. I've heard Freddie talking to him,' Tom explained.

'Well, Freddie, darling, don't go doing any more silly things, even if Billie wants to - promise?'

The little boy smiled sheepishly and wriggled free, joining Ollie, playing with a toy fire engine on the grass.

*

The painting took six weeks and was finished apart from one section behind the main chimney that could only be reached from an inner roof inside the parapets.

'I'm not quite sure how you get to it,' Cameron admitted to the evening drinking assembly.

'Perhaps we can leave that bit for now, until your painter's cramp is better?' suggested Tom.

'Suits me, I've been round the house three times and my arm is killing me. Miranda's complaining her service is overdue.'

'I thought you'd just had the Panda done at the garage?' remarked Belinda, slow on the uptake.

'Yes, but it's **my turn** to be pandered!' insisted Miranda.

Tom quickly changed the subject: 'There are a lot of things we need to be getting on with inside before winter, starting with the loft insulation.'

'Never a dull moment,' thought Belinda, Carla's baby alarm alerting her with a shrill scream.

*

Buttercup sat on the front drive like a forlorn orphan for several more weeks. Cameron made repeated visits to The Mucky Duck asking after Patrick, but nobody had seen him for some time. After her usual reluctance to start, Buttercup was revived and swiftly secreted beneath the pines behind the house; put out to grass like a faithful old bovine.

The dry weather broke and continuous heavy rain reduced the grass to marshland. Buttercup was sinking in the mire. Tom's misgivings about her were eventually confirmed when The Mucky Duck's landlord, Nigel, got wind that Patrick had been arrested in connection with a builder's depot robbery. It was just as well she was lying low - which was more than could be said for Freddie's imaginary friend.

126

CHAPTER ELEVEN

Recipe for Disaster

Autumnal downpours followed the long, hot summer drought and Cameron's paintwork was doing a sterling job keeping out the elements. But nothing could save the Flowers' kitchen from near disaster.

Re-felting the flat roof was top of Tom's list of Running Repairs - 'running' being the operative word. He wanted the exterior finished before winter, though Belinda regretted the roof being left till last, especially with the unpredictable weather. She had asked whether it could wait till spring, but as it was leaking he insisted it going ahead. It would only take three days and be of minor inconvenience. She wasn't exactly enthused to hear that the roofers had been booked for October 13. Checking the calendar hanging above the kitchen sink, she was relieved to see it was a Monday, not Friday. She wasn't usually superstitious, but something about Haggleby Hall made her feel insecure.

There was no cast iron guarantee for good weather, though the day dawned bright and fair, albeit chilly, with possibility of showers by evening. The roofers had agreed to arrive early and work through until middle afternoon. Belinda made sure all kitchen chores were done by 8am. She did not cherish the idea that once the roof was off, the inside temperature would drop to the same as outside, around 64F. Nor was she happy about being beneath the roofers. Just before their arrival, she told Miranda: 'I'm keeping out of the kitchen as much as possible. I don't want a pair of hairy legs come crashing in on me.'

'That could be fun!' her friend predictably replied. 'I could spend all day finding something to do in your kitchen!'

Belinda was grateful that Miranda had invited Freddie next door to play while the roofers were at work and as always, he needed no encouragement. He and Ollie were becoming like brothers, shades of sibling rivalry already creeping in.

When Paddy O'Reilley Roofers arrived, Cameron went outside to instruct the team before he left for work. How she wished he or Tom could have stayed home, but both had busy schedules. Belinda presented Paddy and his three workers with mugs of steaming coffee and, after brief introductions, quickly withdrew. She spent the morning vacuuming and dusting the lounge while Carla contented herself in her baby bouncer clamped above the lounge doorway, hopping up and down and swinging to and fro like Tigger from Winnie the Pooh. When she had had enough, Belinda put her on the mat with her toys, allowing a few more precious minutes to finish the chores.

Braving the kitchen to prepare lunch, it was, unsurprisingly, perishing. Most of the roofing felt should have been stripped off by now and judging by the banging and crashing above, the work was progressing smoothly. Retreating to her favourite armchair in the lounge, she covered herself with a multi-coloured blanket her grandmother had knitted and "plugged in" Carla, tucking into a welcome cheese and pickle sandwich. Suddenly there was a knock on the door and a tangled grey head of hair peered round.

'Oh, ermh', Paddy cleared his voice with embarrassment. 'I'm sorry to disturb you, missus, but could me and the lads have a cuppa when you're finished like? It's a bit fresh up there today…and the tits have had a go at your milk. I've brought it in for you'

She silently cursed Tom for forgetting to put out the box for the milkman. At least Chloe Clutterbuck had made no subsequent appearances. 'Thanks, Paddy, please just help yourself. Tea and sugar are in the jars on the unit, milk in the fridge.' Carla beneath her sweatshirt, suckled on regardless. It seemed that wherever Belinda retreated for a feed, there was always somebody after her for something. Winding her daughter, she took her upstairs for an afternoon sleep. Freddie was still round the Maclaren's, so she afforded herself the luxury of a few moments at her Olivetti typewriter, attempting to piece together her next Potty Poets' creation. But try as she might, the words flowed like heavy duty concrete. Along the corridor she could hear heating engineer Ray Summers and his son, Simon, soldering pipes. The new central heating system was progressing well and she couldn't wait to see the back of the antiquated wrought iron radiators, the ultimate in ugliness against the elegantly designed interior.

Deserting her rising wastepaper basket, she headed to the bathroom, only to find herself ankle-deep in plumbing. At times like this she longed for a downstairs loo! The Maclaren's were fortunate in having one on both floors. But the remoteness of the Flowers' bathroom at the far end of the galleried landing was an inconvenience. It was doing nothing to help Freddie's potty training, or Tom's dubious habit of tinkling behind a tree. Belinda had caught him at it while she was picking rhubarb, but when she tackled him was fobbed off with some lame excuse about human smell discouraging Muntjac! She thought old Ned's recently mentioned tip about stuffing human hair into tights and hanging from branches far more savoury, and would avoid the risk of Tom being caught with flies open! Belinda had a few laddered pairs at the ready for when their regular hairdresser, Caron, next did the Haggleby Hall rounds.

Desperate to relieve herself, she trod precariously along the corridor, largely absent of floorboards. One slip and she could be devoured by a black hole! She spoke to Ray's derriere, painstakingly engaged in aligning copper piping. 'I'm terribly sorry, but can I use the bathroom?'

His cheery face popped up, glad of the diversion. 'Be my guest. It's good to have a stretch.'

Over the weeks he had been coming to the Hall, Belinda had warmed to him. Unlike some of the workmen, he was unflappable and quietly got on with the job. He was also officially registered her knight in shining armour. A few days previously he had gone to Freddie's rescue after he had fallen off his ride-on and cut his head open on the hall floor. Ray had carried him, screaming, to the kitchen table and calmed him while she dressed the wound. Little did she know that her hero was about to prove his worth again. Her return to the typewriter was short-lived, a few minutes later Carla screaming for attention through the adjoining wall. Collecting her from her cot, she dressed her in a thickly-knitted jacket and leggings and before going downstairs, offered Ray and Simon a cup of tea.

The kitchen was uncomfortably chilly, the temperature dropping like a tombstone through the opened roof. She sat Carla in her baby chair with a beaker of juice. Brewing up in the largest pot, she shivered, comforting herself with the thought of imminent central heating. In the hall she called up to Ray to collect his tea, and went outside with a tray and plate of digestives for the roofers.

She was surprised to see them wrestling with plastic covering. 'Are you calling it a day already, Paddy? It's only three o'clock?'

'We've got to pop back to finish another job in East Grinstead, missus. Don't worry; we're covering up the roof, so you'll be a 'right if it rains.'

Looking up, she saw thick black clouds rolling in. 'Are you certain about that, Paddy?'

'Oh yes, be Jesu-z. This lot would keep out Niagara Falls!'

Belinda wished she shared his confidence. A few minutes after his truck had left, sure enough a sudden downpour ripped from the uncompromising sky. From the lounge window she watched the garden deluged by an onslaught of silvery arrows. She doubted the effectiveness of the plastic covering and going into the kitchen to prepare the children's tea, battled her fears. Carla was grizzling and her nose felt cold, so she got her blanket, tucking it round her in the baby chair. She quietened her with a rusk, which usually worked! Miranda was due to send Freddie back at five o'clock, so Belinda started preparing the children's tea. Suddenly, Carla screamed, dropping her soggy rusk on the floor. What had triggered that? There was nothing for it but to pick her up. As she did so, Belinda realised the cause of her distress. Water was dripping on to her forehead, mingling with tears streaming down her reddened cheeks.

'Oh, you poor darling, let Mummy dry you,' comforted Belinda. Pulling kitchen towel off the wall holder, she was horrified to see water coursing down the wall on to the draining board. Dabbing Carla's face and giving her a cuddle, she became aware of plopping noises round the room, confirming her worst fears. She must do something to save her newly-polished parquet floor! With her daughter on one hip, she collected the only bucket, used for car washing, from the cupboard in the outer hall. Two others she possessed were still in the attic catching roof leaks. Tom and Cameron had "borrowed them" the night of a heavy storm, while she was in hospital recovering from having Carla. How she wished that Carl, her daughter's godfather-to-be, was still on site! But he and his boss Barry Bashford had completed the building work weeks before. "Uncle Carl" returned occasionally to visit and Carla always delighted in seeing him, as if the two had bonded the day he helped deliver her in the garden.

Beneath the drips, Belinda started dotting about saucepans, bowls and any other containers she could lay her hands on. Increasing in number and regularity by the minute, the metallic and thudding plip-plops were making music, which in another time and place would have been entertaining. Above the melody a door slammed in the hall and seconds later Freddie appeared, demanding "bic-kits."

'I'm sure you've had plenty already. It's tea time - you and Carla will have to eat in the lounge because the kitchen roof is leaking.'

Freddie thought it all a big game, smacking his feet in the puddles. 'Can I play boats, Mamma?'

'Not now, Freddie! Go and watch Sooty while I bring in your scrambled eggs.'

She put the plate and a glass of milk on his stand-up tray, warning him to be careful. Freddie's food usually ended up on the floor, but that was the least of her worries. Wedging the heavy oak door open, she returned to the kitchen and cooked Carla's eggs in the microwave. Removing them, she suddenly noticed water running down the wall, straight for the electric socket! Dabbing it, she switched off the socket. She could have been electrocuted! Near boiling point herself, she looked up in despair, only to see the ceiling bellying under the weight of water. The rain was still lashing down unmercifully, the thundering sound an eerie underscore in the "Pots and Pans Concerto". 'I just hope this lot holds,' she silently prayed.

The saucepans were quickly filling up and she emptied two. The kitchen wiring was only stapled to the walls and daring herself to look closer, her anxiety mounted. Water was trickling down the Baby Belling socket! How was she going to cook her and Tom's supper? They would have to eat round the Maclaren's. She was livid with the roofers for leaving her and the children "high and dry", or rather, low and rather wet. She suddenly thought of Agatha's story about her aunt and uncle returning from abroad to discover that workmen they had hired to repair the roof had scarpered with the lead. The east wing had been so badly damaged by rain it had to be demolished.

'Oh, why don't you f...ing stop,' she implored the heavens, just as Ray Summers was coming through the door.

'Umh... it's ok, we're all done for today,' he stuttered with embarrassment.

'No, Ray, I didn't mean you, sorry. I was cursing this terrible weather. As you can see, the roofers have deserted us. They've covered the roof with plastic but it's leaking like a sieve. I'm really worried about the electrics.'

'I can't believe anyone could be that stupid!' he exclaimed angrily. 'You'd expect roofers to make sure everything was watertight before leaving a job.'

'I did wonder about Paddy O'Reilley, but come to think of it I do remember one of his men saying he hoped the covers were enough.'

He ushered Belinda into the lounge with the children. 'Now leave the kitchen to me. I have some polythene to cover the wiring.'

Relieved, she picked up the wall phone to ring Tom. Typically, he was out on a job. His father gave her a number to reach him. After several rings, a softly spoken woman answered: 'Boxall and Berry Undertakers.'

Belinda wondered what on earth Tom could be doing at an undertaker's and asked to speak to him urgently. She held for a couple of minutes and fought back tears when she heard his voice. 'Hello, Bellie. Are you OK? Is there a problem? How are our roofing friends doing?'

'They are no friends of ours, Tom! Have you looked at the weather recently?'

'No, can't say I have. I am a bit busy with a stiff right now.'

She almost smiled, but the sorry state of her kitchen was far from amusing. Certainly, Tom's job did sound strange. He was an industrial photographer, but there was nothing industrious about a dead body.

133

'Tom, whatever you're up to, just listen! It's raining cats and dogs here and the roofers have gone. They had ripped the felt off and left plastic covering on, but it's useless. Our kitchen is like The Titanic!'

He gasped. 'Bloody hell - it sounds like the rats have left the sinking ship! Just wait till I get hold of Paddy O'Reilley; walking the plank will be a kindness... and to think he came highly recommended by someone Cameron knows. I suppose that explains it... Get Miranda to phone the garage and get him back pronto. I'll wind up here and be back soon as I can.'

'You must take that Paddy off the job! Our kitchen's a disaster. The parquet floor is ruined, the ceiling's about to fall in, water is going into the electrics - if it doesn't stop raining soon, we won't even have a kitchen!'

'Thank God Ray is with you. The kitchen might be flooded, but at least you have that swimming pool you've been dreaming about!'

'That's not even funny, Tom. We can't afford a new kitchen chair, let alone a swimming pool!'

*

That evening she and Tom shared Spaghetti Bolognese with Cameron and Miranda. At least Tom and Cameron had managed to stop the roof leaking, using tarpaulin the builders had left in the shed.

'I don't want another day like this, ever!' said Belinda, seeking sympathy.

'You won't have to, not if I can help it,' assured Tom, quietly fuming because Paddy O'Reilley was still not answering his phone.

'Most of the covers the roofers put on had blown off,' said Cameron.

'I specifically instructed that idiot to make sure the roof was watertight if he didn't get the job finished.'

Belinda was desperate to change the subject: 'How did you get on with your stiff today, Tom?'

'Hey, steady on there!' cautioned Cameron with raised eyebrows.

'My job was to photograph this dead bloke in a coffin.'

'Ah, that's not to be undertaken lightly.'

'Why were you photographing a dead body?' asked Belinda, licking tomato sauce off her lips. 'It sounds rather gruesome.'

'The client wanted one last picture of her dearly departed, looking all spruce in his best Sunday suit.'

'Ah, that's rather sweet, in a ghoulish sort of way.'

'The deceased looked pretty smart actually; he'd been shaved and the rouge and lipstick worked wonders.'

'Well, I find it all pretty macabre,' said Miranda. 'Once you're dead, you're dead and no amount of cosmetics can make you look otherwise. If you kicked the bucket, Camay, I'd prefer to remember you how you were.'

'You mean pale, red-eyed from too much beer and with grizzly whiskers only trimmed on alternate Sundays,' said Tom.

'Like now,' observed Miranda, tickling his beard. 'Perhaps he's dead already and this is just his ghost causing trouble.'

As if on cue, there was a sudden eerie ringing, lasting a split second. The conversation halted. It came from the old servants' bells in the far corner of the kitchen. A sudden chill filled the air. Surprised expressions were exchanged. Belinda swallowed hard, her heart pounding. No-one dared breathe for fear of upsetting an "unwelcome presence". Then nervous titters erupted.

'Oh, Camay, it's that wretched ghost from number five again. Perhaps he's ringing for some Five Alive!' Miranda joked.

'It's just the wind blowing up from the cellars. That's why it gets so cold in here.'

'If he's drinking Five Alive at least he's a healthy ghost,' said Belinda.

Tom bravely approached the row of brass bells hanging on coiled hooks, each one numbered bcneath. Before his eyes, bell five sounded again and rang several times, as if trying to communicate.

Everyone froze. Belinda shuddered as she recalled Nellie's words about Uncle Milton's spirit haunting Haggleby Hall. When the old woman was mentioning it that hot summer day she and Carla visited her and Ed's cottage, something had distracted her and she had dismissed it. She did not believe in ghosts, not at Haggleby Hall, anyway. Everyone agreed that the house had a warm, friendly 'feel' with positive vibrations.

Tom peered up. 'I can't really see very much, the bells are high up and covered in cobwebs. It's rather weird, though, I have to admit.'

'We've heard it a couple of times before and it's only that bell that rings,' Miranda explained. 'I think someone in room five is trying to tell us something.'

Cameron was his usual sceptical self. 'Perhaps the servant forgot to empty their jerry!'

'There must be a perfectly good explanation for all this. It could be a mouse or Ramrod trying to catch one,' suggested Belinda.

'Which room is number five?' puzzled Tom, thinking practically. No-one knew. 'I suppose I could trace the wires back to find it, assuming they're still intact, but it's not exactly top of my agenda right now.'

Knowing Tom's unending list of "to do's", it would be quite a while. Cameron was most likely right - wind from the cellars.

*

Next morning the Flowers' kitchen was filled with sunshine and it was hard to believe the previous afternoon's nightmare. The rain had finally stopped later that night and the place was starting to dry out. Before Tom went to work he tore down the polythene Ray had wrapped round the electrics.

Back on site, Paddy O'Reilley and his men were forging ahead with felting the roof, having been threatened with court proceedings if the job was not finished swiftly. Paddy had agreed to waive half the bill. Belinda thought he had been dealt with leniently and wanted them all gone as soon as possible. She wished Tom could stay at home but as usual, work had to come first. After waving him off, she put "Thomas the Tank Engine" video on for Freddie to watch, and took Carla upstairs for a nap before setting about restoring her kitchen.

She was sorting out her saucepans when the moment she dreaded arrived; there was a modest knock at the door and Paddy O'Reilley stood there, literally with cap in hand. Glancing sheepishly, he was apologetic: 'I'm really sorry, missus, about the water getting in. We did the roof up good and tight but it did rain buckets. Today's "Sun" said we'd had a whole month of rain in one day.'

'Do you read The Sun every day, Paddy?'

'Ah, yes, indeed I do.'

'But you couldn't have read yesterday's weather forecast.'

He fiddled with his cap. 'Oh, I usually read it over me coffee. I must have been distracted, missus.'

'Distracted by the page three girl perhaps? Had you have taken more notice of the forecast and covered up the roof properly, my kitchen would not now be looking like a condemned, municipal swimming pool.'

Suddenly, as if by fate, plasterboard bellying under the weight of water relented above the diminished figure. The sudden whoosh nearly knocked Paddy over, soaking his bushy hair and overalls. Spurting like a whale, he rubbed his eyes and wrung out his cap. 'I knew rain was expected,

137

missus, but we did cover up the roof. That strong wind tore the plastic sheets off. I wasn't expecting this to happen and then to have such a ding-dong…'

His words made her shiver, thinking of the bell ringing. She glared coldly: 'No, nor were we, Paddy. It was quite a shock to us all!'

CHAPTER TWELVE

Christmas Spirits

Christmas 1986, the first at Haggleby Hall, was indelible in Belinda's mind. Since moving in life had been fraught with building work, but with her kitchen now fully restored and the festive season fast approaching, she was looking forward to celebrating in style. As everything within the mansion was larger than life, it was fitting to have huge Christmas trees gracing the grand sitting rooms. Three of nature's finest, hand selected from the Haggleby Estate by Tom and Cameron, were duly delivered by Bert, the gamekeeper, for a fiver and a pint of Tom's highly potent 'Flower Power' home brew. (Tom had let on to Belinda that Bert had agreed to assist with another festive task, but she had been sworn to secrecy).

The spouses planted the trees in terracotta pots on the front lawn, ably assisted by Freddie and Ollie, and being some 12ft high, took much grunting and groaning to haul through the French windows. The most handsome towered magnificently in the ballroom bay overlooking the front lawn and Tom had to wire together three sets of bulbs to make sufficient impact.   Belinda and Miranda danced precariously on ladders, dangling giant baubles that Grace had bought for a song at an auction. Freddie and Ollie draped glittering stars and cotton wool-bearded Santas they had made with mum's help. Last, but not least, Belinda carefully tied on foil wrapped chocolate novelties for everyone to enjoy after the lunch.

The other Christmas trees took pride of place in the family lounges. Dripping with festive ostentation, they looked spectacular and when the doors adjoining the ballroom were open, could be viewed simultaneously. Tom suspended gold lanterns and chains from the high ceilings

139

and added holly and sparkle to fixtures and fittings. Soon the mansion was looking like Tinsel Town!

The hall he and Miranda decorated in early Victorian style, the period of the house, with freshly cut spruce and holly threaded between the metal stair spindles. Flowing round the capacious galleried landing with its ornate egg and rose carvings and down the stairs to the flagstone floor, the breath-taking sight was one of a traditional Christmas card. Tom regretted not having his camera from work, but it was holiday time, after all.

*

Christmas Eve dawned cold and bright as the families rose early to deal with last-minute preparations. There was the turkey to collect from the village butcher and fruit and veg from Ripe n' Ready farm shop. Then, mince pies to make for afternoon tea, and quite a few being needed as Miranda had invited the whole neighbourhood!

Belinda felt warmed by the thought of this, their first large gathering of the locals. With the huge rooms at Haggleby Hall it was great to be pushing the boat out and they would finally see for themselves the absence of any Hippie commune!

As for presents, the place offered numerous hiding places (although Freddie and Ollie were dab hands at ferreting them out). Belinda fondly remembered her family's previous Christmas Eve; Flowerpots Cottage having been so small Freddie's presents had to be secreted in the garden privy - it was so cold there was a pipe burst and Tom had to keep the fire going all night to dry them. She had found cooking festive lunch in the cramped kitchen a logistical exercise and then, at the table, poor Grandma Flowers had needed shoe-horning in.

Thankfully, Haggleby Hall offered the choice of two huge kitchens and two spacious rooms for dining. Christmas Eve morning Belinda and Miranda were

140

discussing cooking arrangements when the sons burst in. Clutched in Freddie's little fingers were foil wrappers looking uncannily like those Belinda had hung on the Christmas tree.

'On floor,' he announced.

Ollie, with traces of chocolate round his mouth, nodded. Eyeing the pair suspiciously, Miranda remonstrated: 'you little scamps have been pinching chocolates off the Christmas tree, havent' you?'

'Nnh. On floor,' Freddie repeated, shaking his head adamantly.

'Choc'lates all gone,' Ollie wined tearfully.

'We'd better go investigate!' stormed Belinda.

The boys were frogmarched into the ballroom and everyone gazed in disbelief at the big Christmas tree stripped of its chocolate novelties! All that remained was the odd empty foil wrapper.

'I don't believe it. Someone has stolen the chocolates!' exclaimed Miranda. 'I just hope they're horribly sick.'

'Well, it can't have been these two little monkeys. I deliberately put the chocolates out of their reach - and there would be evidence all over their faces.'

'The men wouldn't have taken them …would they?'

'Talking of monkeys, there's another odd thing. Our bowl of monkey nuts keeps going down, but Tom swears it's not him. Freddie can't even manage nuts.'

'I think we must have a nut-craving, chocoholic Christmas ghost!' surmised Miranda. 'All nibbles under lock and key!'

*

The afternoon party had the ingredients for a congenial gathering, but trouble was brewing. In the ballroom Grace served tea, while Miranda passed round her mother's alcoholic Christmas cake. Belinda did the rounds with piping hot mince pies, cooked to perfection for once. Carla was expertly balanced on her left hip, looking adorable in a red Christmas outfit and attracting much attention. Everyone wanted to hear the story of her swift arrival in the garden. It was a great topic for conversation as Belinda's tea grew cold on the fireside table.

Among the many neighbours were Minty and Pearl White, a strange couple who lived at the coach house over the wall. Minty ran his own dental practice and wore a permanent grin, almost as an advertisement. Belinda quickly grew to dislike this nosey-parker, who persisted in prodding her about Haggleby Hall's 'living arrangements'. Desperate to shut him up, she explained: 'The Flowers live on one side of the house, the Maclaren's on the other, with Granny Grace on top.'

Eyebrows raised, he persisted: 'Who actually owns what then?'

'Well, we each own a percentage of the property, worked out on floor areas. It. confuses the district council no end. They haven't got a clue how to apportion the Poll Tax, so they categorise us Flats One, Two and Three - it's a bit of a giggle, really, to think we pay peanuts to live here!'

'Can't be bad - whose part of the house are we in now?'

'The ballroom is shared. We use it for special occasions; high days, holidays, family get-togethers, that sort of thing.'

'The hall is magnificent, whose it that?'

'Oh, that's also communal, though we do have our own separate kitchens, lounges and bathrooms.'

Getting closer to the bone, he probed: 'What about the upstairs?'

Belinda had nothing to hide. 'We have four bedrooms, Cameron and Miranda, three, there's one we share and, of course, Grannie Grace has her own at the top of the house.'

All ears next to her husband, Pearl White chipped in: 'What about the shared bedroom?'

142

'Either family can use it for visitors, though we have to be very careful,' Belinda answered guardedly.

Minty was like a dog with a rabbit. 'How do you mean *careful*?'

Belinda related an episode in which her friend Nancy, being in no fit state to drive home, was invited to sleep in the spare room. 'Unbeknown to us, Cameron and Miranda had also invited a friend, Nick, to stay after a boozy evening. You can imagine what happened…Nancy got into bed with Nick and both were so far gone it didn't dawn on them till morning…'

Minty's eyebrows reached for his receding hairline as Pearl sniffed noisily. Red- cheeked, Belinda wished she hadn't elaborated. Her story would not exactly improve the families' image in the village. Desperate to redress the matter, she insisted: 'Tom and I, Cameron and Miranda are happily married…'

At that moment there was a scream and Pearl leapt on to a footstool near the fireplace, her body quaking as she drew her long tartan skirt tightly round her legs.

'Don't you think you're over-reacting?' Minty said curtly.

'N-no, no I'm not. Look!' She pointed nervously to a plate of half-eaten Christmas cake left on the hearth. 'The-there was a m-mouse on that plate. I - I saw it. It shot off behind the s-sideboard.'

Tom went to Pearl's rescue with a hastily poured double Scotch. 'Please have no fear, dear lady; our scavenger will be dealt with. Miranda, you must tell your mother our mice love her Christmas cake!'

Cameron quickly diverted everyone's attention. 'Now, who would like a quick look round – but I'm sorry I cannot guarantee any more wildlife?'

The tension evaporated as the assembled followed him and Tom good-humouredly into the hall. Belinda and Miranda started clearing away the tea things. In the kitchen

Belinda put Carla in her high chair, saying to her friend: 'I didn't know the men were going to give a conducted tour. I think I've left something rather personal on the bed.'

Oh, well, after our unwanted visitor that will really make their day!' giggled Miranda.

Cameron had salvaged the embarrassing scene, but she was obviously feeling duty bound to apologise. 'Sorry, Belinda, it was a bit cheeky offering to take the neighbours round your private parts without even asking, but we're all rather fed up with the same old questions that really boil down to who is sleeping with who?'

'You're right. It's time we stopped the busy bodies believing this is a Hippie commune and we share husbands. I was undergoing the Third Degree with Minty and Pearl White when that mouse appeared ...come to think of it, it was rather timely!'

Half an hour later Belinda and Miranda met the tour party in the hall and were heartened to learn that everyone was much enlightened after seeing the separate living accommodation. Whatever ice had remained was broken and even Pearl White was giggly, thanks to Tom's double whisky. The mouse incident was forgotten, but on leaving she couldn't resist another dig: 'An interesting arrangement you have here, particularly sharing the spare room, but it must have been simply dreadful for your guests - eerh, Nick and Nancy?'

'Oh, I think they rather liked it, once they'd sobered up and got a good look at each other. It must have been fate - they've just got engaged,' said Cameron, smirking.

*

Waving off the neighbours, the mums hastily went their separate ways to bath the children before the arrival of a Very Important Person, "Father Christmas", who was due to pay the children an early evening visit. Freddie, sharing

144

a bath with Carla, asked: 'Mummy, doesn't Farver Chwismus get stuck up chimddies wiv all dem toys?'

'No, darling, Father Christmas is magical. He can make himself smaller when he has to.' Belinda was amazed at her own quick-thinking.

The little boy could hardly wait to see this wonder man. Squeaky clean and wearing pyjamas and dressing gown, he rushed excitedly downstairs yelling repeatedly: 'Farver Chwismus is coming!'

The welcoming party gathered in the ballroom to await the VIP. To light Santa's way, Cameron had erected lanterns on posts, though no-one was sure whether he would be coming up the drive or down the chimney.

'Have you put carrots out for the reindeers?' Granny Grace asked the boys.

'Lots!' enthused Ollie, 'though mummy says not 'nough for Chwismus dinner now…don't like 'em anyway.'

Carla, fighting to stay awake on Belinda's shoulder, cooed. The boys stood with noses pressed to the windows, desperate to see movement in the coal black garden. Minutes ticked by, the glass misting. Everyone was bursting with anticipation. Suddenly, Freddie, pointing, exclaimed: 'Farver Chwismus dere!'

A faint light flickered in the darkness, hardly visible to the grown-ups. Twinkling, it moved slowly towards the tangled shrubbery Tom had named the Motto Grotto, centring the lawn. A ghostly figure carrying something on its back started to take shape.

'Farver Chwismus! Farver Chwismus!' the boys squealed, jumping up and down ecstatically.

Carla sprang awake, not knowing whether to laugh or cry. As the figure approached they were able to discern a large hooded man with a shaggy white beard, wearing a red cloak and carrying a sack. He was staggering and, after a few yards, lost his balance. The sack flew one way and he the other.

'Ooohh!' the onlookers chorused.

'Toys all broke!' Freddie howled.

'Farver Chwismus hurt. Get doctor!' sobbed Ollie.

'Don't forget, children, Santa is magical. He doesn't feel pain and what he has in his sack will be fine,' Tom reassured them. 'He's probably had one too many whiskies on his rounds.'

They watched as the sad figure rose unsteadily to his feet and struggled to heave the sack back on to his shoulders. Resuming his laboured course, he zigzagged his way towards the front of the house. Tears forgotten, the boys raced eagerly towards the sound of Tom's Heath Robinson-style school bell, hanging by the front door. By the time everyone had joined the boys, they were busy emptying a big sack that had mystically appeared on the threshold.

Playing the game, Cameron asked: 'How did Santa get that sack in? You two aren't tall enough to open the door.'

'Magic!' Freddie reliably informed him.

While the boys were distracted ripping paper off puzzles, crayoning books and toys, Belinda espied Tom, armed with a pint of homebrew, about to slip outside. 'You're supposed to give Santa sherry not homebrew.'

'Shush… this is for Bert, not Santa!'

She glared. 'Don't you think Bert's had enough?'

*

Christmas Day was eventful, particularly as it had snowed during the night for the first time in years. As the hall clock was about to strike six, Belinda was rudely awakened by a weight dive-bombing her.

'Open presents!' Freddie insisted, dragging a pillowcase bulging with brightly wrapped shapes to the bed. While she gave Carla her early morning feed, Tom, half comatose, took him downstairs to see whether Santa had paid a second visit down the chimney. They were soon back, her thoughtful husband carrying mugs of tea, traditionally laced with whisky, and shortbread biscuits. Freddie was clutching two stockings which he and Carla had left hanging empty on the mantelpiece, now stuffed with gifts. Belinda and Tom's bed was soon buried beneath a sea of brightly coloured paper.

In the lounge downstairs presents awaited everyone beneath the Christmas tree. Before the unwrapping ceremony, Belinda asked Freddie: 'Did Father Christmas have his mince pie and sherry?'

The little boy nodded, pointing to an empty plate and glass on the mantelpiece.

'Look, there's Santa's footprint in the ashes!' exclaimed Tom.

Freddie, despite his tender years, was not easily fooled. Struggling with two hands, he lifted Tom's Wellington boot standing by the fireplace and dropped it in the grate. 'Nah, dat's daddy foot.'

'Tom, I told you to put your welly back in the hall!' scolded Belinda.

'Santa must take the same size as me!'

*

Belinda stuffed the turkey and put it in the oven, timed for 2pm lunch. She had opted to do the roast, with potatoes and associated trimmings, while Miranda cooked the vegetables, prepared on Christmas Eve. At 11am Grace appeared, looking smart in a woollen, purple two-piece and silky cream blouse with a bow. She was accompanied by her gentleman friend, Roderick, with whom she had struck a deal over the sale of Haggleby Hall (though nobody quite knew what it was). He was looking dapper in a grey suit with a red cravat and matching silk handkerchief spilling from his top pocket. They were quickly monopolised by the children eager to show off their toys. By mid-day Belinda's parents had arrived and everyone assembled in the ballroom for pre-lunch drinks. To the dulcet tones of Bing

Crosby singing "White Christmas", the families toasted the first of many Christmases in their new home.

Lunch was served in the Flowers' lounge overlooking the front lawns, freshly falling snow painting a winter wonderland. Before Tom's roaring log fire, the four-course meal came together perfectly, plates, steaming bowls and casseroles appearing from all directions. Tom carved the turkey and with Belinda pulled the wishbone. Belinda, with the biggest part, wished for a long and happy future with their friends.

Eating more than their fill, the revellers withdrew to the ballroom to exchange presents. Serenaded by the "phut,phut, phut" of the Flowers' percolator, everyone unwrapped them in turn. Belinda flushed tearing the paper off Cameron and Miranda's. It was a teapot and staring back at her was a man sitting on a loo, pondering the eternal verities. Though not exactly a work of art, it inspired her to start a novelty collection. Tom chortled, opening a brick-sized book called Mansion Makeovers, while Miranda stood poised over Cameron's head with a marble rolling pin from her parents. Grace giggled, flicking through a cartoon book called 'High Fliers', as Roderick, a West Country hotelier, enthused over a video of BBC sitcom, Fawlty Towers.

Cameron's present from his brother had arrived by post from Scotland. When he opened it, he tittered, 'Alistair, always the practical joker!' Everyone was dying to know what it was, but he teasingly re-wrapped it. 'You lot have to wait till later!'

Miranda, dying of curiosity, tried soft-soap: 'Oh, come on, Camay, I'll give you a really special present later if you show us what you've got!'

'Humh, tempting, but you'll have to wait, like everyone else. Tell you what; I'll give you a clue. Let's say it will drive me up the pole!'

'As if you aren't already! Come on, what is it?'

148

He winked quizzically. 'Ah, the answer's blowing in the wind.'

'It doesn't look like a Bob Dylan album to me, more like hankies or a scarf.'

'Hey, keep your nose out! You'll find out soon enough.'

After the grand lunch followed by liqueurs and chocolates, grandparents were just starting to nod off when Tom loudly announced: 'Roll up, roll up! Cameron and I have a *little* party piece for you.'

Belinda was intrigued but nervous about his promise of some "hot entertainment" on Christmas Day. She had quizzed him about it all week, but he would not elaborate. Cameron had been known to drop his trousers after a few beers and Tom for going in drag to a fancy dress party. But with grandparents and young children present, they wouldn't do something like that, would they? As they left the room she inhaled deeply, praying they would have the sense to 'keep it clean'. All went quiet for a few minutes and then the front door slammed.

'Don't tell me, they've buggered off to the pub,' said Belinda's father grumpily.

'I think it's closed, Dad.'

The door opened and with fistfuls of trumpets, Cameron announced: 'Ladies and gentlemen, presenting our special house-warming present!'

It was none other than a hefty chunk of tree trunk. 'In true traditional style, a Yule log for The Old Hag's festive fire!' declared Tom.

After much struggling they managed to heave the gnarled stump into the ballroom fire, using their feet to wedge it on small logs, which immediately lost all trace of glow. The only roar was of laughter from the onlookers. But the merriment quickly turned to coughs and splutters as smoke billowed into the room. Despite the husbands' efforts to remove the offending lump, it was stuck tight (and there smouldered for the next three days!).

'I think the wind must have changed,' Tom tried to explain.

'If this is yours and Cameron's idea of not needing to stoke the ballroom fire for the rest of Christmas, we are not impressed!' bellowed Belinda.

The French doors were opened and a cold wind sliced through the fog like a guillotine.

Grandparents collectively elected for home, Grace and Roderick retreating upstairs to her flat. Miranda suggested a bracing walk for those remaining, to clear their lungs. Unusually, the husbands agreed without complaint. Although it had stopped snowing, the ground was starting to freeze, so the walk was hasty. After a couple of miles and frozen to the core, they headed back.

Cameron stopped everyone at the top of the drive: 'You know I'm all at sea after opening Alistair's present.'

'You're probably still recovering from the effects of smoke,' said Miranda, teeth chattering.

'I think the walk's freeze-dried my lungs, but now I can show you what Alistair bought me. I did say it was blowing in the wind.'

Looking across to Haggleby Hall, everyone burst with laughter. Flapping from the flagpole was the Jolly Roger.

'Let's head back, me hearties, I'm chilled to me skull and crossbones! And Polly, get the kettle on - or you'll go flying off the plank!'

The fresh air had done the trick, festive spirits were rekindled. Fortunately, the wind had changed and the ballroom fire was behaving itself with a reticent lick of flame.

*

Putting Carla in her cot that evening, Belinda was feeling restless. She left Tom and Freddie watching Captain Hook and went in the kitchen to clear away the supper plates. Suddenly, her heart skipped a beat. Something darted

150

rapidly across the floor and a tail vanished behind the dishwasher. She grabbed a torch kept handy for Haggleby Hall's regular power cuts. Shining the beam behind the machine, all she could see was a straggle of wires, a piece of half eaten toast and a Lego brick. She must have imagined it.

Next night she saw it again; just a flash of movement. It continued to visit nightly, as bold as brass, suddenly appearing from behind the lounge bookcase, making a beeline for the sideboard and vanishing. The antique piece of furniture, with its carved dogs' heads and game birds, made for a hunting lodge, provided the perfect setting for a 'Tom and Gerry' scenario. Tom's attempts to trap the mouse by placing a pile of books at both ends of the sideboard, failed miserably. "Wily Whiskers", so named, was spotted on several occasions running under the kitchen door, round the sink unit and disappearing behind the dishwasher.

The unwelcome visitor was there every night of Christmas week and assumed the culprit of the vanishing tree novelties and nuts. Tom bought a mousetrap and one night before bed set it with cheese, placing it on Wily's route. But the cheese remained untouched, as did a fresh piece the following two nights. Someone Tom knew had told him that mice loved chocolate. A piece of Cadbury's was duly placed under the spring. Next morning the chocolate had gone, so had the mouse.

The game of "Tom and Mouse" continued. On New Year's Eve he tried a tip from a rat-catcher Cameron knew from The Mucky Duck, to set the trap with a squashed After Eight. Mice were unable to resist the minty chocolate and while lingering to lick off the gooey mess – snap! It couldn't fail. But it did. Either Wily Whiskers didn't visit that night, or managed to resist the temptation to be lured to certain death. Instead, the creature had taken to exploring the Flowers' kitchen. In a drawer, he reduced paper doyleys to wedding confetti and under the sink, gnawed into Belinda's Fairy. Tom reckoned the green soap for cleaning his collars and cuffs would be good for inner mouse cleanliness, but his joke did not amuse Belinda.

Emergency talks were held over a beer on how they could get rid of Wily once and for all.

'We could try dragging Ramrod round to yours,' suggested Cameron, 'but it's not his territory and *he'll* be the one skulking behind the dishwasher!'

'That's Wily's route, Ramrod will find him impossible to resist!' conjectured Tom.

Miranda suggested a humane trap. 'The mouse is enticed into this box by some tasty bait and the door slams down. You can then drive it down the road and let it out.'

'What's the point of that? It can still wander back,' said Tom.

As the days passed he had to admit that Wily Whiskers had got the better of them! Then, one Sunday morning, he got up with Freddie and, as usual, they went downstairs to make tea. As he opened the kitchen door, there lying before them was a little brown creature with paws in the air!

When Belinda was greeted with tea, Freddie burst in, sounding tearful: 'Mumma, mouse dead!'

She struggled to hide a smile.

Tom explained: 'Wily must have followed his usual route; from the bookcase, across to the sideboard, along the back, under the kitchen door and then…slap bang into your radio on the floor.'

'Well, obviously I'm more attuned to catching mice - my radio is far more effective than any mouse catcher you have come up with!'

He looked defeated. 'Think I'll just stick to alligator-wrestling from now on!'

Joking apart, she hoped Wily's demise would put an end to the strange goings-on at Haggleby Hall.

CHAPTER THIRTEEN

The Oddie's

January 1987 was recorded as having the coldest spell in southern England since January 1740. People called it a "Siberian Winter". Snowfalls were accompanied by bone-chilling winds and sub-zero temperatures, but the families were snug. The loft had been fully insulated just a few days before Christmas, with the help of a government grant. Tom had expected various cash hand-outs to be available for a Grade Two Listed property but was bitterly disappointed. With so much work still to do, budgeting was paramount, but at least the couples had a lifetime's practice.

Ray Summers' central heating installation with industrial size convectors and radiators was heating the place like nothing ever had before. The humidity was soaring and everything felt damp, even the settee cushions, as the fabric of the building started drying out. Needless to say, Belinda's "triffids" (Tom called her much loved plants) thrived.

A sizeable Calor gas tank tucked away in the rear garden serviced three boilers in each of the kitchens. With the help of zone-controlled heating and thermostats, bills were expected to be manageable. When the monthly gas delivery arrived, Freddie and Ollie loved watching the driver attach the lorry's umbilical cord to the tank. In the three-quarters of an hour it took to fill, their little inquisitive minds pumped the poor driver with questions and it was Belinda's job to keep the coffee flowing. The gas was delivered monthly, but shortly before December's was due, it ran out and a bone-chilling weekend was endured without heating or hot water. From then on, Tom made sure to check the tank gauge regularly.

153

Deep snow kept everyone indoors, then one afternoon Belinda and Miranda, going 'stir crazy' with the children, dragged them out. Freddie and Ollie were desperate to try out a sledge, found in one of the outhouses, on little slopes on the front lawns. The wind was biting and Belinda's ears and nose ached with cold, while Carla, appearing snug in snowsuit and mittens, kept grizzling. It wasn't long before the boys, with soaking wet gloves after a snowball fight, begged to go back inside.

Despite being confined the children had ample room to burn their energy. Among favourite activities was 'camping' in upturned clothes horses covered in blankets and playing hide and seek in all sorts of obscure places, French window shutters, the outer hall cupboard, beneath the stairs to name but few. Equally exciting was launching plywood planes from the landing and having dens in huge cardboard boxes left by Ray Summers, in the hall.

The drive was impassable so for a few days Haggleby Hall was completely cut-off. They may as well have been in the middle of the Arctic, but Belinda felt safely cocooned in their ginormous 'igloo'. The white shrouded grounds contrasting an azure blue sky were breathtakingly beautiful and the air was pure and serene. Initially, being housebound was a novelty, but was short lived as supplies started running out. It didn't take long to discover how reliant everyone was on the outside world.

One morning, after more heavy snow, Belinda was draining the last bottle of milk when Mr Gubbins from the dairy rang. He breezily announced that his driver had not dared attempt the drive and had left her delivery at the bottom. Hailing the joys of country living, she went in search of Tom. He was on his two-week festive break and she eventually found him sitting on the bedroom floor opening a chunky box he had been storing for months under the wash basin.

Belinda was intrigued: 'I was wondering what was in that. It looks like a huge TV screen.'

'Didn't I tell you? It's a Tatung Einstein computer. It belongs to a client, who couldn't get on with it, so I promised him when I had time I would have a go.'

'You think you can get your head round that? It took you ages on that little black box thing you had at Flowerpots?'

'Oh, you mean the Sinclair ZX81.'

Back in the early 80s Tom had spent hours on the device, heralded as the first affordable home computer. It had seemed a waste of precious time then and she dreaded the same thing happening again. 'You and your boys' toys; can't you find something more useful, with so much to do around the house?'

'I just thought with a few days off, I would have a bit of fun. Mark my words, Bellie, computers will be our bread and butter one day!'

'If you say so, clever dick, but they'll be no bread and butter if you don't go and collect our delivery from the bottom of the drive before it is snatched by scavengers or starving motorists!'

Sulking, he went into the hall to wrap up warm; having decided not to invite Freddie, battling the snow alone would be hard enough. As Belinda busied herself in the kitchen, she glimpsed two heavily-clad strangers walking past the window. Surprised to see any sign of human life, she went to investigate. Tom was already opening the door to a dumpy figure in a beige duffle coat and striped tea cosy hat. Through a muffled scarf, a female voice greeted them: 'H-h-hello, I'm Astral Oddie and this is Edgar. We're your "gate-keepers".'

In the hall they all shook hands. It took Belinda a few seconds to cotton on who they were - the neighbours from Haggleby Lodge!

'Sorry we couldn't make your Christmas tea party,' said Astral. 'I did leave a message with your aged retainer.'

'Oh, you mean Fred Crum our butler.'

'Yes, he was very helpful. How many years has he been with you?'

'Since we bought an answerphone – you could say he's recorded "Tom foolery"!'

'Oh forgive me. I didn't realise…that's brilliant.'

The lanky gentleman folded back his anorak hood revealing thick greying hair tied in a ponytail. Beside him was a sledge carrying a large box. He spoke with a polished accent: 'I think these groceries belong to you.'

Tom invited the couple in and over steaming mugs of coffee, asked: 'How are you enjoying your retirement, Mr Oddie?'

Edgar insisted on being called 'Eggie' - Freddie's word for his favourite breakfast - which made Belinda smile. 'I spend most of my spare time in the garden. It's not huge, just a couple of acres, but the rhododendrons and azaleas are a picture in the spring. I would be delighted to show you round when the weather improves.'

'He hybridises some magnificent specimens,' said Astral excitedly, 'but he's too modest. He's had several registered by the RHS.'

'Are you a keen gardener, Tom?' asked Eggie. 'You've certainly done a great job in tidying the grounds. The former owners had let them go rather. I'm sure I can help you out with a few plants to add a bit of colour.'

'It's more of a labour than a love, but your offer would be most welcome.'

'And how about you, Mrs Oddie, are you retired?' asked Belinda.

'Astral, please… I'm still working part-time at Horley hospice.'

'Oh, are you a nurse?'

'A family bereavement counsellor, not what some would call the happiest of jobs?'

'Tell them about your other work,' urged Eggie.

She brushed her hand uncomfortably through her peppery curls. 'I'm sure they don't want to hear about all that.'

'You should be proud of your special gift!'

'Not everyone wants to know.'

'Go on, try us,' invited Tom.

'W-ell,' she faltered, 'I've just finished training as a spiritualist.'

'How interesting; I assume bereavement counselling and spiritualism complement each other?' Belinda commented.

She smiled coyly. 'In a way, but I try to keep my roles separate.'

'Astral was the seventh child of the seventh child,' Eggie chipped in. 'Been psychic since she was knee-high to a duck, but best keep it under your hat with the people round here.'

'Tell us about it,' endorsed Tom. 'Half the village thinks *we're* hippies.'

Eggie's eyebrows rose: 'Really? We're not ones to listen to gossip. Thinking of flowers, there used to be some stunning borders on your front lawn here.'

While the men were discussing more earthly matters, Belinda invited Astral to tell her about her spiritual gift.

'I can go into a shop that to you would look empty, but to me is full of people.'

'How do you mean?'

She rubbed her hands, choosing her words. 'Well, I can see people who have passed over.'

'Fascinating; it must be difficult knowing where to queue!'

She laughed. 'No, I'm used to it. It all started when I was a child. My granddad came to me on several occasions after he died.'

'Weren't you frightened?'

'No, it was lovely to see him with his gentle smile, as if he'd never gone. Well, he hadn't really. I remember feeling something warm on the back of my hand.'

'Oh?'

'When I was a nipper he used to put his warm pipe on my hand. I used to hate it, but he was only being playful.'

The story triggered one Belinda had to tell: 'One dark evening, as a girl, I was walking home from my friend's; we'd been revising for exams. I saw this black figure, a man in a long cloak, wearing a funny-shaped hat, standing under the street light. He looked very strange, certainly not of the world I knew. I was frightened and ran all the way home. A few years later - I was doing a project on the history of my village - and I read that a thatched cottage near the spot where I had seen him had been a Quaker Meeting House in the 17th century. There was a picture and I realised he was dressed just like the Quakers.'

'I bet you were quaking at the knees!' Astral joked, 'but it sounds very likely that you saw an apparition.'

'Or someone waiting for a lift to a fancy dress party,' said Belinda, making light of it.

It was snowing again and as the visitors were in no hurry to leave, she offered to make more coffee. In the kitchen Astral told her about when she was a young girl, her mother taking her to look at a new school, 'While mum talked to the headmistress I was sent to play with the children. I remember this girl dressed in sportswear, as if she was ready for PE. She showed me how to jump - much further than anyone I have ever seen before. She was so light on her feet she seemed to float above the playground. She could have been an Olympic champion, but I suspect she was more your paranormal athlete playing her own games.'

'You mean she wasn't for real?'

'On the other side, yes.'

'She was a spirit?'

Nodding, she said: 'It sounds like you have certain sensitivity, Belinda. I've recently started meetings for people interested in spiritualism. You're welcome to come and join us.'

'N-no, that sort of thing is really not for me. I'm more of a God person and I'm not sure our vicar would approve. Tom and I go to the village church. We are having Carla christened soon.'

'We never had our three christened. Sadly, they have all flown the nest now. We do miss them. Eggie and I rattle around in the lodge, but we'd never move because of his beloved garden. You must come down for tea.'

Belinda nodded enthusiastically and he, half listening, interrupted: 'You're very welcome, but wait until the azaleas and rhododendrons are out.'

Suddenly, Carla's baby alarm erupted. It sounded like someone beating merry hell out of her activity centre, with a cacophony of bells, rattles and squeakers. Baby screams went into overdrive. Belinda was furious: 'Oh no, Freddie's woken her up. Wait till I get hold of him!'

She flew upstairs, Astral following. In Carla's room there was no sign of Freddie. Belinda noticed it was icy cold. The activity centre on the end of the cot was silent. Who could have caused such a din? Carla, blotchy-cheeked with tears, lifted her arms pleadingly. Belinda rocked and shushed her comfortingly, but it took some minutes to calm her and she remained unsettled.

'There's no sign of Freddie. He must be hiding,' said Belinda.

'How do you know it was Freddie?' asked Astral.

'Well, it couldn't have been Carla - the activity centre is fixed to the outside of her cot.

'What about the other little boy?

'Ollie? I doubt it. He and Freddie are forbidden from playing up here when Carla is asleep. They know they'd be in big trouble if they did.'

Astral eyed her curiously, shivering.

'Carla's room is always the coldest in the house. I sometimes wonder if we have a ghost though the house seems to have *good* vibes.'

'Humh?' remarked Astral, thoughtfully.

Suddenly, a wind-up monkey on the chest of drawers started banging its cymbals, making both women jump.

'It does that sometimes of its own accord,' explained Belinda. 'Carla's nursery rhyme book plays 'Twinkle Twinkle Little Star' in the bookcase. It's not supposed to unless someone opens it, and I'm sure her toys move around… of course, it could be the boys.'

Astral's prominent eyes grew wider. 'Perhaps it's vibrations …'

Belinda was eager to hear more, but Carla's grizzling cut her short. 'I'd better take her down for lunch.'

'Is it alright if I stay here for a few minutes?' asked Astral.

'OK, but don't get colder than you are already.'

When Astral re-joined her, Belinda was feeding Carla fruit dessert. 'Is everything all right?'

'It is very cold up there. I sense something else.'

Puzzled but reluctant to hear more, Belinda offered her a warming sherry. While Astral took over the feeding spoon, she went into the lounge, asking Tom to pour one for everybody. After a few sips, the conversation drifted on to the boys.

'Those two get into all sorts of mischief,' said Belinda. 'Remember all that heavy rain before Christmas? The drive flooded, which it had never done before. We watched the water heading towards the front door and we thought the main had gone. When Tom went over to investigate, he found toy trucks, bricks and stones blocking the drain. The boys had been playing quarries… poor Tom's become paranoid about drainage!'

Astral smiled: 'Ah, the joys of sons; we have two and our daughter was a tomboy.'

Belinda wanted to confide in her about Freddie. 'He has this imaginary friend. Children sometimes do, don't they? Last summer, small as he was, he *actually* climbed a ladder twenty feet up to the scaffolding. He said his friend Billie was up there and wanted to play. Freddie was barely two-and-half and I would never have believed he would do something that dangerous. I nearly died seeing this little pair of red Wellingtons on the ladder. It was just as well Tom was working up there and managed to coax him up without panicking him. But it really scared us all…'

'Humh' said Astral. 'Perhaps he just wanted to see his dad? You are right, though, children do have imaginary friends and we adults can't possibly know whether they are based on somebody they actually know or are just in their head.'

'This might be a strange question but do you think they can see things that we can't?'

Astral was animated. 'Well, young children are more sensitive to spirits than adults because they have only recently crossed over from the other side and unlike grown-ups are completely open-minded…'

Eggie, coming into the kitchen ear-wigging, cut her short. 'Darling, I'm sure our new neighbour doesn't want to hear about that sort of thing. Watch it, Belinda; she'll be having you down to one of her meetings to commune with her 'special guests!'

'I sometimes wonder if I have ESP,' said Belinda, 'but it does bother me that Freddie needs an imaginary friend when he has Ollie.'

'Oh, he's very real to Freddie,' said Astral, cryptically.

*

That evening Tom and Belinda told Cameron and Miranda about their neighbours. 'Oddie is a good name for them,' said Tom.

161

'Eggie Oddie - sounds like one of Miranda's omelettes,' joked Cameron. 'You say he's an expert gardener. Do you think he'll come and scramble through the brambles with us, with his machete?'

'If he's got time, his couple of acres obviously keep him busy; though he has offered to give us some shrubs and show me how to plant them.'

'He's very educated, no doubt - he reels off all these plant names in Latin - but he sounds obsessed with gardening,' said Belinda. 'He gardens in the dark, heaven knows how - by floodlight I suppose?'

'They're certainly an odd couple', endorsed Tom. 'Astral is a bereavement counsellor and a spiritualist - a strange combination.'

'I think they complement each other,' said Belinda, reiterating her earlier words.

'Do you think Astral's egghead husband uses a spirit level when he's gardening?' chuckled Cameron.

Miranda grimaced. 'Astral sounds the ideal person if you want to contact a dead loved one. Camay, if you popped your clogs first would you keep in touch?'

He shaped his hands over her bosoms. 'Sweetness, however could I not touch you - dead or alive?'

Belinda had something to get off her chest and told them about the incident earlier in her daughter's bedroom. 'Carla seemed terrified. She was looking straight through me towards something or *somebody else.* I think she was spooked by another presence.'

'Did you ask her what she saw?' quizzed Tom.

'No, she's only a baby, Tom, but Astral thought there was another presence.'

'That's poppycock! You really don't believe in that sort of thing?'

'Well, she is a spiritualist.'

Miranda had heard enough. 'Well, we all had a *lovely* morning. We had a snowball fight and did Freddie tell you, we made this brilliant snowman? You two must come out and see it tomorrow.'

'Oh yes, he was full of it at bedtime.' chirruped Belinda. 'Were the boys with you the whole time… they didn't go off upstairs, even for a few minutes?'

'No. When we came in we were all so cold I made hot chocolate and we sat by the fire watching a video.'

'There you are then. If it wasn't the boys knocking seven bells out of Carla's activity centre who or what was?'

'Urban spacemen, probably,' mumbled Cameron, disinterestedly.

'Or someone from the *astral plane*!' joked Tom.

Belinda shivered, feeling the blood drain from her face. 'What if the place is haunted? And the baby room of all places.'

'You don't really believe in that nonsense, do you, Bling?' scoffed Cameron, using the affectionate nickname he had given her.

'There's a logical explanation for everything,' reassured Tom.

'Like the bell ringing,' said Miranda, unthinkingly.

Tom and Cameron exchanged knowing stares. Belinda knew they were hiding something. 'What about the bell-ringing?

'Tell Belinda about that night she and the children were at her parents and you came round for stew, Tom?'

'Oh yes, Randy, your dumplings were lovely!' exclaimed Cameron, attempting diversion.

'Camay; I'm talking about the bells - you know, "I can't stand the bells!" Some bloke called Quadi-moto said it in a story about Notre Dame, I think?'

'Quadi-moto - sounds a great name for a Japanese car!'

'I think she's talking about the story of Quasimodo, the hunchback of Notre Dame,' explained Tom.

Belinda couldn't bear any more. 'Stop beating about the bush, you lot! What did you find out, Tom?'

He sighed. 'I didn't want to worry you, Bellie, but you know the old servant's bell we heard ringing in the kitchen, bell five? Well, we traced it back to the airing cupboard in the children's ante-chamber.'

'You did, how?'

'Cameron and I went upstairs to have a look at the airing cupboard - I'd had this idea about using the space for an en-suite for the children - and we found this old bell-pull inside. When I tried it, Miranda heard bell-ringing in the kitchen, just like that night we were all in there.'

Belinda's spine tingled. 'OK, but *who* was pulling the bell that night we heard it?'

Tom shrugged. Cameron quickly changed the subject: 'Great idea of Tom's; an en-suite for the children's rooms, don't you think? You could say it was a flash in the pan.'

'Or perhaps you flushed out something rather unpleasant!' she warned fearfully.

'I bet it was that big fat mouse giving Ramrod the run-around,' reassured Miranda.

'How come the bell pull is inside the airing cupboard, Tom? An odd place, don't you think?'

'No, it isn't. In the house deeds the children's rooms were originally one and when   it was divided and the airing cupboard put in, the bell pull was left inside. But, don't worry, Bellie. I'll take the damned thing out!'

'And while you're at it, get rid of Carla's activity centre? I can't go through all that again -nor can she!'

CHAPTER FOURTEEN

Brush with Fear

Freezing weather persisted till middle March and after being confined to the house for what seemed an eternity, Belinda took her first walk round the garden with Carla. She was just big enough to ride in the buggy Tom had recently bought, which, though second-hand, was much easier to wheel about than Freddie's old pushchair. Baby buggies were relatively new on the market and a new one was a luxury they could not afford.

The thaw had set in at last and being outside was uplifting. All around them dripping water was making a melody of its own. Belinda was amazed to see weeks of accumulated snow vanishing rapidly and she and Freddie were well prepared in their Wellingtons for the pools of water dotted about them. The snowman Cameron, Miranda and the boys had built was still remarkably intact. His carrot nose had disappeared, probably devoured by wildlife, but the moth-holed, plaid cap was lying sodden on the memorial stone that Belinda had happened upon last summer, while in the throes of having Carla. She wrung it out, splashing the inscription. Brushing water off with her gloved hand, she recalled Tom mentioning that he had wire-brushed it just before the snow and the inscription could now be read in full.

BILLIE BLEWETT
June 5 1957 to October 13 1965
Flying with God's angels
Rest in peace

'I wonder who Billie Blewett was?' she said aloud. The surname she had not heard before and the word "flying" suggested a bird. Birds didn't have surnames, though. She thought of poor Monty, originally Uncle Milton's parrot, which had escaped after its cage was knocked over by Ramrod, never to be seen again. She doubted it would have survived the harsh winter.

'My fwend's Billie,' answered Freddie, scraping the stone with a stick. 'He plays wiv me sometimes. He likes Mr Snowman … but mamma, nose gone!'

There was that name again; Billie, it was starting to haunt her. A lump rose in her throat recalling the terrifying day last summer when Freddie was lured up the ladder by his so-called imaginary friend.

'Can we put new carrot in? And Billie wants 'is 'at back on.'

'Oh, does he? Tell Billie we can't because Mr Snowman is melting. He might have lost his head by tomorrow.'

Freddie's face crumpled.

'Mr Snowman is only frozen water and when he sees the sun he goes back to liquid again. We'll build another snowman next winter when it snows.'

Tears filled his eyes. 'Don't want him to go.'

'He has to darling. He's melting like chocolate does in your mouth… if you're a good boy you can have some when we go back in.'

As if somebody flicked a switch, his little forlorn face lit up and he started skipping wildly, dodging this way and that, and giggling, as if playing catch with a mate. Did the mention of chocolate change his mood, or was his imaginary friend running circles round them?

Whatever game was being played, perhaps it was time she and Tom put a stop to this "Billie". The question was, how?

*

Watching the changing seasons in the secluded oasis of her home gave Belinda ceaseless pleasure. Having six acres was a privilege and she loved strolling round them

166

when the opportunity arose. As trees, shrubs and plants popped their buds there was an air of expectancy and thoughts of another glorious summer in their new-found paradise warmed her. Her favourite spot was the side garden with an aged mulberry tree. Beneath it during winter a fleet of snowdrops bobbed their floral sails, closely followed by a contrasting flotilla of purple and yellow crocuses. She was excited to see new signs of life in the mulberry tree. Tom's attempts to revive it by piling nutrient-rich soil over its semi-prostrate trunk were proving effective and she lived in hope of a bumper crop of fruit for summer puddings.

Like the house, the long-neglected garden was showing its appreciation at being taken in hand again. The rhododendron hedge running along the west side was a mass of purple flowers called "Ponticum", which proliferated along the Sussex lanes. The front lawn's "Motto Grotto" of rhododendrons splashed glorious crimsons, pinks and whites across their tangled emerald canvas. Eggie, their neighbouring garden authority, said the shrubs would have been even better had they not suffered bud blast during the freezing "Siberian" winter. At its coldest she would always remember the morning she went into the kitchen to find the laminate coating on her cupboards either cracked or lying in slivers on the floor. Tom, having a severely limited budget, had scraped off the remaining plastic and sprayed the fronts green.

Mother Nature, likewise, was carrying out her cosmetic work as the dull, winter green lawns wrapping round the house slowly took on a vivid vibrancy. Belinda watched the gnarled wisteria plaited untidily along the front and side of the house slowly transform from a jumbled brown mass of twigs into breath-taking spills of slate blue pendulums. Their fallen flowers billowed like confetti in the hall and kitchen, keeping the vacuum cleaner on overtime.

167

Behind the outbuildings with two sheds, a stone-built garage and former game pantry, the walled kitchen garden played host to a vintage crop of Japanese Knotweed. Tom had tried weed killer and hacking it down, but it persisted with a jungle-like vengeance. Whenever she saw it she thought of Uncle Milton, still missing after all these years. Her imagination began running riot again. Could his remains be underneath the thick stubborn stems? But surely the police would have thought of that when carrying out a search? If they hadn't and Belinda was right, Tom could be in for a nasty shock when he started resurrecting the walled garden for growing fruit, vegetables and flowers. He was feeling inspired by a BBC programme they were watching called The Victorian Walled Garden, which followed restoration work at Chilton Foliat, in Wiltshire.

When Belinda and Miranda didn't feel like a trip to the supermarket they would buy fresh produce from a smallholding on the other side of Haggleby Road. They walked down there with the children two to three times a week, buying items priced on bits of cardboard and leaving money in a tin under the stall. Sometimes they saw the elderly couple who ran it, Bill and Beth, who lived close by in a bungalow owned by the estate. To the children's amusement Beth wore Wellington boots slit down the back and they called her "Mrs Flappy Welly."

*

Life at Haggleby Hall brought the Flowers' and Maclaren's much closer to nature. Occasionally, when Belinda walked on the surrounding farmland she espied deer, which catching sight of her, swiftly vanished. It was a thrill to see them sometimes on the drive, though the poor animals obviously felt otherwise. At night their endearing faces captured in the car headlights were enchanting, though within a few seconds they would spring over the fencing as light as air and be gone. Her Ford Fiesta travelling up and down often encountered pheasants, inevitably when she was in a hurry. The males' sleek, bronze-speckled, blue-tinged feathers were beautiful, but the pea-brained birds darting aimlessly before her wheels were infuriating.

Sometimes she would see a pair of French partridges strutting around the garden, pecking everything in sight. Tom called them "Ropandum Eaters" - another term from his alternative dictionary - so coined after the birds decapitated a thriving collection of Snakes Head Fritillary he had lovingly planted in his new rockery. He had built it behind the line of conifer trees right of the front lawn, having utilised the bank of an old swimming pool he had discovered after clearing a tangled pile of brambles that must have been running riot for years.

One day Belinda was sitting on the lounge steps engrossed in writing her next Potty Poets verse when something tickled her toes. It was a French partridge and her surprised cry alerted Bootsie, a golden retriever the Maclaren's were minding for old friends. The dog bounded across the lawn, hot on its tail feathers, but to no avail as the startled creature shot over a hedge.

Having Bootsie about the place was a mixed blessing. He had a strange fetish for footwear, which had inspired his name, and sorely tested everyone at Haggleby Hall. Leaving a pair of boots or shoes around was fatal because invariably one would go missing. Whatever size, Bootsie was not proud when the urge to grab one came over him. Periodically, the odd item was discovered under a shrub when Tom was gardening or in a remote corner of the house when Belinda and Miranda were cleaning.

Within Haggleby Hall's walls were other testing life forms. In spring the children's bedrooms were always invaded by lacewings, though the delicate green flies were more of a nuisance than harmful. They were shortly followed by strange, minute insects which looked like black specks and sat motionless on windowsills. Tom christened them "Snurgle Beasts", which made them sound fierce but, oddly, they did nothing short of disappearing as mysteriously as they had come.

The garden at night could be incredibly noisy, despite the blissful absence of traffic and tranquil rural surroundings. On one occasion Belinda was rudely awakened by a blood curdling cry, which sounded like murder being committed.

'Don't worry, darling, it's only foxes making love,' Tom assured her.

'It sounds like he's strangling her!'

Another night an eerie flapping noise disturbed them. Belinda was terrified. She thought an evil spirit was in the room. When Tom put on the light a startled bat was circling over them. She took refuge beneath the bedclothes while fearlessly he crossed its path to open their two windows wider. The disorientated creature quickly vanished into the night, but just as they were settling down again, it reappeared with a mate. They played chase, round and round, in and out of the windows, and it took some time for Tom to shut them out.

As spring rolled into summer the families had another countryside nuisance to contend with, this time man-made. Crow-scarers were primed by Ripe n' Ready Pick Your Own farm to go off at the crack of dawn and explode half-hourly till dusk. Every morning they awoke Belinda and as she drifted off again, the next bang guaranteed her fully awake. The fields surrounding Haggleby Hall were dotted with the pesky machines and she was not the only one getting ratty. Tom had a word with Chris Brown, the farm owner, who agreed to reset the devices, but this only delayed their wake-up call by an hour. Then the estate's gamekeeper, Bert, dropped in and over a pint of homebrew Tom asked for his help. Thankfully, within days the crow-scarers were replaced by scarecrows!

170

A summer highlight was celebrating the families' first anniversary at Haggleby Hall. A barbecue was held on the back lawn, with foundations of the demolished wing which served as a perfect patio. Miranda made a cake in the shape of the house, with cream coloured walls, crenulations and iced doors and windows. It was filled with Ripe n' Ready's strawberries and washed down perfectly with champagne. But living in the country was not all strawberries and cream. In hot dry weather the upstairs rooms were invaded by big black flies. They came off the fields, sat on the walls during the day and as the temperature fell, crawled through the ill-fitting windows, even when closed. Spraying and vacuuming up the currant-like clusters became an evening ritual.

Flies weren't the only menace in the house. Something sinister was definitely at work in Carla's room and this time it was Tom who witnessed it. One Sunday, full of enthusiasm after a week's caravanning holiday at East Wittering, he set about painting over the blue birds on the wallpaper. He whistled as he worked, dipping his brush into the paint can balanced carefully on top of the ladder. At lunchtime Belinda did a roast, accompanied by a bottle of red wine, which was not such a good idea. Afterwards Tom, in good humour, returned upstairs to resume the painting and when she had done the washing up, she went up to check his progress.

'That's looking so much better, darling. I'm sure Carla will love it, especially when we put up some friezes. But I'd watch that paint can if I was you - it looks a bit dodgy on top of the steps.'

Half an hour later she was making tea when he burst through the kitchen door, fulminating: 'Don't you dare say I told you so, or I'll throttle you!'

Back upstairs she stopped dead at Carla's door. 'Good God, Tom, what have you done?'

The paint can had fallen on to the floor, still upright, but the heavy impact had splattered emulsion over the carpet and across Carla's new little bed, spraying her Mickey Mouse duvet and cuddly animals bright apricot.

'Tom, why didn't you cover the bed before you started?' she remonstrated.

'Because I wasn't planning on spilling paint and nor did I! Believe it or not, I had nothing to do with that can falling off.'

'I suppose you're going to tell me the wind blew it off.'

Angrily, she shunned his embrace as he tried to reassure her: 'We can wash Carla's "cuddlies". Emulsion is water based, it will wash out.'

There was so much mess Belinda didn't know where to start clearing up. On auto pilot, she stuffed the sodden toys into the plastic linen bin and carried it to the bathroom. How could she begin to explain to Carla what had happened? Still fuming, she marched downstairs. Freddie and Ollie were busy playing with Duplo on the kitchen floor, too engrossed to acknowledge her. She unbuckled Carla from her bucket chair, parked beside them. Bracing herself for an emotional outburst, she carried her upstairs, praying for divine help. Thankfully, inspiration came in a flash.

'Carla, Daddy thought he'd paint your "cuddlies" to match your new room, but mummy thinks they look silly so I thought we could give them a bath and make them look colourful again.'

The toddler's face lit up as her tiny hands clutched the side of the bath, eagerly awaiting the sight of her precious toys taking a dip. One by one Belinda tossed them in - Tricky Ted, Spotty Dog, Ellie Elephant, Jazzy Jeff, Marcus Mouse...but to no avail!

Carla suddenly started screaming. Perhaps their appalling state had finally registered? But far from being upset, she wanted to join in the game. Belinda, not thinking twice

172

about her pretty cotton dress Tom's parents had bought for her first birthday, moved the bin over and the little girl squealed excitedly, plunging her favourite bear, Snowy, into the apricot-stained water.

'I don't think your "cuddlies" will ever look the same,' said Belinda - 'they'll be even better!'

Her daughter whooped with delight. It was one of the greatest games ever.

*

That evening relations in the Flowers' household were somewhat frosty. Belinda was exhausted after spending an hour-and-a-half in the bathroom, but at least Tom had removed the ruined carpet, promising to replace it the following weekend. Carla, having said 'goodnight' to her cuddly animals pegged on the washing line, had happily gone to bed with Ollie's favourite bear, Talky Ted, which he had loaned her for the night.

As Belinda was going downstairs Miranda appeared, inviting her and Tom round for a consolation drink. In the Maclaren's kitchen Tom sat clutching his beer tankard, looking sheepish, and the conversation inevitably turned to the afternoon's events.

'I hear your decorator's been rather clumsy with the emulsion, Belinda. I'd sack him if I were you,' Miranda sympathised.

'That would be a kindness, believe me.'

'Perhaps we should have given that "quick one" at The Mucky Duck a miss,' Cameron unthinkingly let on.

Belinda was livid. 'You didn't go to the pub, did you, Tom? And you had that wine at lunchtime. No wonder you knocked the paint off. You were drunk!'

'We only popped out for a swift one, Bellie - painting's thirsty work - but I wasn't drunk. I swear that paint falling off was nothing to do with me or the booze.'

'You'll be telling me next that some weird magic was at work.'

'Well, I was using "Magicoat", but it happened while I was in the loo! I heard this bang and when I went back it was on the floor. I couldn't believe it. I'd left it perfectly balanced on the ladder.'

'Perhaps it was one of the boys?' suggested Miranda.

'Impossible, they were downstairs playing on the kitchen floor.'

'Bootsie could have gone up there, though he doesn't normally go your side of the house,' volunteered Cameron.

'No, he wouldn't have got in. I distinctly remember closing Carla's door to keep the smell of paint out of Freddie's room.'

Belinda was unconvinced. 'Whatever happened, Tom, there'll be no more boozing while you're decorating!' She had to admit she had never known him lie to her. He would always hold up his hands when in the wrong.

Memories of strange happenings in Carla's room flooded back and fear swept through her. Should she share her thoughts with the others? They would joke about it, but anxiety was getting the better of her. 'I…I know this may sound whacky, b… but supposing what happened was some supernatural force?'

'You mean one of those polka ghosts that dance round the room hurling things about?' suggested Miranda, looking deadpan.

'I think you mean *poltergeist*', corrected Tom, smiling.

'Th…that's what I meant,' agreed Belinda, not daring to repeat the word.

'I think you're getting a bit paranoid, Bellie. There must be a more down-to-earth explanation, but I can't think of one just now.'

Her anger welled up again. 'You're always so sceptical, all of you! I'm telling you there's something nasty at work in that room. Carla will have to sleep with us for now.'

174

'Hey, I'm sure there's nothing to worry about. Let's just put it down to one of those things,' suggested Miranda. 'Now, why don't you stay for a bite to eat?'

'Then we could play Ollie's new game, "Spooks Alive"!' suggested Cameron, tactlessly.

Belinda was inconsolable. 'Sorry, Miranda, I'm not hungry. You can stay, Tom. I'm going to ring Astral. See what she makes of this.'

CHAPTER FIFTEEN

An Ill Wind

Belinda was inexplicably woken from a deep sleep. It was pitch black. The landing light she and Tom always left on for the children was out. 'Power cut', she thought dismissively; nothing unusual in the remote area where they lived. She was just drifting off again when an eerie roaring noise outside woke her with a start. It sounded like the wind, but somehow different. She had never heard anything like it before. Her heart was beating rapidly. She must have been dreaming. Tom was still snoring, perhaps it was that? She pulled the covers over her ears. Shivering more with shock than cold, she snuggled closer, spooning her knees into his sleeping body. She felt warm and secure. She started drifting off, when there it was again. Wide awake, she reached for her bedside lamp. The switch clicked uselessly. This time Tom heard the noise too. 'What the hell was that?'

'God knows, but we've lost the power.'

Her heart was thumping as he sprang out of bed, opened the door and fumbled in the darkness for the emergency torch clipped to the landing wall. He flicked the beam across the room. Thankfully, Carla, whose bed was now in the far corner of their spacious bedroom, hadn't stirred. Everything looked normal, but it was far from it outside. In the distance they could hear rumbling like thunder, which rapidly gained momentum and within seconds a blood-chilling wail encapsulated the house. Suddenly, the door burst open and a small voice quivered: 'Mum-my...dad-dy...fwightened.'

Hugging Freddie tightly, Belinda assured him: 'It's all right, darling. It's only God moving the furniture, though He could have waited till tomorrow. Come into bed and have a cuddle while Daddy has a look.'

Tom went over to the window, shining the torch into the night. 'It's only the wind, but it sure is a stormy night.'

He stood silhouetted against the pale moonlight for a few minutes, watching the ravages of nature. Freddie snuggled down with Belinda and, secure in her arms, was soon fast asleep. But she remained fully alert and a few minutes later there was another meteoric onslaught. The room seemed to shake.

'Oh God, Tom, there it is again!'

'Is Freddie asleep?' he whispered.

'Yes, I think so.'

'Try not to wake him, but come and look at this!'

Carefully extracting herself from the bed clothes, she gingerly approached the window. At that moment another whirling cry, even louder, splintered the silence. She could hardly bring herself to look outside, imagining an army of black faceless riders charging towards them, flourishing weapons. A shrill whistling pierced her ears like a warning something terrible was about to happen. She wanted to hide, but there was nowhere to go. 'Th-that's the worst storm I've ever heard. What the h-hell is going on?'

Tom drew her towards him, holding her tightly. 'It's OK, Bellie, just very strong winds. Don't worry; we're safe in this house.'

She forced herself to look through the window and was astonished to see the line of tall cupressus trees swaying like African tribesmen in a war dance, their feathered headdresses moving frenetically.

'I've never seen a…anything like this before. I w…wonder what it is - a tornado, a whirlwind or something. It's really s…scary.'

He stroked her hair reassuringly. 'Don't worry. It will blow over. This place has survived all sorts of weather for a good couple of centuries. Let's get back to bed. There's nothing we can do till morning.'

Tom shone the torch on the bedside clock. 'It's only a quarter-to-two; let's try to get some sleep.'

Belinda huddled in the warmth of her motionless son, awaiting the next freak gust. It came as she was drifting off. The room seemed to be floating effortlessly, up, up and away. She saw herself looking out of the window across a moon-sprinkled landscape; hills and dales, fields and hedges, sleeping towns and villages, fast forwarding at high speed. It was surreal. Suddenly, everything stopped as if in suspended animation; no noise, no movement, complete stillness. Then she was falling, plummeting earthwards, down, down, until, interminable seconds later, there was an explosion of bricks, dust and mortar. She must have been thrown clear by the impact because she was now outside, looking up at the ruins, convinced she was Dorothy in The Wizard of Oz. She desperately tried to prise her eyelids apart, snap out of the nightmare, run away, but her legs wouldn't move.

She was lying by a railway at the back of beyond, a train was whistling in the distance. Wheels were clattering on the tracks, louder and louder, nearer and nearer and suddenly it was upon her. A steel monster hurtled passed, snorting clouds of steam. The wind in her face forced her eyes closed. Beads of sweat were on her brow. She was groaning with frustration, locked in sleep, then a distant voice: 'Wake up, Bellie! You're dreaming.'

An almighty crash dragged her back to reality. Rudely awakened, her heart was pounding. She heard Tom say, 'A tree must have blown down,' but she struggled to respond. Again Tom got up, clicked the torch and exclaimed: 'Look, at the carpet!'

She rose to her elbows, bleary-eyed. In the spotlight the aged, sickly-green and pink carpet was rising and falling as if breathing. It was a spooky sight.

As always, Tom applied logic: 'The ballroom is beneath us. The French doors must have blown open and the wind

178

is coming up through the floor. I'd better go and close them.'

She was desperate to get up for a few minutes, reset her mind after her nightmare. 'I'll come. The children are dead to the world and there's no way I'm going back to sleep.'

Putting on dressing gowns, they followed the torch beam on to the landing. The stairs were feebly lit by a red emergency light, installed when the house was leased as a children's home. They crossed the hall into the ballroom. As she stood by the doorway Tom drew back the heavy velvet curtains from the first French windows. Faint moonlight spilled through, but the doors were closed! He followed the torch beam to the far French windows. Such was the length of the room that she could see little, but his voice echoed: 'And they're shut. Curious!'

Returning, his light reflected the grand piano and beneath it Grace's aged Christmas cactus hanging limply over its wrought-iron basket like a huge sleeping spider. Everything was as it should be. 'I'll check the rest of the downstairs; you'd better go back up in case the children wake.'

As she climbed the stairs, the emergency light cast eerie shadows through the balustrades. She chastised herself for feeling jumpy, but was ill-prepared for what she suddenly saw. A strange, translucent glow was moving outside the children's door. She stopped dead, hardly daring to breathe. Her eyes strained to discern what appeared to be the figure of a young boy dressed in short trousers, shirt and pullover. He was moving slowly along the landing and seemed to be beckoning. Instinctively, she followed.

He turned into the Maclaren's corridor and seemed to pass through the door to Grace's flat. Belinda was shaking with fear as icy cold enveloped her. It was difficult to be quiet, even on tiptoe, the aged floorboards squeakily announcing her tread. She was suddenly aware of her proximity to Ollie's room and prayed he wouldn't hear her. How would she explain herself? Looking through the half-glazed door going up to Grace's flat, she watched the illuminated figure rise and vanish somewhere near the top. It was fortunate that Grace was away at Roderick's hotel. Belinda so wanted to go up, but how could she? Being directly above Cameron and Miranda, she was bound to wake them. It was amazing the household had not been disturbed already. But this was the back of the house, in the lee of the storm and all was silent.

Returning, she passed the children's rooms, where she had first seen the boy. Had he come from Carla's room? She hardly dared contemplate it, but was hugely relieved their daughter was in with them and, remarkably, hadn't stirred so far.

Back in bed, Freddie was still curled up as she had left him. She slithered beneath the clothes, feeling the comforting warmth of his body. The wind seemed to have abated and she lay there in complete darkness, mulling over what she had just seen. Was it all a bad dream? Tom rejoined her, sounding baffled: 'It's really odd the doors hadn't blown open. The wind must have whipped up through the floorboards.'

'Is e-everything else OK?' She tried to sound normal but her experience had unnerved her.

'Inside, yes, thank heavens, though I dread to think what dramas await us outside.'

Belinda was shivering. He took her in his arms. *She had* seen a boy; no question, though in what form? She had to speak to Astral as soon as possible. She had recently confided in her about the paint can episode in Carla's room and her friend had promised to visit and put her psychic powers to work. Now it was doubly urgent.

*

The following morning was bright and breezy, though the wind had lost its strength. After such a traumatic night Belinda felt muzzy and in greater need than usual for her

180

first cup of tea. But there was still no power. She would have to settle for orange juice. Torture! The central heating had not come on either, which being gas-fired puzzled her until Tom explained that the boiler needed electricity to fire it.

The family was up promptly, clad in thick jumpers, jeans and body warmers. She was amazed at how Freddie had slept through the rest of the storm and Carla, completely through, oblivious to the worst winds Belinda and Tom had ever known. As they all sat chomping cereals, Tom said: 'I've just seen Miranda in the hall. Strange, the Maclaren's didn't hear a thing, but their bedrooms weren't facing the wind.'

Belinda heaved a sigh of relief, thankful they had not heard her in the night. She would have to find the right moment to tell them she had seen a ghost. But how could she when she hardly believed it herself?

'They were relieved Grace was staying with Roderick,' continued Tom. 'She'd have been wobbling about like a bowl of blancmange up in the flat.

Belinda wondered how Grace would have reacted had she seen the "presence" invading her home. Did everyone see ghosts or just people with certain sensitivity?

'Mum-ma, blonge!' chirped Carla, a fan of chocolate blancmange.

Tom picked up his lunchbox. 'Storm or not, I must try to get to work. I've got an urgent job, but if I can reach the motorway I should be OK. I'll be back early this afternoon to check the roof and help with any clearing up.'

He pecked her cheek. Belinda was annoyed. How could he even consider work at such a time, urgent or not? At least Cameron was staying home to check for damage. She took the children upstairs, closing the stair gate behind them. Through the bathroom window she saw Tom's car going up the drive. He was being over- optimistic, but that was him. As she washed Freddie and Carla in cold water,

181

she pictured the face of the boy. He had seemed agitated, as if he had wanted her to see something. No, she had not imagined it.

When they returned to the kitchen, she switched on the radio for the eight o'clock news:

'Thirteen people have died and dozens have been injured in the worst storms ever recorded in Southern Britain.

Most were victims of falling trees and buildings as winds overnight reached 94mph in London and 110mph in the Channel Islands, resulting in an unprecedented number of emergency call-outs.

In Dorset two firemen were killed attending a 999 call. In Dover five people died, including two seamen in the harbour.

A number of homes had their roofs blown off, while along the South Coast boats and yachts have been extensively damaged.

On the Isle of Wight, Shanklin's near century-old pier was destroyed. In Folkestone, the crew of a Sea Link ferry was blown aground and the crew had to be rescued. In Jaywick, Essex, a caravan park was totally destroyed.

Insurance companies are preparing themselves for huge pay-outs as householders begin filing claims.

Earlier this week the Meteorological Office forecast the strengthening of a depression over the Atlantic, which last night BBC weatherman Michael Fish assured viewers would course along the English Channel. But it swept across the south coast and its devastating impact was entirely unexpected'.

Belinda could not believe her ears. The previous evening she and Tom had observed the lounge barometer needle rapidly plummet from "Change" to "Stormy", so how could the weather forecasters have got it so wrong? She remembered the wind strengthening during the afternoon,

182

twigs falling across her and Miranda's path as they walked with the children, the air invigorating.

The morning was different to any other. Without power an uncertainty filled the house. She couldn't do the washing, vacuuming, cooking and many other household chores. It was like being transported back to Victorian times, pre-electricity - liberating, yet restricting. How long would the supply be off? She feared it could be weeks. She had to ring the electricity board. Of course, the phone was dead!

Within a few minutes Tom returned. 'So you didn't make it,' she announced smugly.

'I met Cameron coming up the drive, shaking his head. He said there were several trees down. We're not going anywhere for some time.'

'We're imprisoned, cut off in our own home. What now?'

'It'll be OK, Bellie - we have two hunters and two gatherers. We'll survive.

The radio droned on as she rinsed the breakfast dishes under the tap, half listening to a voice saying the last time winds of such velocity hit the South East was in 1703. 'Would you believe it?' she exclaimed, not expecting an answer from Freddie, busy building a Lego tower, and Carla sucking toast. Tom had gone back out to check the roof and re-appeared half-an-hour later, shaking his head. 'We've lost quite a few tiles so I know what Cam and I will be doing for the rest of the day. We'll put back what we can, but we'll have to get roofers in.'

'Not that shower we had in before!' She shuddered at the memory of her flooded kitchen after the idiots had removed the felt on the flat roof above her, inadequately covering it just before heavy rain.

'No need to fret, Bellie. Paddy O'Reilley and Co will not darken our doorstep again. Anyway, the main roof will be a more specialist job.'

183

Tom had taken her up to the main roof, which was inside the castellations and perfectly safe as long as one didn't stand too near them. It was accessed through the glass door at the top of Grace's stairs. Visualising the illuminated figure of a boy for the umpteenth time, her head was swimming with questions. Where did he go at the top of the stairs? Did he simply vanish, go along the corridor, or pass through the door on to the roof?

Tom could see she was anxious. 'Are you all right, Bellie? You look as white as a sheet?'

She drew breath nervously. She would have to tell him sooner or later. 'There's something I have to tell you.'

'What, darling? What's wrong?'

'I don't know how to put this, but last night, after I left you and went back upstairs, I saw something really weird.'

'Everything was really weird last night.'

'Yes, wasn't it, but it was nothing to do with the wind. Please don't think I'm going mad, but … I saw a ghost; at least I thought it was. It looked like a young boy. A strange light was moving along the landing. I watched it going over to the Maclaren's and followed it to Grace's door. It went straight through it and up the stairs, disappearing into thin air!'

'Oh, Bellie, are you sure it wasn't a dream? You were very restless. You kept tossing and turning. I'm surprised Freddie was sleeping so well next to you.'

'I know what I saw, Tom.'

'Why didn't you tell me last night?'

'I didn't think you would believe me and I didn't want to risk waking him.'

His eyes searched hers, contemplating the enormity of her words. 'Thinking about it, everything starts to make sense. Maybe Freddie does see his "friend", Billie. He certainly put him in danger that day up the ladder … and it could be Billie behind all the strange goings-on in Carla's room. Now, do you believe me about the paint can?'

184

'Billie!' Freddie chortled as the Lego tower clattered to the floor.

Tom and Belinda exchanged anguished looks. 'I think we should go and see Astral right now!' he urged.

'When, the drive is impassable, remember?'

'I think we could walk down there, try and get through. Anyway, we'd better see if she and Eggie are still in one piece. And we mustn't forget to check on our other neighbours. I'll pop up and see Nellie and Ed later, if I can get up there.'

They were donning coats and wellingtons when the Maclaren's filed into the hall.

'You'll not get very far without a chain saw,' scoffed Cameron.

'We're at least going to try and reach Haggleby Lodge, see if the Oddie's are OK,' insisted Tom.

'We'll come with you,' offered Miranda.

Belinda was dismayed. She didn't want to speak to Astral with the Maclaren's present. She would have to find a way. As they left the house the sun smiling down was uplifting. The wind had lost its strength, but was still bracing. At a glance everything looked normal, but Cameron's words focused them on the force of the storm: 'There's a tree down in the pine walk. It's completely covered the greenhouse, but would you believe it, not one pane of glass is broken!'

Belinda said: 'You should have been over our side of the house; it sounded like we were under attack by screaming banshees. And there were these strange clinking noises overhead.'

'They were the roof tiles, but we should be able to claim for a new roof on the insurance,' said Tom optimistically.

'A sudden windfall', Cameron punned.

'That's not funny - but if it means we get a new roof,' agreed Miranda. 'Grace said the other day there's not much

185

left in the house fund, so our new kitchens and bathrooms will have to wait, boo-hoo!'

Such concerns paled into insignificance as a scene of devastation loomed before them; upended trees lying across the drive, branches smashed to smithereens, leafy debris scattered in wild confusion. Getting through it was a major battle. Carla had to be air-lifted over each casualty, while Freddie and Ollie squealed with glee each time they needed swinging over. To them it was a game, but to Belinda each stricken tree had been put to death, the leaves still full of life clinging on unknowingly.

A gap in the hedge looking across the field stopped them in their tracks. Belinda was choked to see an aged oak that had dominated the landscape for some 200 years on its side.

'How the mighty fall,' said Tom sorrowfully.

Near the bottom of the drive, one of the horse chestnuts that had supplied the boys with conkers blocked their path, but everyone managed to squeeze through a small gap between its upended root ball and the wrought iron fence. The road, usually busy at eleven in the morning, was eerily silent. It looked as if there had been a global attack. Fallen trees blocked the road and telegraph poles had been ripped up like matchsticks, their wires coiled round fragmented tree branches.

Belinda pondered nature's irony of a late autumn, the weight of so many remaining leaves aiding the freak winds to loosen the trunks. The beautiful rural scenery everyone had taken for granted would never be the same again. She felt breathless with anger. How could Mother Nature play such a cruel trick? How could God allow centuries of growth to be snuffed out like a candle? "War of The Worlds" and "Earthquake" flashed through her mind. But this was no disaster movie; this was for real and the reality hit the pit of her stomach. She could only remember a huge sense of loss once before, when her beloved grandfather

186

died suddenly on the eve of his golden wedding. Only this time she was grieving for the countryside that she had cherished all her life.

Remarkably, Haggleby Lodge, which was surrounded by trees, appeared to have survived unscathed. Tom went on ahead; picking his way through to the Oddie's to check on their welfare. Everyone was relieved when he returned a few minutes later, reporting the couple were fine, though Eggie was lamenting the loss of some prized specimens in his garden. In need of cheering up, he had invited them all in for coffee. Belinda prayed for an opportunity to have a quiet word with Astral.

The children were poured blackcurrant juice and Eggie set to work boiling water on a Primus Stove. Freddie and Ollie were fascinated to see him undo a little cap on the side, pour in methylated spirits and pump a knob, creating a bright blue flame. 'It's not high speed gas, but it will boil water.'

Steaming cups of coffee were passed round.   'This is nectar!' Miranda exclaimed, gulping gratefully.

'Talking of sustenance, what are you going to do for cooking? You are electric, aren't you? It could be off for some time,' warned Eggie.

'Good   question,'   responded   Belinda   as   Miranda shrugged.

'I have a couple of camping stoves in the attic. I'll go and dig them out.'

'I need a quiet word with Astral,' said Belinda, seizing the moment.

'I'll need some help, why don't you chaps come upstairs and give me a hand? I have some toys up there the boys might like.'

'Oh, will you go, Tom? I'm tired after going up and down roofs and battling through jungle!' protested Cameron.

Curiosity aroused, the boys followed, leaving Carla playing alone on the floor, who immediately started whimpering. Miranda scooped her up, settling at the dining table and feeding her a biscuit. Sighing, Belinda resigned herself to the Maclaren's having to hear her story. She unburdened herself nervously without interruption.

'You should have woken me. I would have seen the little devil off the premises,' uttered Cameron from behind "The Horley Mail."

'Oh, Bellie, that's really scary! Two *living* boys in the place are hard enough. I'm not sure how I'd cope with a dead one,' remarked Miranda.

At last the Maclaren's seemed to be taking her seriously! Belinda felt as if a weight had been lifted from her shoulders. Astral, appearing unsurprised, chose her words carefully: 'Some places retain spirits of people who have passed, but cannot move on; if someone has died suddenly in tragic circumstances or, for one reason or another, cannot be at peace. This child is a restless spirit and he is desperate to tell you something.'

Cameron asked: 'If this kid came to a bad end, why does he have to hang around us? Can't we just ask him to go haunt somewhere else?'

Miranda expressed excitement. 'To think we have actually got a ghost of our own. It shows how much history there is to the place. We should tell people. We could open the house to the public, make some money.'

Belinda cringed. 'You are joking! I don't think this should be advertised - exorcised more like, or whatever Astral can do to rid us of this... this child.'

'You could consider asking Rev Makepeace for an exorcism,' suggested Astral, 'but I think this spirit needs to tell us something. I would suggest a meeting first, just between us to see what he has to say.'

Belinda swallowed hard. 'A séance you mean?'

She nodded. 'I'd be happy to help. If you all agree, I'll come up to the Hall as soon as the drive is cleared. I will need to bring a few things in the car.'

'That could take quite a while,' remarked Cameron. 'And don't ask me to play crystal ball or whatever. The only glass I'll be looking through is a beer glass.'

'If you preferred not to participate, you'd be very welcome to commune with spirits of your own choosing,' Astral amusingly replied.

Miranda sighed. 'I'm not sure the road to The Mucky Duck will be open for a while either, Camay, so you'll have to be content with a whisky in the wood shed.'

CHAPTER SIXTEEN

Medium Wave

With no electricity or telephones, it was all hands to the pump. Tom and Cameron repaired the roof best they could, salvaging tiles the boys helped round up in the garden. As for getting out of the drive, a chain saw was top priority. Knowing them to be in great demand, Cameron wasted no time in battling the few miles on foot to Tree Sculpture, in Crawley. He managed to buy the last one, returning from his tortuous trek with reports of fallen trees across most country roads.

The whirring of wood sawing filled the air from dawn to dusk. Firewood was plentiful, but without central heating the house was dropping colder by the day. The power could be off for weeks, so Tom made it his mission to find a generator. This would have to be brought back by car, so the drive needed clearing as quickly as possible. Besides, if they couldn't get to the shops soon, they would all starve! They also needed a launderette and to get to friends for a bath. Heating saucepans on the camping stove was wholly inadequate, especially when the children had come in filthy after playing in the garden.

Tom kept the log store topped up with fallen wood - there would be enough to keep the home fires burning for years! Fireplaces in all sitting rooms were working overtime and everyone looked forward to suppers by a roaring blaze. Candles were out in force and Tom commissioned an oil lamp previously used as ornamentation in the lounge. Belinda loved its soft warm glow, which seemed to offer reassurance that everything would be all right.

For Belinda and Miranda the days were challenging, with household chores taking twice as long without power. Washing had to be done by hand and floors swept manually. Now they knew how their grandmothers had felt at the end of a long arduous day with no mod cons to lighten the load.

It took Tom and Cameron several days' chain sawing to clear the drive, so Astral's meeting was delayed until late the following week. As her visit loomed, Belinda battled foreboding. She detected an element of scepticism in the ranks, especially Cameron, and everyone seemed reluctant to talk about it. There was little opportunity anyway, with them all so busy, which was probably just as well. At least their unwelcome "house guest" had gone quiet for the moment.

Belinda had always believed that those "on the other side" should be left in peace and the idea of a séance conflicted with her religious beliefs. But it was the better of two options, as she felt that an exorcism to rid this lost soul would possibly not fulfil everyone's morbid curiosity about what he was trying to say. It was compelling and, as Astral had warned them, he might continue to haunt them until somebody listened. Deep down Belinda believed that the meeting was crucial if the two families were to remain at Haggleby Hall. Besides, it was unhealthy for Freddie to continue regarding "Billie" as his friend and more concerning was the spirit's increasing mischief. Where would it all stop? "The pestiferous one" - as Tom labelled him - was making their lives unbearable and only Astral could help put an end to it.

The evening of the meeting finally arrived and the children were put to bed without the usual prolonged ritual. Freddie's story was short and sweet and Carla drifted off after a single round of "Twinkle Twinkle Little Star".

Everyone assembled in the ballroom, dressed in thick jumpers and sweatshirts. The room was chilly, despite a fire burning earlier, as Astral had instructed Tom to let it go out, also to use a minimum of candles. Belinda felt strange; it was usually filled with warmth, a bright and happy place for sharing drinks and jokes with family and

191

friends. She thought of her fellow members in Mid Sussex Potty Poets, who loved the ballroom venue and tonight's meeting suddenly seemed completely potty! She could hardly believe it was happening herself. Following the storm, the group's last gathering had been cancelled. Without a poem to write and preoccupied with current events, she had penned a few words to "the pestiferous one" to help relieve her anxiety:

WILD CHILD
Who are you from an unknown place?
Tell us you name. Show us your face.
Playing games and causing scenes,
Tormenting us all, for what means?

Naughty boy, you are such a tease,
Making us feel so ill at ease.
Yet you are but a young child,
Poor lost soul just running wild.

This place is no longer your home.
Return to where the spirits roam
On "the other side"- far away!
But first, what do you have to say?

For the meeting everyone took a seat round the Flowers' big, oval mahogany table, which Astral had asked to be positioned in the centre of the ballroom. Belinda sat between Tom and Miranda and joining them at the last minute were Grace and Roderick, who had flown back from the West Country that afternoon. A taxi driver had managed to get them home from the airport, despite the difficult roads.

As expected Cameron was not present. He could be forgiven for having nothing to do with Astral's "shenanigans", as he called them. He, of all people, was usually game for an adventure. But this was no adventure and with the road up to The Mucky Duck newly opened, no-one could blame him for pursuing his first Harvey's brew in ages with "more down-to-earth" company.

They all sat in silence waiting for Astral to begin and it was strange without the usual banter. Belinda's stomach was fluttering with apprehension. She imagined how butterflies must have felt when she as a child used to catch them in a jar. She would keep them for a while, admiring their beauty and when she tired of them, would open the lid and shake the jar, watching the odd survivor fly away. But more often than not, their wings remained closed, never to fly again. Her remorse had never left her. But here in the present moment there was no getting away. She desperately wanted life to be normal again, to be back in the lounge snuggled up to Tom on the settee and chatting by candlelight, as they had come to do after the children were in bed.

Astral took her seat inside a black cabinet, ferried up the drive in Eggie's estate. It had curtains pulled across and she asked: 'Is everyone ready to begin?'

Once there was complete stillness, she welcomed them and said: 'Now, you know why we are here and I am very aware that for all of you this will be your first encounter with those "on the other side". Please remain quiet unless spoken to and respond calmly if a question is put to you. I am hopeful my spirit guides will do their best to help us and by the end of the evening we are enlightened by this meeting.'

She asked Tom to blow out two candles, leaving the room eerily dark. As Belinda's eyes became accustomed to shadows in the far corner, the memory of the translucent figure she had seen on the night of the storm made her spine tingle. Astral's words focused her: 'Now, please hold hands, close your eyes and concentrate hard.'

Belinda clutched Tom's clammy fingers in her right hand and Miranda's cool palm in her left. Minutes ticked by interminably, the only sound was gentle breathing. Desperate to speed the meeting through, Belinda battled to clear obtrusive thoughts. Roderick fidgeted on a squeaky chair, otherwise silence prevailed for some minutes. She was just beginning to think it all a complete waste of time when a rattling noise behind her made her jump. She shivered. It was the tambourine Astral had left on the floor. Both Tom and Miranda's grasp tightened. Suddenly, a deep male voice boomed: 'How! Running Bear welcome you and will bring others to speak.'

He had to be one of Astral's spirit guides, a North American Indian! Belinda smiled wryly. Miranda stifled a nervous giggle. Feet shuffled beneath the table. The room fell silent again, everyone hardly daring breathe. Then, slowly, a ring of light appeared. On the table Astral had placed a cardboard cone with a fluorescent band around the bottom, which had previously been held to the Flowers' oil lamp to energise it and summons the spirits. Everyone gasped as the light slowly circled them. Suddenly, a Cockney boy's voice rang out: 'Cor, ain't I clever? …never done that before!'

'Tell us who you are,' Running Bear prompted him, gruffly.

After slight hesitation, he announced: 'Billie…Billie Blewett - a good name for a boy who can blow a fancy light round, don't you reckon?'

Belinda wanted to laugh, partly to relieve the tension, but stopped herself.

'Who among us do you wish to speak to?'

'That nice lady wiv the short brawn 'air.'

Despite an icy chill Belinda's cheeks flushed. A sudden lump came to her throat, but the words tumbled out: 'You mean me, Belinda, Freddie's mum?'

'Yeah, that's right.'

194

'Are you... the...the Billie on the memorial stone outside here?'

'Yeah, that's me... but I don't like it out there.'

'Shouldn't you be sleeping with God's angels?'

'Nah, not me, nevur liked sleepin' and I'm no angel.'

There was an awkward silence.

'Tell everyone why you are here, Billie?' urged Running Bear.

Hesitating, the boy started gabbling: 'I like birds - used to go up on the roof and watch 'em flyin', but wasn't s'pose to. Last time, I'd got in trouble with 'ole Ma Mudd, the guv'nes. She was gonna cane me for stealing Johnny Brown's chocolit. He of'en 'ad chocolit from his gran, but was too mean to give me any! On the roof it was very windy, 'ard to stand up. There weren't any birds... I wanted to go back, but then...'

The voice stopped. The tension was unbearable. Tom asked: 'What happened next, Billie?'

Terrified, the boy hesitated, then his words were gushing: 'There was this really strong wind, blew me off it did. Then I fell, but I didn't bounce.'

Belinda was desperate to relieve his stress: 'It's OK, Billie; you're here with us now. You're safe.'

Silence again. Just as everyone thought they had lost him, he resumed his chirpier voice: 'You're a kind lady, not like me Ma. She never wanted me. When we lived in London she used to 'it me... but she could sing and she were a luvely dancer. I use to watch 'er when she took me to her work at the theatre... I nevur had a Pa, not that I remember. After Ma died I was sent 'ere. Nobody would play wiv me... Fred plays wiv me now, 'e's me friend.'

'I know you like playing with Freddie, Billie, but sometimes your games are not very nice.'

'Yeah, sorry, but we do 'ave fun, 'im and me. He's lucky 'aving you as a muvver and 'aving a sister an' all. They 'ave nice toys.'

'You like their toys, don't you, Billie?'

'Yeah, I love Fred's plane screaming round... and the bells on Carla's cot, I love the noise. Why 'ave you taken them away? Was it cos of me?'

'I'm afraid so. You like ringing the old servants' bells, don't you Billie?'

'Oh yeah, can you hear 'em?'

'Yes, we all hear them.'

'Is there anything else you have to tell us, Billie?' urged Belinda, aching to get to the bottom of what he was trying to say.

'It was me who took the chocolits, cos it was Christmus... but can't eat 'em no more.'

'Don't worry, you're forgiven'.

Sensing the energy dropping, Tom forced the question: 'Tell us why you're still here, Billie?'

'I like it. I like playing wiv the toys.'

'You like Carla's room, don't you, Billie?' prodded Belinda.

'Yeah, that was my room. I loved it, least I did till her Pa painted it.'

Tom bristled. Belinda squeezed his hand to shush him.

'I liked them birds on the wallpaper, but can't see 'em no more. They're stuck underneaf now... stuck, like that poor bloke up there...' The voice was fading.

The cryptic words begged response. 'What bloke? Up where?'

'C...can't tell ya....' the voice was barely audible.

'Billie, don't leave us!' There was so much more she wanted to know.

Running Bear took control: 'The energy's dropping. Sing! Sing!'

Without hesitation Tom burst into the Sixties song she remembered Lonnie Donegan singing:

"My old man's a dustman,

He wears a dustman's hat,

196

He wears cor-blimey trousers
And he lives in a council flat…."

Everyone round the table joined in. Belinda found it surreal hearing one of her favourite childhood songs, but it had the desired effect as the boy responded happily: 'I like that song, Ma used to sing it…'

She was desperate to keep him talking and asked, 'Was it you, Billie, who made the paint can fall off the ladder in Carla's room?'

'Yeah, sorry missus, I didn't want the birds painted, see?'

'I know you were cross about Carla's wallpaper, but it is her room now, not yours and you like Carla, don't you?'

'Yeah, she's sweet. Sorry I made a mess, but, hey, I gotta go now. This geezer I told you 'bout is waiting to come through.'

There was no time to think. She had to let him go. 'Goodbye Billie, it's been nice talking to you'

Grace, silent till now, was sensing another presence. Her usually calm voice had an uneasy edge: 'Who is there?' She had to repeat herself and an older man's voice came through, sounding distant: 'I have a message for Trix.'

Belinda wasn't aware of anyone in the room by that name. Then, to her complete surprise, Roderick spoke. His stuttering, greatly improved over time with Grace's patient assistance, was again pronounced. 'Is th-at r-really you, Uncle?'

'Yes, my boy, how are you? Caught any whoppers lately?'

'I…I am well, Uncle, th-thank you, but I…I don't f-fish now.'

'Ah, dear Trix, that's a pity. You loved fishing. Remember when we used to go out in the boat?' The voice, filled with sadness, wavered. 'The old boathouse, it's….'

'I'm really sorry about the b-boathouse, Uncle. W-what happened to you? We were all so w-worried?'

'I got stuck up top, me boy. Bloody door slammed shut. Could'nt get out…'

'Stuck, where Uncle?'

'Behind the chimney pots, remember, you came up with me once? You were the only one who knew my secret hideaway.'

'Secret hideaway, I d-don't remember?' said Roderick, desperate to make sense of it.

Suddenly, there was a flapping sound. Something seemed to be circling above the table. Belinda thought it was a bat, but it suddenly started squawking: 'Pieces of eight… bugger off, vicar…,' repeating the words over and over.

Belinda couldn't believe her ears. It was Monty, Milton's blasphemous parrot! Miranda gasped, suddenly realising that her charge had not survived the great outdoors after all. The unwelcome disturbance seemed to trigger groaning noises from the cabinet.

'Our medium cannot cope with more visitations!' warned Running Bear. 'She is getting very tired. We must bring this "experiment" to a close now. Thank you, everybody, for allowing us to work with you.'

Tom fumbled in the dark for the matches and located a candle to light. There was a   sense of anti-climax as faces stared blankly, trying to take in the enormity of the last few minutes.

*

A warm glow from the Flowers' oil lamp was reassuring. Tom threw more logs on the lounge fire and everyone gravitated around it, chilled after such an unnerving experience. As he and Belinda passed round stiff drinks, Cameron appeared, looking uneasy. Unusually, he sounded reticent: 'Did you, umh, manage to tune in OK?'

'It wasn't a case of turning on the radio, Cameron,' replied Miranda sharply.

198

'Sorry I wasn't on your wavelength, Randy.'

'Well, you can make it up to us by taking Astral and her equipment home. She's had a hard evening. Get her back quickly - that is, if you are in a fit state to drive.'

'Perfeckly OK,' he said, stomping off.

Everyone felt dazed, but with a few sips of alcohol the conversation slowly gathered pace.

Grace was concerned about Roderick. Not only had his stuttering regressed, he looked pallid, as if in shock. 'How are you feeling, dear?' she asked putting her arm around his shoulder.

'I - I'm c-completely at a loss to understand w-what Uncle was t-talking about.'

'I'm sure it will come to you,' she assured him.

A few minutes later Cameron returned and sensed the subdued mood: 'Well, if this is what communing with the spirits does you'd have been better off up at The Mucky Duck with me.'

'We had to give it a try, mate,' Tom insisted.

Miranda briefly explained the meeting's events, commenting: 'Believe what you want, Cameron.'

'Just as I said, it's all a load of poppycock - and look what it's done to you lot. You all look wrecked! More medicinal treatment, Tom, keep the homebrew flowing!'

'You're drunk, Cameron!' stormed Miranda. 'You'd soon change your tune if you'd have been in there with us!'

'You don't believe in all that séance rubbish, do you? It was all a "put up" job. Didn't you know Eggie was hiding in the corner doing special effects?'

'Hardly, Cameron, he returned home after dropping off Astral. You really should have been with us. We saw lights and things moving. Voices were talking to us...'

'Now you two, everyone's entitled to think what they like,' cut in Tom. 'If Cameron doesn't believe it, that's his prerogative. I must say I was pretty sceptical to start with, but now I've seen it for myself...'

199

Cameron slumped into an armchair, confused. Grace, knowing he would eventually come round, questioned Roderick further. 'What do you think your Uncle meant about being up behind the chimney pots - Heaven, perhaps?'

He shrugged solemnly.

'Sounds like a riddle to me,' suggested Tom. 'Did Uncle Milton sometimes speak in riddles?'

'I don't r...r-recall him doing that.'

Cameron lit his pipe, sucking noisily and enveloping everyone with smoke. 'Chimney pots - that is potty! Perhaps your Uncle was a chimney sweep in a former life?'

'Well, it certainly looks like *you* could do with one!' coughed Miranda, waving a hand to disperse the greyish haze.

'One thing's for sure, there's no smoke without fire,' said Tom.

Miranda dabbed her eyes with a tissue. 'Is Cameron's pipe getting to you, too?' Belinda asked.

'No, I'm used to that. It's poor...poor Monty. He...he really is dead! I cannot tell you, Roderick, how sorry I am he got out and flew off.'

'Perhaps Monty got stuck up the chimney looking for the old man?' Cameron conjectured flippantly.

Belinda didn't know whether to laugh or cry, but he did have a point. The meeting had left them no further forward in learning what had happened to Uncle Milton, but at least now they had something to go on. Astral had been right, "tuning in" to Billie.

CHAPTER SEVENTEEN

Hidden Secrets

Belinda drew back the curtains and opened the shutters, illuminating the ballroom, which had been eerily dark the night before. Everything felt normal again. Astral's meeting all seemed like a bad dream.

She had woken to the sound of a taxi going down the drive, Roderick and Grace having left early to go flying again. With so much else happening they hadn't said where. At breakfast Tom expressed surprise: 'Those two seem to spend more time in the air than down here.'

'Can you blame them with the state of the roads?'

'They're probably off to France to get away from this mad house. Roderick certainly looked like he needed it after our get-together.'

'Perhaps they are off to Gretna Green!'

'Oh Bellie, you're such a romantic. I can't see Grace tying the knot again. She's far too independent.'

Belinda had noticed the chemistry between them and believed otherwise. Her feminine intuition was rarely wrong. 'They are certainly spending a lot of time together. He's either here or Grace is down at the hotel, helping in the office, and they're always flying somewhere.'

'Well, we all know Cameron thinks Roderick a lady's man. Even you had your doubts after your strange experience in his room that day we were looking round the place.'

'I can't be sure it was him with a woman. All I remember was this high-pitched giggling. It sounded like a woman, I suppose.' She peeled the shell off Freddie's egg. 'Now I've got to know Roderick, I think Cameron's wrong and is being over-protective of his mother - even she notices it. Grace and Roderick are just good friends. She has helped him enormously with his speech, though you wouldn't

201

have thought so last night. Hearing from his uncle like that must have been a real shock.'

'I don't want to talk about it right now with little ears flapping!'

But she *needed* to talk. 'The children are too young to understand. You must realise, Tom, this business is not doing them, or us, any good. We've got to pursue it further or this place will remain haunted for the rest of our lives and I for one will not be staying.'

'I agree with you, Bellie. We have to make sense of it. I've been thinking it might be a good idea if you and I popped round to the Haggleby Estate Office to see if we can dig up anything about the house. I've heard the office has an impressive archive and there might be something to give us a lead. I could try charming Kitty Titmus, the estate clerk, into letting me have a look through the records. I could say I was helping an author client researching country estates in the South East.'

'Good thinking, darling. This morning would be ideal - Miranda is taking the children for a walk up to "Ripe n' Ready." ' Her mind was still buzzing with the meeting. 'Do you think after last night Billie might let us be?'

'Now what did I say about little ears flapping?'

Freddie certainly wasn't listening. Engrossed in a delicate operation to remove the white from his hard-boiled egg, he announced gleefully: 'Look mummy - ball.'

'Yes, Freddie - and as you often find with mummy's eggs, you can bounce it on the floor,' replied Tom, rubbing his blonde curls.

It was Belinda's turn to be annoyed. 'Cooking perfect eggs on camping gas is not the easiest thing. When are we going to get the power back on? It's three weeks since the storm?'

'It shouldn't be long. Hundreds of power workers have been drafted in from all over the country. We could ask at

202

the estate office. They might know more about repair works in the area.'

As she cleared the breakfast table, something squashed underfoot. She scraped the egg yolk from her slipper and wiping the children's hands, promised them: 'After we've brushed your teeth you can walk up to the farm with Miranda and choose a pumpkin for Hallowe'en.'

'Did you know Hallowe'en is also known as All Souls Day?' asked Tom, a fount of knowledge, as he packed the dishwasher.

'No. So why do we carve ugly faces in pumpkins and dress up like witches, vampires and ghosts?'

'It's really to do with praying for the souls of people in purgatory, to help them atone for their sins.'

'I sometimes wonder if we're in purgatory. Perhaps we need prayers for lost souls here?' she suggested.

'One lost soul is enough. Let's hope we can help Billie - and Uncle Milton.'

*

The estate office was only three-miles but with the usual route still blocked, Tom had to go the long way round. It was the first time they had ventured that way since the storm. She was sickened to see the dramatically changed landscape. Travelling up Wood Hill she lamented the fate of the loveliest and oldest trees. Some had completely toppled over, others were leaning, some snapped in half like broken pencils, while others were completely stripped of branches. Hedgerows were speared by splintered branches and telegraph poles were askew, their wires coiled by the roadside, awaiting the repair teams.

Smaller tree trunks had been removed from the carriageway for single vehicles, with piles of timber stacked alongside. Bigger trees partially remained. It would be months before everything would look normal again.

Despite nature's mutilation, Belinda was relieved to have some respite from the house's strangely oppressive atmosphere. Haggleby Hall didn't feel like home anymore. The meeting had left her restless and irritable. She envied Cameron's simplistic view that it was all "a load of bunk", but like everyone else she was convinced there were hidden secrets waiting to come out. Who knows what they might discover at the estate office? She hoped it would not be all a waste of time. At least she and Tom were showing Astral their support. Any doubts and they could lose a good friend. Deep down, Belinda had had enough. If she and Tom didn't turn up anything, the families would have to talk. Perhaps it would be simpler if they did consider selling the house? But the whole thing had gone too far, hadn't it? They had put so much time, money and energy into Haggleby Hall, the home of their dreams - and nightmares.

*

Belinda sat in the car while Tom went to speak to Kitty in the estate office. The large, Victorian brick building hung with red Sussex tiles and a grey slate roof looked like a row of former estate workers' homes. When Tom finally beckoned her in, he introduced her to a buxom brunette wearing a low cut blouse and tight skirt around her generous hips. Belinda wondered what charms Tom was using to be allowed into the archives.

The woman had a pleasant, albeit nosey manner: 'Haggleby Hall must be a fun place to live. I bet it has lots of history. People say it's haunted. Have you ever seen a ghost?'

'Oh, just the odd spirit,' Belinda shrugged, hoping Miranda hadn't been blabbing to her friends about Billie, or it would be twice round the houses by now.

Kitty's prominent eyes grew wider: 'Really! What have you seen?'

'Just figments of my wife's imagination,' dismissed Tom, desperate to quell any rumours.

Kitty led them up a short flight of stairs and along a corridor to a large room with an oak refectory table, wooden office chairs and metal filing cabinets. Shelves stacked with dusty, black box files lined two walls. She briefly explained the filing system and before leaving, asked Tom: 'You'll get in touch about photographing my pair, then?'

'I'll call you from work, when I've got my diary,' he replied awkwardly, closing the door on her.

'You have some "glamour work" to do, then?' Belinda jealously probed, unable to resist the question. Tom had been known to exercise his photographic skills in such directions, which Belinda disapproved of, but it paid good money.

'Don't worry, Bellie. I don't think Kitty would even make page 3 of Littlewoods catalogue. She's asked if I would photograph her two-year-old twins, pain in the bum but it's the only way I could get her to agree to us seeing the archives. We're supposed to have the express permission of the estate manager, so this has to be hush-hush.'

They extracted a box file each from the shelves and sat at the refectory table. The next two hours were spent ploughing through documents, maps and photographs detailing Haggleby Estate's land, properties and associated items. A blue folder containing historical information focused Tom's interest. Reading through, his voice was intermittent: 'A country mansion built in 1780 for the dowager of Henry Fielding-Winters, of the Sussex land-owning family...in Victorian times it was loaned to the community as a poor house, when it was known as Charity House... during the First World War it was a convalescent home for soldiers recovering from their wounds...'

His excitement mounted: 'Hey, according to this, Milton Fielding-Winters inherited Haggleby Hall on the death of his father in 1932. His mother had died two years previously.'

Belinda's brain started calculating. 'Roderick told us Uncle Milton was born in 1911, so he would have been 21 - it was literally "the key of the door"!'

'He and Elizabeth had a son, didn't they? I seem to remember Agatha mentioning him once.'

'Come to think of it, she did when she showed us round the house. I think she called him, James.'

'That's right. Didn't she say he went to Australia and married a girl out there? It's funny we've never heard Roderick talk about him?'

'Yes, that is strange. Uncle Milton disappeared in 1973. I wonder why Haggleby Hall didn't go on the market sooner?' puzzled Belinda.

'I suppose because he was not officially declared dead? I believe Aunt Elizabeth wanted to sell the place much sooner. She was struggling with its upkeep, but legally her hands were tied. Eventually, when the sale was permitted, Roderick and Agatha had to deal with it because of her state of her mind. We came along at the right time. With Elizabeth's ailing health, the money was desperately needed to pay for her nursing care.'

'Do you think she bumped off Uncle Milton; put arsenic in his tea and buried him under the Chinese Knotweed?'

'So that's why it grows so well! Seriously, Roderick told Grace that after Milton's disappearance the police really put Elizabeth through it, but they couldn't pin anything on her and, of course, there was no body. Because of it all she had a nervous breakdown and subsequently lost her marbles.'

'Lost her marbles, how convenient!' exclaimed Belinda, pouring them a glass of water each from a jug Kitty had left.

'Don't be cynical, Belinda! Milton was a ladies' man by all accounts, but Elizabeth was devoted to him. It's all rather sad, really.'

Half-an-hour later, after further shuffling of papers, Belinda was about to call it a day when Tom came across a reference to Haggleby Hall being rented to a London council as a children's home in the Sixties. He summarised: 'The kids went to Haggleby village school, though apparently it caused some upset in the local community. There were stories of bad management at the home, with children being ill-treated and - hey, listen to this - the tenancy was terminated following the tragic death of a male orphan in 1965.'

'That must have been Billie! It's the year on his gravestone,' she reminded him.

'When you think about it, our home does have a chequered history.'

'And, no doubt, we are becoming part of it - the Hippies of Haggleby Hall!'

Tom's eyes gleamed with anticipation. 'Whatever part, it does look as if the old place is looking to us to fill in the missing details.'

He unfolded a yellowing architect's drawing of floor plans, dated 1961. 'This was probably done when the property was put on the rental market.'

She watched Tom's finger trace the outline. 'There's the missing wing on the Maclaren's side, where we can still see the foundations on the back lawn. Wow, it looks like there used to be an octagonal ballroom above the kitchens and cellars! And there is the former drive to the stable block and coach house, which Elizabeth had converted into homes.'

Belinda held up an old photograph she had come across earlier, showing a clock tower in the stable yard. 'It's a pity that's no longer there!'

Tom's attention returned to the drawing. 'From this we know there have been quite a few changes to the Hall. The Maclaren's sitting room is marked as the billiards room and our kitchen, the conservatory. And look up the main stairs; it proves my theory about Carla and Freddie's bedrooms originally being one with a door straight in from the landing. The ante-chamber and airing cupboard must have been created when the room was divided.'

'Probably when it was rented as a children's home,' she conjectured.

Tom's finger hovered over the top floor. 'I didn't know there were so many attic bedrooms. Originally these would have been for the servants.'

'I wonder when they were converted into the flat. Roderick might know?' suggested Belinda.

'That's weird,' said Tom, burying his nose in the plan. 'I didn't know that little room was there, with a door leading from Grace's bedroom.'

'I wouldn't expect you to know Grace's bedroom intimately, but come to think of it, I don't remember another door – perhaps there's a secret room?'

'It might have been blocked up. We must have a look, with Grace's permission, of course?'

'Yes, we must, as soon as possible,' agreed Belinda, eyeing her watch. 'We have to go now. Miranda's insisted we're back by one. She's doing lunch.'

*

Cameron was on the front terrace puffing his pipe pensively. He was watching the boys excitedly batting a ball swinging on elastic from a pole he had sunk into the lawn. He beckoned Tom and Belinda over: 'Just in time for a beer!'

'It's a bit nippy out here, isn't it, Cam?' she said. The boys should have their coats on.'

'Oh, they're keeping warm with my new toy. I've been instructed by the Memsahib to entertain them while I stand here waiting for a lady visitor.' He poured two beers from a jug on the table. 'I hope it's not that wretched woman from the WI. She's such a pain in the derriere, always asking Miranda to bake a cake or run a goldfish stall or something.'

Belinda turned her coat collar up against the cold wind. 'The trouble with Miranda is she doesn't know when to say "no".'

'She does when she's got *one* of her headaches.'

Ollie stretched his arms to Cameron, seeking a cuddle: 'Daddy... cold. Go in now?'

'Your mother said we've got to stand here and look out for a pink flying elephant.'

'Efelunts not pink.'

'The ones with big ears are.'

'What old flannel is your father telling you now?' asked Miranda, approaching.

'Mummy, do pink efelunts fly?'

'No, darling, *elephants* can't fly, any more than pigs can - don't believe everything your father says!'

Confused, Ollie pulled "Sniffy" from his pocket, a strip of mangled fur he carried as a comforter, and held it to his nose.

'It's getting late. I hope nothing's happened to Lavinia,' said Miranda, checking her watch.

'Is pink piggy not coming?' asked Ollie.

'You mustn't call her a pink piggy, even though she may look like one!'

'Mummy, can we have a piggy?'

'Good idea. We can fatten it up for Christmas and roast it!' teased Cameron. Ollie sniffed his fur again. 'Talking of food, can we go in? I'm starving and it doesn't look like the elephant is going to turn up.'

He offered his son a shoulder ride as consolation. Suddenly, a small plane whined its approach and within seconds a Piper Cherokee swooped overhead, narrowly missing the parapet with its coat of arms. Belinda glimpsed two people inside, but it was gone before she could be sure.

'Grannie!' Ollie shouted excitedly.

'Mum doesn't fly that dangerously. There was a bloke at the controls,' observed Cameron. The truth suddenly dawned ... 'Don't tell me it was her fancy man - not Rodders? Since when could he fly?'

Miranda feigned ignorance. 'Didn't Grace tell you, she's been helping Roderick learn - and he's just got his Private Pilot's Licence, so he can go solo?'

'I bet you chaps knew all along she was helping him and you never said a word?'

'I know nothing,' said Tom truthfully.

Belinda shook her head: 'nor me, honestly.'

The Piper came round for another circuit, this time comfortably clearing the parapet. She could discern Roderick piloting and Grace waving, and waved back.

'You had all this planned, with lunch and everything,' Cameron chided Miranda.

'Grace and Roderick only let *me* into their little secret the other day,' she admitted. 'Your mother didn't want us to know she had made a deal with Roderick to sell us the house on condition she helped him learn to fly.'

'So that's how she clinched the deal - and I thought he just wanted his wicked way with her'

'Camay, you should know that's not true. Grace and Roderick clicked right from the beginning. If anything, it was her finding him a qualified instructor and helping to teach him that brought them together.'

'I bet it's more than flying lessons Mitts has given him.'

'But you have to hand it to her; if it wasn't for Grace we wouldn't be here.'

'In more ways than one!' teased Tom.

Cameron displayed his "little boy hurt" look. 'Why didn't she tell me herself?'

'Because she thought if you discovered the bargain they'd struck you'd be angry.'

'Randy, as if ... now what's that about Rodders going solo? Are we're getting shot of him at last?'

'Certainly not, Grace is very fond of him, so you'd better get used to it.'

Belinda, usually amused to hear Cameron winding up Miranda, was pre-occupied with her and Tom's morning. Taking him aside, she whispered: 'Shall we say something about the secret room?'

'Later!' he shushed.

Cameron thumped his empty tankard on the table. 'What's that about later? You two will just have to wait. I'm popping down the cellar to fetch that bubbly Miranda's been dying to open. Amy Johnson and Biggles deserve a toast!'

CHAPTER EIGHTEEN

Out with a Bang

In a moment of aberration, Belinda had agreed to join St Saviour's Church choir for Christmas. She had not sung in public since school, though she enjoyed singing and frequently burst into song when nobody was around. One day, while washing up, she was belting out "The Hills are Alive to the Sound of Music" when someone knocked the kitchen door, and she was committed before she could say, "Edelweiss". The most unlikely person, Reverend Makepeace, apologised for intruding, but wanted an urgent word. She expected another prod about the Bell Tower Fund, but for once was wrong.

'I've just been up the drive to visit the Gregory's, Ed's not well again. Nellie told me about your…ermh …"spiritual squatter". I wondered whether I could be of any help; talk to the Bishop about a special service, perhaps?'

She was completely taken aback. She often visited the Gregory's for eggs and, having known Ed was ill, had been to see him the previous day. While there, she had confided in Nellie about Billie. The old woman was like a mother and Belinda thought she could tell her anything in confidence. Nellie must have let it slip.

'I'm sure Mrs Gregory was exaggerating, vicar. You know how people gossip about Haggleby Hall being haunted, but we won't need divine intervention, thank you.'

He looked confused, but did not labour the point. Instead, to her complete surprise, he said: 'I heard you singing, Mrs Flowers. You have a good voice. St Saviour's is short of choristers for Christmas and we do so like to put on a good show at Yuletide. Would you mind joining us for the season of goodwill?'

For once she was completely lost for words, but how could she refuse, particularly as the Flowers and Maclaren's had only been able to make a modest contribution to the church fund? The thought of moral blackmail welled up in her again. Little did the vicar or anyone else realise that "the Hippies of Haggleby Hall" were effectively as poor as church mice, their every spare penny devoted to bringing the old place up to scratch. A dip in the economy was not exactly helping Tom's business either. But singing didn't cost anything. She might even enjoy it. 'I'll come as long as it's only for Christmas **and** can you please keep what Nellie said to yourself? The last thing we need is another rumour going round the village.'

Later, she struggled to explain to the others why she had agreed to become a temporary chorister. She could hardly believe Tom's words: 'Well, that's most commendable, Bellie and, do you know, I have been thinking for some time about having a crack at bell-ringing?'

Miranda's comment equally surprised her: 'I'll join as well if you like. I love belting out carols and could do with something to tickle me tonsils at Christmas.'

'I thought you used wine and G n T, Randy. God help us!' exclaimed Cameron.

Many a true word spoken in jest, but the thought of The Almighty's support at such a difficult time was comforting. Besides, it could be fun.

*

Late for their first Friday night choir practice, Belinda and Miranda took their places with the sopranos at St Saviour's Church. The choristers were singing "Good Christian Men Rejoice!" and as Belinda battled through a line of carol books, she could feel the eyes of choir mistress Millicent Merryweather following her. She wanted to explain that having to feed the children, get them to bed and arrive at church on time for 7pm had been impossible,

213

especially after Carla being sick from too much chocolate pudding.

It was not a good start, but at least the "new recruits" were distracted from thinking about the following afternoon, when Tom, Cameron and Roderick were being let loose in Grace's bedroom in search of "the secret room". Belinda couldn't understand why she was feeling so apprehensive. As Tom said, it was highly unlikely they would find anything. Whatever happened, it might help get their tumultuous lives back on an even keel; a comforting idea in the run-up to Christmas. But after all they had been through would life ever be the same again?

On Belinda's right was a young woman called Sally, who had a lovely voice. Left of her was Angela, a woman in her Fifties, whom she knew from the village, but she seemed to be singing from a different song sheet. Belinda struggled to keep her left ear turned off to scale the top line without sounding flat. The church felt uncomfortably cold, despite wearing her moth-balled, cable-knit sweater and thick tights beneath her denims. Hitting high notes with teeth chattering was challenging. She soon discovered Sally's secret; a hot water bottle tucked under her anorak, which she passed along the line for quick hugs.

Choir mistress, "Millie", was a plump Scottish woman, discordantly dressed in shapeless, emerald green track suit bottoms and a brightly patterned, orange woolly jumper that screamed at her untamed, curly red hair. Her daytime job was teaching music at a school for delinquent children, and at the end of a long week, with a disparate bunch of choristers, her sharp temper was understandable. Belinda quickly discovered that her bark was worse than her bite and her dry wit her saving grace. "Miss Heavyweather", as she was known, was a stickler for note-bashing. She sorely tested church organist Peter Piper, who had to play every crotchet and quaver repeatedly for the singers to come anywhere near the perfection she expected. No wonder the

214

choir was short of singers, thought Belinda, flagging on her seventh attempt of the "On Jordan's Bank" descant. Millie glared at the sopranos through thick, black-rimmed glasses, her pop-eyes daring them to get it right - or, as Angela whispered, they could be polishing the church brass for a month!

As everyone was fumbling through copious sheets of music for the next carol, Andy Chantry filed sheepishly into the basses, bleating on about London trains. Millie held up her hands: 'Andrew, we are not interested in why the 5.45pm was cancelled or that you had a Swiss Cheese Plant sticking in your ear on the 6.15pm.'

Andy flushed, flicking through his music sheets despairingly. 'Sorry, Millie, but I haven't got that carol. I wasn't here when you handed it out last week.'

'That's because you were late last week.'

'Promptness is next to Godliness,' quoted an alto, Verity, obviously a "Miss Goody Two Shoes."

'If this talking doesn't stop, you'll stay until midnight,' stormed Millie, unable to take much more.

'It'll be good practice for Midnight Mass,' commented a bass.

Halfway through "O Little One Sweet", she complained: 'You sound as sweet as lemons, and Andy, stop grating!'

'That Swiss Cheese Plant didn't help,' he muttered.

Eventually, when Millie decided it was sugary enough, she stopped everyone to make an announcement.

'With a bit of luck she's leaving,' Angela whispered.

'The Bishop has very kindly agreed to attend our carol service this year, so we must be on top form.'

Everyone groaned. Halfway through "O Come all Ye Faithful" Millie waved her hands, yelling: 'Stop! Stop! Half you lot sound anything but faithful. Basses, think of your lovely ladies at home and sing with a smile on your faces!'

'Not if I think of mine,' said one.

'Think of your mistress then,' suggested another.

Alto Heather complained through chattering teeth: 'It's too damned cold to think of anything. I need a double Scotch at The Mucky Duck.'

The next carol was "In the Bleak Mid-Winter". As Belinda shuffled her pages, a hot water bottle landed in her arms. It was Angela's: 'Pass it on to Linda. Her hands have gone blue.'

Two verses in, their "task mistress" urged: 'Give it some welly! You're two feet deep in snow.'

'No wonder Linda's cold,' said Miranda, sparking Belinda's fears of being given their marching orders.

'Wellies aren't allowed in church,' insisted Verity, thankfully taking the spotlight off them.

"The Angel Gabriel" was obviously new to the choir, hesitant voices conflicting with Peter Piper's key plonking.

'It's supposed to sound angelic. Mary's just given birth to baby Jesus; the music is light and gentle, not heavy and lumpy like donkey do-dos!' instructed Millie.

Belinda couldn't feel her feet, let alone her vocal cords, but the thought of singing "Silent Night" warmed her - that was until Millie announced they would sing it in German at the churchwarden's request. This received a cold reception.

'He won't even hear it - he's going to Berlin for Christmas,' grumbled a bass.

'It's enough to drive you up the wall,' said Walter, next to him.

'My father would turn in his grave if he knew I was singing in German,' said a voice behind.

Millie insisted everyone at least attempted the words on their sheets. After a predictably mangled rendering, she asked despairingly, 'Does anyone speak German?'

Tenor Hans, a former prisoner of war, married to a woman in the village, raised his arm. 'I still have my helmet. Shall I wear it when we sing this?'

Suddenly, a telephone rang through the darkness. 'It's the Almighty, right on cue, and thankfully, multi-lingual,' joked Mickey, the choir's comedian.

'I didn't know we had a phone,' said Sally.

'There's one in the vestry, but I thought the line was dead,' puzzled Millie, rushing off to answer it.

The choristers took a well-deserved breather, the topic for debate being the warmest drinking hole afterwards. Two minutes later the choir mistress reappeared. 'It's Telecom. They want to talk to a Fred Wilkinson. I've never heard of him. Have any of you lot?'

'He used to be church treasurer, but died some time ago. Better go and tell them,' urged Andy.

'I've no time for this. You go!'

Pleased for respite from a somewhat interrupted "Silent Night", he dashed out, only to return a few minutes later: 'The Telecom man said St Saviour's hasn't paid the phone bill for two years and wants to talk to somebody in authority.'

'About the time poor Fred passed on,' said bell-ringer Bill, who, like Belinda, had been roped into the choir.

'He'll have to hang on till we've finished,' said Millie, 'We'll wind up with "We Wish You a Merry Christmas."'

Everyone rose to the occasion like a bevy of boozers at a Bavarian beer festival, gaining rare approval from Millie at last!

Saying "The Grace", Belinda felt uplifted. Being bamboozled into singing was not so bad after all. She had not laughed so much in ages. Perhaps The Almighty was working in mysterious ways?

*

Grace needed little persuasion in allowing the men to search her bedroom for "the secret room". Belinda and Tom were beside themselves with curiosity, Roderick eager to get to the bottom of his uncle's message, while Miranda worried about damage that might be caused. Cameron was his usual cynical self, but reluctantly agreed to play along.

Having decided to do some early Christmas shopping, Grace left and everyone assembled at the bottom of her stairs, the men tooled up for action. Although there was still no electricity and Tom couldn't find a generator for love nor money, Cameron had, thankfully, managed to "acquire" one a few days before. It chugged away on the front door step, Tom having rigged it up to the supply for lighting, sparking the gas boilers and running a limited amount of electrical devices.

As the men climbed the stairs, Miranda shouted after them: 'Do be careful with Grace's wall. Don't you dare make a mess, Camay, or there'll be no marital services for a month! I've promised your mother her room will be ship-shape by the time she returns.'

The women and children filed down the kitchen stairs to don anoraks and wellingtons. Guy Fawkes Night was being celebrated the following Wednesday, so Belinda and Miranda had agreed to make a guy for the bonfire they had been building from storm debris. Belinda supplied a moth-eaten jacket of Tom's, Miranda an old pair of tartan trousers and a pipe of Cameron's and Grace, a woolly hat and scarf. The activity took place in the game pantry, overlooked by Grace's flat, which proved a fitting place for the children, who found stuffing the guy with newspaper balls a huge game. As the figure took shape, Ollie cried: 'Look, mummy, man!'

'Yes, he'll certainly set the world alight!' Miranda's pun raised a groan from Belinda.

Banging could be heard from the flat, though the guy makers were so engrossed they hardly noticed. Eventually, with legs and arms tied, he was finished - but there was nothing for his feet!

'I know, Tom's old wellies - he keeps complaining they're leaking. I'll buy him a new pair for Christmas,' said

Belinda. Going to find them, she welcomed the excuse to go into the house and check on the men's progress. The banging had stopped. They might have found something! Removing her wellingtons, she slipped into the Maclaren's kitchen and went up the back stairs. Quietly ascending the flight up to the flat, she could hear distressed voices on the landing. She paused and listened.

'I-if only the police had knocked through the closet when they searched for him they would h-have discovered the little room on the other side.'

'They wouldn't have thought to do that, Roderick. We wouldn't have if Belinda and I hadn't seen the floor plans,' said Tom.

'The police obviously hadn't checked the roof thoroughly either, or they would have found the roof door behind the chimneys,' said Cameron.

'I must admit I have never noticed it when I've been up there,' said Tom.

'Nor me. It's difficult to see and not easy to get to. I wonder why old Milton went up there. It's a pokey hole. Did you see that pile of gentlemen's magazines and whisky flask on the table? Perhaps he was just doing like any ordinary bloke, escaping to his garden shed to get away from "her indoors".'

Roderick suddenly remembered: 'Of course... u-uncle took me up there once. He...he... told me it was his den where he went for a quiet puff of shag. Aunt Elizabeth re-refused to let him smoke his pipe in the house.'

'After this, how can I ever enjoy my pipe again?' asked Cameron, dolefully.

'What are we going to tell the girls?' asked Tom.

'Tell us what?' demanded Belinda, confronting them.

Three surprised faces stared grimly. 'Bellie, we've...found... Tom's voice trailed off.

'You've found...him?'

219

'Yes, I'm afraid so - or, rather, what is left of him,' said Cameron gravely.

His words unleashed an emotional cocktail; shock, sadness, relief, resignation. At least the findings confirmed that the spirit world was working with them. There was so much Belinda wanted to say, but her only words were 'Poor Uncle Milton!' as tears filled her eyes. Tom's strong arms embraced her; his voice was shaky but stoical: 'We're assuming the remains in that old rocking chair are Uncle Milton's. They're certainly human and if we are to believe what he told us at Astral's meeting…'

Roderick was choked. 'To th… think he's been up there all th… this time and we never knew.'

'And just the other side of mum's closet,' said Cameron, shocked.

Tom's practical brain was at work. 'As the closet is walk-in, I can only assume it was originally a dressing room linking a box room, but I wonder why the doorway was filled in?'

'Perhaps somebody didn't want the old man to be found?' suggested Cameron. 'But there was still the roof door.'

'But look how long it took us to find it.'

'Poor Aunt Elizabeth - she doesn't even k-know what time of day it is, let alone who uncle was!' cried Roderick.

Belinda gave him a consoling hug, which seemed pitifully inadequate. 'It's probably just as well.'

'Because of her state of mind I doubt the police will even contact her,' said Tom. 'I'd better go and call them.'

Cameron held up his hand. 'Hang on! You know, we could save us all a lot of aggravation if we kept this to ourselves. I have an idea…'

Belinda gasped. Cameron's ideas could be brilliant, and ridiculous.

'We could put poor Uncle Milton in a bin liner and give him a proper send-off for Guy Fawkes!'

She couldn't believe his words, let alone his insensitivity. In Miranda's absence she wanted to kick him. 'You have to be joking! If we didn't report this we'd all be locked up, besides think of Roderick!'

Cameron apologised, but she was too preoccupied to notice. Did Milton simply go up to his den for a quiet smoke, sit in his rocking chair and die, or was there something more sinister? Would they ever know?

'Did anyone notice that broken skylight above the chair and all those feathers?' asked Tom.

'Don't tell Miranda, but they looked remarkably like that wretched parrot's', Cameron answered solemnly.

'Monty must have known his owner was below!' deduced Belinda, remembering Milton's beloved pet flying over the roof-top the day Rev Makepeace and his wife came to tea.

There were footsteps on the stairs. The conversation stopped. It was Grace back from shopping, looking tired. Cameron offloaded her bags and ushered her into the kitchen to explain events. Seconds later they re-emerged, she rushing to comfort Roderick. 'What terrible news! Your poor uncle! What can one say? To think, every time I went into my closet...'

Attempting to lighten the mood, Cameron teased: 'We've had to demolish it, Mitts, but have no fear we'll build you another and send your clothes to the dry cleaners!'

'Don't listen to him,' comforted Tom. 'We only knocked a few bricks through and we took your clothes out first. When Cameron shone his torch we could see another room with a door to the roof.'

Fighting the temptation to clout Cameron, she said: 'A secret room, well! It's most upsetting to think poor Uncle Milton died in there, but at least the mystery is solved at last!'

But was it?

*

221

St Saviour's carol service was a week before Christmas. Tom helped ring the bells - having started Wednesday night practices a few weeks before - and the choristers sang their hearts out, aided by tots of sherry from Millie. The event was enjoyed by all, despite a little drama during the processional carol as Walter nearly set fire to Andy's surplice with his candle while filing into the pews.

'Thank God Angela had that bottle of water with her,' said Miranda, taking off her robe.

'It makes a change from a hot water bottle,' Belinda replied. 'I don't think anyone noticed, though I did hear the basses complain it was slippery in the back row.'

'Well, it obviously kept them on their toes. Millicent said they excelled themselves.'

If life on "the other side' was to be believed, even Uncle Milton was able to share in the joyous occasion. A few weeks before, his remains had been finally laid to rest at a quiet family funeral in the church's garden of remembrance. Following his discovery, Tom did notify the police and a forensic team went over the scene with a fine tooth comb, but found no evidence of "foul play". An inquest had yet to be held.

After the service Belinda and Miranda joined their families at the back of the church for mulled wine and mince pies. Reverend Makepeace sauntered across and greeting them, hinted: 'It has been suggested your lovely grounds at Haggleby Hall would be ideal for the Sunday school's Easter egg hunt. What do you say?'

Belinda winced, but it was a sure sign "the Hippies" had been accepted by the community at last!

Cameron, never missing an opportunity replied: 'We'll have to think about that, vicar. Now about that Frog-Eyed Sprite you mentioned for your daughter's twenty-first...'

CHAPTER NINETEEN

Prime Exposure

St Saviour's Easter egg hunt was a calamity. The date had been agreed by everyone, but Tom had clean forgotten a shoot booked in the ballroom that very day. It was for his best client, Lily's Frillies, and it was only when he glimpsed the New Year work diary that he noticed the double booking. His father kept the diary and Tom cursed him for getting "passed it". He had tried to reschedule, but too many people were involved and the photographs were urgently required by the printers, working months ahead for the autumn/winter catalogue. Tom had asked Rev Makepeace to consider moving the hunt from Easter Saturday to the following weekend, but he was adamant it remained part of the organised festivities. There was nothing for it but to let both events go ahead.

'Haggleby Hall will be a bit like that TV series "Upstairs Downstairs", but think of it as "indoors outdoors",' said Tom, attempting to quell the others' misgivings over a lunchtime drink.

'More like "inside out" if the models get their undies the wrong way round,' joked Cameron.

'Seriously, you lot, I am lacking inspiration - any ideas for the set would be welcome. My brief is to create a festive setting with an intimate atmosphere, plenty of movement and room for imagination.'

Belinda was worried about children ferreting around within sight of scantily-clad women. 'There's plenty of room for imagination, Tom, and mine is running riot. They'll be trouble!'

Cameron suggested: 'While you take the young ladies, so to speak, Belinda and Miranda could lead the kids into the Motto Grotto and lose them for a bit.'

'With ideas like that, we'll be leading you in there and tying you to a thicket,' warned Miranda.

'A bit of "dwyle-flonking" wouldn't go amiss,' said Tom, using his unique vocabulary.

'I still don't understand why this shoot can't be re-booked. It is Easter Saturday, after all. It's supposed to be a public holiday,' protested Belinda.

Tom was unbending. 'Lily's Frillies are treating it like any ordinary working day and everything's too far advanced to change. The PR company has already made arrangements with the agencies, models were booked months ahead; altering people's schedules at this stage is impossible. Besides, this job's worth a lot of money and the way business is, I can't afford to lose it.'

'Any ordinary working day - there's no way it is going to be that!' exclaimed Belinda.

'Don't worry, I have a cunning plan,' said Tom, using Baldrick's saying from BBC TV's "Black Adder."

Cameron imitated Baldrick: 'We can blow up the garden, my Lord, so all the Easter eggs will be smashed to smithereens and the little children will have to find worms wrapped in silver paper instead.'

'No, you idiot...I am going to create a night time setting with the curtains drawn, so no-one in the garden will have the faintest inkling of what's going on inside.'

'It sounds fine in theory, Tom, but there is one fly in the ointment,' Belinda cut in; 'our kitchen will be buzzing with children painting Easter eggs.'

'Everything's arranged,' explained Miranda. 'I am supervising the little artists with my friend, Jenny, and as Nellie is bringing the eggs, she'll be here to hand them out.'

'The place will be a hive of activity with all those gorgeous birds parading next door!' Cameron remarked.

'There will be one feathered variety,' Belinda informed them. 'Nellie is bringing Chloe Clutterbuck to add to the atmosphere, who will be in a cage in the corner. We think she'll inspire the children.'

'You won't need red paint, then,' said Cameron. 'The little monsters are bound to go poking their fingers in!'

'Provided the ballroom doors are kept locked and women and children stay in the kitchen, everything will be just fine,' Tom reassured them.

'Balls'... uttered Cameron, prompting Miranda to stamp his foot. 'Owh, Randy! I was jokingly about to suggest balls and chains to keep them in the kitchen!'

'You've been watching too much Black Adder!'

Belinda had profound misgivings. 'It had better work, Tom, or we'll be excommunicated by the church!'

'Of course it will work, Bellie.'

'Well then, as you know the garden better than anyone else, you can assist Miranda and me with hiding the Easter eggs the day before.'

'Oh, why can't the boys help you? I've got enough else to do.'

'Because they'll be taking part in the hunt and would then know where the eggs were hidden, silly.'

'We need a Plan B in case it rains,' suggested Miranda.

'That's easy; you and the kids wear anoraks. I'll stay inside and help Tom with the young ladies,' volunteered Cameron.

'Oh no, you don't, Camay! As you're so good at painting you can help the children with their eggs. They won't need a ball and chain with you there!'

*

Easter Saturday dawned bright and dry and was unusually warm. God must be smiling on us, thought Belinda, as she and Miranda laid tea tables on the front lawn. The previous evening eggs had been hidden in the least likely places, and Belinda feared they wouldn't all be found - and might melt! One egg she hoped would remain undiscovered she had secreted in a little gap beneath Billie's memorial stone. She had put it there especially for him. He was a chocolate lover, how could she leave him out? She knew she was being ridiculous, but he had seemed so real! Surely now, having had his say, he was at peace? He had not appeared since Astral's meeting.

Tom spent all morning setting up photographic equipment. Everyone had taken a part in recreating Christmas Eve in the ballroom, even the children making ornaments for the tree. The real Xmas had barely passed and having to drag out all the decorations again was a pain! A freshly-cut pine, as always supplied by Bert the gamekeeper, was positioned in its usual place and hastily adorned. Spruce and pine cones lined the mantelpiece and holly was stuck behind pictures and around table candles.

'The children are totally confused - they don't know whether it's Christmas, Easter or New Year!' chortled Miranda.

'They're not the only ones,' Cameron agreed.

During the hunt Belinda had agreed to help the Mothers' Union with teas on the front lawn. Cameron had been let off the hook from helping Miranda supervise egg painting. Tom thought his services would be better utilised as photographer's mate and fire stoker.

Miranda had reluctantly agreed, warning him: 'One foot out of line and there'll be no nookie for a year!'

Belinda added her weight: 'Remember, when you two paint the cellars this summer you could find yourselves locked in!'

At mid-day cars and taxis started arriving, dropping off models and staff from Lily's Frillies and its PR agency, Limelight Unlimited. With such propensity to go wrong, Belinda was praying the young ladies stayed out of the limelight. When everyone had assembled in the ballroom, she listened to Tom's briefing on the afternoon itinerary. 'Now, as we have an Easter egg hunt going on outside,

226

there will be a lot of children running around, so nobody must leave the shoot between 2pm and 5pm, except to use the Maclaren's downstairs loo. It's through those double doors, across the sitting room and down the corridor near their kitchen.

'*On no account* use the door to the hall, or the one into our lounge which leads into the kitchen where kids are painting eggs. They don't need to see half-naked ladies parading around.'

'*Under no circumstances* open the curtains in here as this would not only affect the pictures, it could land us in all sorts of trouble with the Sunday school.'

Belinda went outside to help Rev and Matilda Makepeace welcome a succession of cars spilling out children, who quickly started running riot in the garden. Fortunately, Sunday school teachers and parents were supervising and in case of any problems, Bert was to oversee the hunt, on a promise of home brew afterwards. She greeted Carla's godfather, Uncle Carl, who with girlfriend Melissa had offered to accompany her daughter, Freddie and Ollie on their search. Soon the grounds were teeming with excited boys and girls, vanishing in, and reappearing from shrubberies and leaving no stone unturned in their quest to find Cadbury's eggs. It did not take long to reveal the sharp-eyed chocoholics, proudly clutching their finds in brightly-coloured foil wrappers. While the children were busily engaged, mums and dads sat at the tables to enjoy tea and homemade cakes. Belinda was delighted to see such a good turn-out, including two members from Mid Sussex NCT's Potty Poets.

Jacqueline, pouring her daughter orange squash, joked: 'Now our children are out of nappies, it's time we renamed ourselves "Potty-*trained* Poets."

Lizzie said: 'We might have our mad moments, but at least our literary efforts are improving. It's time we dropped "Potty" altogether.'

227

Belinda had to agree; it was not the most charismatic of names. Between pouring teas, she attended a steady trickle of sticky brown faces with oodles of moistened kitchen towel. Halfway through one, she was asked for more tea by Rev Makepeace, who added: 'This is a tremendous success, Mrs Flowers, and such a perfect setting! We must make it an annual event.'

Suddenly picturing Tom's models posing behind the curtains just a few feet away, she cringed. Extracting herself, she headed back to the house for more milk. In the kitchen it was pleasing to see so many boys and girls flourishing paint brushes, embellishing eggs with a myriad of patterns. She hardly dared look at her floor. She'd worry about that later. Deciding to spend a penny, she headed across the hall to the Flowers' upstairs loo, where everyone from the Easter egg hunt was being directed.

She was aghast to see the Maclaren's hall door open! Tom had given strict instructions it was to stay locked to keep the two parties separate. On the threshold three boys were teasing models queuing for the loo.

'What on earth is going on? You boys get outside!' she stormed.

A brightly made-up, pigtailed girl in a dressing gown complained: 'Oh, Mrs Flowers, I'm bursting. Someone's been in the loo ages!'

The door was slightly ajar and Belinda gingerly popped her head round. There was a feathered squatter on the toilet lid, looking smug! 'I've heard of a flash in the pan but this is ridiculous,' she muttered. Chloe was supposed to be in her cage! Someone must have let her out while Nellie's back was turned. There was no time to worry about the Maclaren's unlocked door; she must fetch the old woman from the kitchen. Closing it, she instructed those who couldn't wait to use the upstairs loo.

There was no sign of Nellie. Miranda was busy intervening between two children fighting over the biggest egg. Her friend Jenny was cleaning up spilt paint, but told her: 'She's just popped back to get Ed's tea. Oh, and Chloe's escaped. Somebody must have opened the cage while our backs were turned.'

'Tell me about it,' said Belinda, wishing that Pru, Carla's health visitor and hen chaser extraordinaire, was in the house. No-one was available to help and immediate action was called for. Belinda grabbed a jacket off the coat stand but when she returned to the loo, it was engaged. Someone must have let Chloe out!

She could hear the Maclaren's adopted golden retriever, Bootsie, barking wildly. The hen suddenly popped out from beneath the long hall table, with the dog in pursuit. Chloe, terrified, flapped into the kitchen, causing chaos, with eggs and children going in all directions. Belinda prayed the din could not be heard in the ballroom. Tom would be furious!

The hen circled the table, pursued by Bootsie, and joining the chase she felt like a headless chicken herself. Two circuits later and back in the hall, the ballroom door suddenly opened and a young woman wearing a black negligee, yelled: 'It's so bloody hot in there I need a fag.'

'You're supposed to leave by the double doors inside!' shouted Belinda, torn between stopping her and apprehending the animals.

'Tom's shooting in front of them. I can't get through.'

Chloe flapped past, straight into "Christmas Eve". In frantic pursuit, Belinda's ears were filled with cacophonous screams as the hen ducked and dived round the furniture. Women in silky underwear and frilly nighties scattered in all directions, huddling in corners, mounting chairs, cowering behind curtains. Belinda wasn't sure who was most scared, the models or Chloe? Tom's face was scarlet as he just managed to save a lighting umbrella from falling over. One thing was certain, he was angrier than she had ever seen him.

'Get that bloody creature out of here!' he boomed above the confusion.

'Let it out! Let it out!' a model shouted.

Cameron peeled back the velvet curtains and opened the French doors. Chloe instantly shot out in a fit of feathers, followed by Bootsie. It was sod's law that most of the Easter egg hunters had arrived back and were congregated around the tea tables. The terrified hen took off, landing in the remains of a bowl of whipped cream. As the dog jumped against the trestle table, it immediately toppled, taking cups, saucers and plates with it. Biscuits and cakes went flying, along with Chloe, whose creamy rear, resembling white lacy undies, quickly vanished into the Motto Grotto.

As Cameron closed the curtains as quickly as he could, Belinda couldn't bear to watch. She prayed that those around her had not seen too much of the indoor activity. She couldn't face going back in, fearing Tom would blow all his fuses, set lighting and all! Two Mothers' Union women helped her reassemble the fallen tea table and pick up crockery. They were surrounded by animated voices.

'Cor, did you see that?'

'I thought that chicken was a goner.'

'I could have sworn I saw some women wearing nighties and Santa hats.'

'I'd go back to the doctor about those tablets, if I were you, Marjorie.'

Belinda had to smile. Thankfully, it seemed that in the time the curtains were open, Chloe and Bootsie's double act had been the main focus of attention.

During the clearing up, who should emerge from the shrubbery than Bert, smiling, with Chloe firmly tucked under his arm.

'Thank God, you've caught her!' said Belinda, relieved.

Carla, trotting across the lawn on her reigns towing Uncle Carl, chirruped: 'Mumma, look eggs!'

'Lovely, darling, and here's the chicken that laid them,' she said, introducing Bert and Chloe.

Thanking Bert, she added: 'I only wish you'd have been in the house. You might have caught her before it was too late.'

'She's certainly ruffled a few feathers, but no harm done.'

'I only hope you are right.'

Nellie came up, carrying Chloe's cage. Soon the hen was back safely inside. None of it had been the old woman's fault, but Belinda just had to let rip: 'Chloe certainly let the cat out of the bag. No-one was supposed to know about Tom's photo-shoot. You'd better get her home before she becomes tomorrow's lunch.'

Nellie, red-faced, stormed: 'I bet it was that Bobby Robbins who let her out. He's a little devil. I'd already ticked him off for feeding Chloe liquorice allsorts. Wait till I see his mother.'

Belinda noticed several families driving away, probably not too impressed. She was relieved Freddie and Ollie were otherwise occupied playing with children waiting to be picked up, for she had to go and face the vicar and his wife. They were helping Miranda clear up the mess. With her heart in her mouth, Belinda struggled to find words: 'I am so, so sorry. I cannot apologise enough to you both and to everyone for this, this catastrophe.'

Miranda quickly put her out of her misery. 'It's alright. I've already explained how the photo-shoot clashed with the Easter egg hunt and that Tom couldn't call it off.'

To Belinda's surprise, Matilda Makepeace said: 'Please don't worry, Mrs Flowers. I think you were very good to have us all and it's been such fun.'

The reverend smiled wryly. 'Tom did ask me to change the date. If only he had said why, I would have quite understood. The unbilled entertainment was a total surprise, but the hunt was our best turn-out ever and the takings will certainly help our roof fund.'

Miranda announced that Lily's Frillies were donating £200 to the church. 'They're delighted that Tom kept clicking away while the chicken was on the loose. They're reckoning on some terrific pictures.'

'What about those poor young ladies?' Matilda asked.

'I've heard they're getting extra pay.'

Freddie ran up, shouting: 'Mummy, Mummy, Billie says fanks for Easter egg, but 'e can't eat chocolate no more.'

'*He can't eat chocolate anymore,*' she corrected, realising that Billie was still in evidence and hoping Rev Makepeace hadn't cottoned on.

*

After restoring the house to order, the Flowers and Maclaren's gathered for a well-earned drink. The ballroom was back to the present day - even the Christmas tree had been chucked out. Everyone wanted to quickly move on from the day's events, especially Tom. Shattered, he cupped his beer tankard, insisting: 'No more shoots at Haggleby Hall, or I'll end up shooting myself!'

Cameron looked puzzled. 'I can't tell you how sorry I am about opening the curtains, but it's the hall door that beats me. Who would have unlocked it? And the key's missing.'

'Search me,' said Miranda, shrugging.

'A good place to start; can I look now?'

'This is no time for joking, Camay.'

'Perhaps you should have taken the key away?' suggested Belinda on hindsight. Her thoughts returned to Billie; did he lock the door? She scalded herself for even thinking it.

'It's as well Grace decided to stay up in her ivory tower. I wonder what she would have made of it all?' asked Tom.

'You know Mitts; she's a woman of the world. There's not much rocks her boat,' said Cameron.

Belinda wished she could keep on an even keel, but with life as it was at Haggleby Hall, that was impossible. It would take time to recover from the day's events and now she was starting to feel jittery about an extraordinary meeting Grace had called between them. Scheduled later that week, it was something to do with finances and Belinda knew the news wasn't good.

CHAPTER TWENTY

Tightening "the Knot"

The day of the meeting was full of surprises, including an unknown visitor. Belinda was in the kitchen when she saw Cameron pull up in Goldie, his Rolls Royce. With him was a tall, casually-dressed, middle-aged man with ginger hair and whiskers. She was sure she had seen him before, but couldn't think where. Nellie also called. As Belinda greeted her at the door, the old woman dropped something into her hand; the key to Cameron and Miranda's hall door. 'I found it in Chloe's cage. I haven't a clue how it got there, but I wouldn't be surprised if it was that Bobby Robbins. I'll box his ears if I see him, though I doubt it'd do any good.'

At least that was one mystery solved and the Maclaren's would be pleased to have their key back.

When Belinda and Tom had joined everyone in the ballroom, Cameron introduced his guest: 'This is Alistair, who is down from Scotland for a few days. Sorry about the cloak and dagger stuff, only we wanted to surprise Mitts.'

'You certainly did. I nearly choked on my tea and madeira!' exclaimed Grace.

Belinda should have realised he was Cameron's brother; she had often dusted his photo on the ballroom piano. He shook her and Tom's hands enthusiastically, saying with a Scottish lilt: 'delighted to meet the Old Hag's "other half", though how you two put up with *this one*' – he pointed to Cameron - 'I simply can't imagine.'

Greeting Roderick, he asked: 'How's the flying? It was great to have you and mum come up to The Highlands and see us at Killabeck Lodge. We really enjoyed having you.'

'Yes, we enjoyed it too. The salmon were biting well that weekend. How many did we catch between us, well over a dozen wasn't it? Thank you for showing us round the estate.'

Belinda handed out coffee. Tom assured everyone that once the business was over "something stronger" would follow. Grace yelled for quiet and opened the meeting.

'As you are all aware, the Old Hag's Sinking Fund was set up with profit made from our property sales, to pay for renovation work. It has done very well, but £40,000 doesn't go far and I am sorry to say that the fund has just about reached rock bottom. The repair work has cost more than we expected and with no extra money forthcoming, we've got to decide where to go from here.'

She paused to sip her coffee. 'At least the exterior is done, the central heating is in and the loft is fully insulated, but we cannot finance the rewiring, new bathrooms and kitchens or any interior decorating. If we ignored "prettying-up" the place for now, there is still the question of maintenance. Now the building work is finished we were hoping to be watertight, but there's still damp in my fireplace wall, so will have to be investigated further. Also, as you know, one of the ballroom bays is still leaking and Tom tells me the cellars are sitting in a couple of feet of water…'

'What! I'd better check on that vintage wine down there,' exclaimed Cameron.

'As I was saying' continued Grace, 'we must come up with some money-making ideas, or I am afraid we'll have to call it quits.'

'I could do the football pools. I was always good at taking the results for grandpa,' Miranda offered.

Tom lamented: 'I would happily put some cash into the fund, but I've had another poor month at work.'

Grace's words hit Belinda head-on. How could it have got to this? They had come so far. She felt numb, powerless. 'Perhaps I should go back to work, but I wouldn't wish Carla on anyone, even you, Miranda.' Her friend smiled gratefully.

'It hasn't been a great spring for car sales, either', said Cameron, arms folded defensively. 'There's nothing for it, Miranda, you'll have to sell your body.'

Grace, having gone through the domestic accounts, said Haggleby Hall was just about breaking even, but warned: 'All we need is another bad winter. We can barely afford to pay the bills now, let alone do repairs. We're holding on by the skin of our teeth and we simply can't carry on.'

Cameron posed the rhetorical question: 'You mean the Sinking Fund has sunk and we can no longer keep the Old Hag afloat?'

There was stunned silence. Seeing the glum faces, she conceded: 'At least we have some control over the situation, unlike certain recent events. Thankfully, our unwanted house guest appears to have, in a manner of speaking, gone to ground at last...'

Grace looked at Belinda, who conceded: 'I'm tempted to agree, but it is probably best to let sleeping spirits lie.'

'I must say we are all indebted to Astral and, of course, to you and Tom for digging around at the estate office and putting two and two together, even if my bedroom closet suffered as a result. I cannot go to my clothes rail without thinking of poor Uncle Milton, but at least he is finally at rest. Now, before we get down to brass tacks, Roderick has a couple of announcements.'

His voice quavered: 'Although I was unable to get to Uncle's inquest and Aggie chose not to go, I managed to speak on the phone to the coroner, who was satisfied there was no evidence of foul play. He concluded that the roof door, though rotting, was solid and had stuck fast. It most likely slammed shut and the handle came away in Uncle's hand, as it was lying near his remains. The medical report said he had a heart condition for years and the fear of being trapped most likely precipitated a heart attack. The coroner returned an open verdict.'

'That means nothing could be proved one way or the other,' said Tom, stating the obvious. Belinda was intrigued. Was it really closure?

Miranda said sorrowfully: 'Uncle Milton must have tried banging, but I suppose as the flat wasn't occupied, nobody would have heard him?'

'Look everyone, the case is now closed and it's time we stopped "banging on" about it!' said Cameron, impatient to move on. Belinda kept her doubts to herself.

'Shall I carry on, Rod?' asked Grace considerately. He nodded sadly. She continued: 'Well, at least now it's dealt with, and *we* have to decide on *our* verdict. I know that with this very sad business we have come close to selling the Old Hag, but with the property market slowing down, now is not a good time.'

'This place could be on the market for months,' Tom pointed out. 'Imagine us having to look for three separate properties again in the hope that everything would come together? And moving costs money. We've barely been here three years and I doubt the house will have increased that much in value. I just don't need the aggravation the way business is right now.'

'The Motor Mart could be doing better, as Mum well knows,' said Cameron. 'Looks like we'll have to pawn the family silver unless someone has a brainwave.'

'All is not lost,' said Grace, enthusiastically. 'While Roderick and I were staying with Alistair at the hunting lodge, we had a good talk and came up with some ideas.'

'Indeed! So what have you three been cooking up?'

'Just listen, bro'!' Alistair scowled.

Grace continued: 'Are you familiar with corporate hospitality?'

Belinda had vaguely heard of it, but couldn't explain it.

'You mean staging fun and games for business people?' offered Cameron.

'I suppose that's one way of putting it.'

'Is corporal hospitality to do with hospitals for army officers?' asked Miranda to despairing sighs.

'The word is "corporate", cloth ears!' Cameron corrected.

'Corporate hospitality, it's quite a new concept, isn't it, where a company pays for its staff to compete as teams in organised activities to help increase productivity?' suggested Tom.

'Yes, loosely speaking,' replied Grace. 'You know how we've sometimes said that the Old Hag would be a great place for staging sporting events, business conferences and so on? Well, we could do it, invite companies to activity days here. Rod and I think we could make quite a lot of money.'

She invited Alistair to explain how corporate hospitality worked at Killabeck Lodge. 'As some of you know, we run some great days out; hunting, shooting and fishing for private and corporate groups, and it more than keeps us in whisky. Why not do something like that here, with activities suited to what you have available? There's quad biking, rowing, fishing, paint-balling, micro-lighting - you have two pilots here - there are endless possibilities?'

'Our six acres wouldn't be big enough, though Haggleby Estate might play ball if we negotiated renting some of their land,' suggested Cameron.

'Great idea!' chorused Grace and Alistair.

'These activities are all about team building,' aren't they?' asked Tom.

'That's right. It's all to do with bonding - individuals performing in groups for the greater good of the company,' explained Alistair.

'Sounds good to me; so all we have to do is play the perfect hosts and lead these pursuits, making sure nobody kills themselves or each other, and the money comes rolling in?' queried Cameron.

'That's the gist of it; team building at Haggleby Hall.'

'Not so very different from what we do now!' said Miranda.

Shall we put this new venture to the vote?' asked Grace.

Belinda hesitated. What were they all letting themselves in for now? Her stomach knotted at the thought of being swept along again, like the Christmas when Cameron sowed the seeds for co-owning a mansion. But there was more choice then, and the idea of giving up everything they had struggled to achieve was too depressing to contemplate.

Following the general consensus, she reluctantly raised her hand.

'Ok, you lot, looks like we're going for it. Drinks all round!' announced Tom.

'Oh rather, but first Rod has something to ask my boys, said Grace.

'Oh - what's that?' they chorused suspiciously.

Roderick fumbled for words. 'I...I... that is, we... would you two mind awfully if I asked for your mother's hand?'

'Feel free, but be warned, Mitts packs a pretty hard punch!' Alistair joked.

Cameron feigned shock. 'What, I always thought a lady kept her hands to herself! But I'm sure she'll be very gentle with you, Rodders. Open the bubbly, a twin toast to the happy couple and corporate hospitality!'

*

The day Grace and Roderick "tied the knot" was mixed for Belinda. The June wedding went like a dream, but as if there was not enough drama, with the corporate hospitality idea swiftly progressing, she found herself entrusted with a shocking secret.

239

As temperatures climbed in a cloudless sky, she and Tom dressed the children; Freddie in "big boy's" grey trousers and pinstripe tie and Carla, looking like a little princess, in maroon velvet dress, with lace-trimmed collars and cuffs and black patent, buckle-up shoes. Ollie was sporting a long, tartan pair of trousers, crisp white shirt and matching dickie bow (the same plaid as Cameron's and Alistair's kilts). Each of them was presented with a bag of Jelly Tots on the promise they would sit quietly in the Flowers' lounge, watching a Disney video, while the adults got ready.

Miranda helped Grace to dress, while Cameron gave Goldie, the bridal car, of course, a final polish and attached ribbons. Belinda supervised the caterers laying up a three-course celebration meal for 50 in the ballroom. It was ideal having two kitchens to prepare the food, the caterers arriving with a salmon mousse starter (the salmon fished by Alistair on the Killabeck Estate), Black Forest gateau and everything else imaginable, right down to ice buckets and lemon squeezers. That morning Belinda had taken delivery of 50 chicken breasts for the main course, coq-au-vin, which went in the ovens as the wedding party left. It was an excellent trial run for the days ahead, when Haggleby Hall was to become a venue for corporate guests.

Grace in her bridal apparel looked like an elegant film star, her slim figure tastefully enhanced by a fitted linen, lilac-coloured dress and jacket and matching picture hat. Alistair was to give her away and Tom to drive them both in Goldie, following a swift lesson behind her wheel the night before. The incongruous sight of Tom's chauffeur's cap with his morning coat and cravat was amusing. Belinda only hoped he would remember to switch it with his top hat for the wedding.

Predictably Roderick was edgy, but had practiced his vows countless times, fondly hoping to minimalise his stutters. Cameron, driving him in a classic Daimler saloon for the ceremony at Haywards Heath register office, insisted on leaving in plenty of time, so they could have a stiff drink at The Mucky Duck first.

All went like clockwork. Belinda had never attended a register office wedding before and was surprised how relaxed it was, without the formalities of a church wedding. Afterwards, the procession of cars headed for St Saviour's Church, Haggleby, for a blessing. Rev Makepeace, whose policy it was not to marry divorcees (Roderick being one), conducted a heart-warming service, which more than compensated.

The church was half full, mainly with relatives and friends. Belinda had noticed a good-looking stranger sitting at the back. She assumed he was a family friend, totally unaware of the big part he had played in Roderick and Agatha's early lives. Unlike a church wedding service, Grace arrived on Roderick's arm, which was just as well! For there was a sudden flurry of activity at the back of the church (Belinda couldn't see much from the choir pews, where she was waiting to sing) and a voice said somebody had fainted. She prayed it wasn't Grace, who had mentioned at breakfast she had been too excited to eat.

The organ continued playing and everyone returned to their seats, though where were the happy couple? She suddenly spotted Grace with Miranda, but there was no sign of Roderick. Perhaps Cameron had been too generous with "doubles" at The Mucky Duck, or the momentous day, climaxing a roller-coaster few months, had proved too much? She was to learn later that Roderick had fainted after seeing "the stranger". Fortunately, after a glass of water and some fresh air, he recovered and an uplifting service by the Rev Makepeace followed, with organist Millicent pulling out all the stops.

CHAPTER TWENTY-ONE

As One Door Shuts...

At the reception, Belinda, Tom and Freddie shared a table with Roderick's sister, Agatha, and husband, David, who had arrived from Wales that morning. The stranger in church, a tall, tanned man with sun-bleached hair, sat next to Belinda, looking nervous. She offered her hand, saying: 'Hello, I'm sorry, have we met before? I'm Belinda Flowers, one of the inmates of this lunatic asylum.'

'No, I don't think so, delighted to meet you. I'm James, James Fielding-Winters, a ridiculous name for somebody banana farming in one of the hottest parts of Australia, but it's an old family name in these parts.' His Ozzie twang was much evident as he continued: 'I think I caused a bit of a kerfuffle in church.'

'Really, in what way?'

'Rod took one look at me, his long lost cousin, and fainted, poor fellow. I think the surprise was too much for him. We hadn't seen each other in years. I didn't mean to stop the service.'

With the arrival of the salmon mousse, it took a few seconds for his words to register; this was Milton and Elizabeth's long lost son, James, whom she vaguely remembered Agatha mentioning as having left the family home under a cloud some years previously. Belinda couldn't remember why. 'Oh, right. Is that why he fainted? You must have caught Roderick at a vulnerable moment, though I wouldn't feel too bad, he's been a bag of nerves and I dread to think what Cameron and Alistair have been pouring down him all morning. So, James, tell me what attracted you to "down under" - a passion for bananas?'

He laughed. 'Call me Jay. No, good heavens, it was this gorgeous Sheila, who became my wife.' A smile glinted from his olive complexion.

'Sheila, is that her real name? It's generic for women out there, isn't it?'

'Absolutely right - my Sheila is called Suzy.'

'She's not with you today?'

He shook his head. 'Someone had to stay and look after the plantation, or rather what is left of it.'

She wondered what he meant by "what was left of it?", but thought it inappropriate to ask. 'That's a shame. So you came over specially to see Roderick tie the knot?'

'I couldn't possibly miss it. I recently got back in touch with Aggie and she wrote and told me about the wedding. She knew I was coming, but I wanted to surprise Rod.'

'You certainly did, James, 'er, Jay. So how many years has it been since you were here?'

'More than I care to remember; it was the early 70s.'

She remembered 1973 as the year Milton had vanished, but thought it best not to mention it. Agatha, sitting opposite, interrupted: 'I see you two are getting to know each other. Sorry I should have introduced you. Belinda. I don't know if you remember me mentioning my cousin, James? We virtually grew up together after Roddie and I came to live here.'

'I think you did.'

Agatha's eyes twinkled with obvious delight at seeing him after so many years. 'We had some great times, didn't we, Jay, building camps, having picnics with food cadged from the kitchen, playing hide n' seek, croquet on the lawn and, best of all, fishing with your father.'

He flinched. 'Yes, poor father.'

As the main course arrived, she asked: 'Did you get in touch with your mother's nursing home, Jay? I am sorry to say she is not good. If you go and see her, don't be surprised if she doesn't recognise you. She has good days, when she is quite lucid, and bad days, when she thinks I am her sister or her old friend from the WVS.'

'I will go and see her, Aggie, of course.'

Belinda was keen to hear more about the old times, but Nellie suddenly tapped her on the shoulder. 'We can hear Carla on the baby alarm. I think she wants her mummy.'

*

Following tea and wedding cake later that afternoon, Grace and Roderick exited in style in a helicopter. Belinda heard it arriving overhead while feeding Carla in the kitchen. Quickly wiping her daughter's jam-smarmed face, she carried her outside to look for Tom, who was keeping an eye on Freddie and Ollie playing on the side lawn.

'Quick, they're going!' he cried.

They headed round the front, just in time to see the happy couple exit the French doors, trailed by well-wishers. Grace looked striking in a mint green two-piece suit, white silky blouse and navy and green hat. Roderick was his usual dapper self, wearing a navy blazer with brass buttons, cream flannels and pinstripe shirt. The couple gave a round of hugs and from the general din Cameron shouted: 'Now you two have joined "the Mile High Club" don't do anything we wouldn't!'

'No holds barred, then!' yelled Miranda.

'Those two get worse', thought Belinda, joining the well-wishers.

Eggie, standing next to her, remarked: 'Grace and Roderick certainly make a handsome couple. They seem well suited.'

'It's wonderful to see them so happy after all Roderick's been through. I'm sure they will be very good for each other,' agreed Astral.

The helicopter slowly lifted, fanning the assembly. To everyone's amusement, slowly unfurling from its rear was a banner with bright red letters: "GRACE AND ROD JUST MARRIED."

'Where's the honeymoon?' asked Eggie.

'I did see it in my crystal ball, but I shouldn't say - it's supposed to be secret, 'Astral answered.

'If you mean that chipped one, you know it's not always spot on.'

Once the excitement had died down Belinda decided to take Carla for a pre-bedtime walk. Halfway down the drive, a little gate that followed a cinder path to the lake invited solitude after the eventful day and she absently wandered through.

Approaching the lake she was reminded of Grace's ingenious proposal for corporate hospitality events; it was large enough for various water activities. Although the idea had taken Belinda some time to accept, she was enthused by a new challenge for the Haggleby Hall team. Especially as it meant they could stay in the house they had all come to love.

Her thoughts were curtailed by a dark figure emerging from the trees. Momentarily unnerved, she quickly reassured herself that it was a fisherman heading off. The late afternoon sun suddenly illumed him and she was relieved to see it was James. He waved and smiled: 'You're a bit off the beaten track with your daughter, aren't you?'

'Yes, I guess I am, but I needed to get away for a while and Carla needs calm before bedtime. She's been pretty good really, but after all the excitement she's overtired. I think she's dropped off, thank goodness.'

He grinned. 'Oh, children, they're too technical for me. I'm much more in tune with horses. They can be bloody minded, but they're OK as long as you show them who's boss.'

'I suppose you use horses at the plantation?'

'Yep, they're a darned sight easier than vehicles for getting around.'

'I tried riding, but it seemed horses always wanted to get me off. You're right, though, babies aren't always a piece of cake. Much to Miranda's amusement I try doing everything by the book, but babies don't read manuals.'

Despite his laugher, she detected sadness in his eyes. 'Do you have children?'

'No, we had all the tests but Suzy couldn't conceive - just as well, really, bringing up a family on a banana plantation in the Australian outback wouldn't have been ideal, especially with the nearest town forty miles away.'

Belinda noticed a bench by the old boat house: 'Oh, look, there's somewhere to sit. It must have just been erected by the fishing club. Shall we?'

Obliging, James gazed at the old boat house on the other side of the lake: 'I used to spend hours there as a boy.'

'It must be very hard for you coming back, Jay, after so much time?'

'In some ways yes, but I knew I would return one day…'

She expected him to go on, but he seemed to relapse into a sombre mood.

'At least your father is now at rest.'

'Yes, I paid my respects earlier, before the wedding blessing.'

'I know you and your cousins shared some special times with him. What happened must have been very hard for you all.'

His smile flickered. 'He was not my real father, you know?'

'No, I didn't.'

'Mother was widowed when I was two and a couple of years later she met Milton. She came from a good family and although they didn't fully approve, he took us both on. When I was young he was a good father to me and Rod and Aggie, who came to live with us after their parents' tragic death. He was strict and principled, but his heart was in the right place.'

246

Chattering geese were fast approaching and they watched as the arrow-shaped gaggle glided effortlessly on to the water.

James continued, choosing his words carefully: 'Father always had a bit of a wild side, but when his brother and sister-in-law died in a train crash, he was devastated. It didn't exactly help his state of mind either. He liked other women and with mother I think he felt neglected. She always seemed wrapped up in her own little world, didn't have much time for him... there was another woman, you know?'

'I know, Jay.'

'I saw them together once... I swear mother knew about them. She tried confiding in me, but I never let on. Father made me promise. She never stopped loving him and chose to turn a blind eye. I think more women did in those days. But it must have been hard.'

He stared solemnly across the water, gripping himself as if cold or holding something back. Belinda could hardly believe the difference in the bright and breezy character with whom she had chatted at the wedding meal. 'This place, is it spooking you out?'

He shivered. 'I guess ... I think I need to settle an old *ghost.*'

'That word, it's a bit too close for comfort, Jay.'

His face tightened. 'Aggie acquainted me with *all that* and how father was found. I could hardly believe it. I thought she was spinning me a yarn - sorry, that's a bit rich referring to a sheep farmer's wife! I shouldn't joke, especially after what you've all been through - and it's my fault!'

'What do you mean *your fault*? You were thousands of miles away.'

'No, I was here the day father died,' he gulped. 'I was the last person to see him alive.'

Belinda could hardly believe her ears. Nobody had mentioned James being at the house that day. She thought he had left years before. Her imagination started running riot, fear sweeping over her. Was she about to hear a murder confession, or be silenced for being in the wrong place at the wrong time? Carla started whimpering and instinctively she stood: 'I... I must be off. It's getting close to her bedtime.'

'Don't go for a minute. Please hear me out. I've never talked to anyone about this before and I need to *now*.'

She picked up her daughter, shushing her and returned her to the buggy. As Belinda reluctantly resumed her seat, James words were gushing: 'That day I came here I was completely unannounced. I was in the UK to attend an international farmers' convention. When I arrived at the house mother was in the big drawing room - I think you call it the ballroom - busy hosting one of her women's groups, so I went looking for father. I knew he was around because his Bentley was in the drive. I searched every room but couldn't find him, and because it was pouring with rain, it was unlikely he was in the garden. Then I remembered his secret den - Rebel's Retreat, he called it. To my knowledge, I was the only one who knew it existed. He used to go up there for a quiet smoke. Mother couldn't stand his pipe; it was forbidden in the...'

Suddenly, a lone fisherman emerged from the trees. They waited till he had past, bidding them a cheery "Good evening."

'So you went and saw him?' she urged him on. He was dumbstruck, so she prodded: 'It must have been very difficult, arriving unannounced after some years away?'

He nodded and hesitating, elaborated: 'Father certainly didn't welcome me with open arms and the conversation was very awkward. There was obviously going to be no forgiveness. It was very hard. I cut to the chase and explained that I was facing financial ruin because much of the banana plantation had been wiped out by fire. I told him I was considering returning to England and asked if he could help Suzy and me to make a new start... but he was having none of it! I got angry and knowing about his affair, I threatened to expose him. He was livid and ordered me to get out.'

Belinda listened compassionately as he fought back tears. 'I must have been mad going back. He had cut me off years before, after I gave up my job in the city to start a new life with Suzy in Oz, so what did I expect? When he said, "never come back" I wanted to thump him. But I never lay a finger on him, I swear.'

Feeling safer now, she took his hand, soothing him. He had to finish the story: 'As I left I slammed the roof door, hard ... but on my life I never realised he would be trapped inside. I just walked away ... and the stupid old fool was sentenced to death.'

'You were ordered to go, so you did,' she comforted, passing some of Carla's tissues.

When he had composed himself, she said: 'Well that confirms the police's findings about the door, but you can't blame yourself for what happened. He riled you, you slammed the door and the handle came away. It must have been loose, anyway.'

'If only I had known...'

'But you didn't.'

'Aggie told me he had no strength in his hands, arthritis you know, he must have struggled with the handle...'

'No, I didn't realise.'

Full of remorse, James stared into nothingness, head bent. Belinda suddenly noticed Carla had nodded off. Not wanting her sinking into a deep sleep so close to bedtime, she said: 'I really must go.'

As she went to get up, he held her arm. 'Please stay, just a minute or two. I need to tell you how sorry I am for burdening you with all this. You're so easy to talk to... I couldn't live with it for the rest of my life, not telling anyone.'

'Did you tell Suzy?'

'No, I couldn't bring myself to. I haven't told a living soul until you. I had no idea that father had died up there that day. The family hadn't known I had gone there, and were unable to contact me because they had no idea where I was, not until I got in touch with Aggie a few weeks ago, when she told me. That's when I heard about Roderick's happy news.'

'So here you are,' she said, strangely wishing he hadn't returned. Their conversation would weigh heavily in her mind and not wishing to prolong it, she said: 'I must take Carla back now. It's getting past her bedtime and Tom will be wondering where I am.'

'You do believe me, don't you, Mrs Flowers? I had to tell someone.'

She nodded, trying to hide the anger she was feeling, as much with herself for failing to realise where her probing might lead. 'I do understand, Jay, but it has come as a shock to me. I thought the whole episode was behind us, after all we've been through.'

'I am extremely sorry, but Aggie told me you were the one most involved …'

'That wasn't through choice, James, there were things happening I couldn't ignore. But telling me of all people, it's not as if I am family or anything.'

'You *are* part of the extended family! I can't bring myself to talk to Rod or Aggie and I'm not sure they would believe me. I can assure you I wouldn't have said anything if I felt I couldn't have trusted you.'

'Have you been to the police?'

'Is there anything to be gained by it? Would they believe me?'

She shook her head, refusing to even consider it. Perhaps it was best to let it be? The case was closed and reassuring herself there was no indication of anyone else involved in Milton's demise, she grabbed the buggy and left. James accompanied her in silence, Carla grizzling all the way.

*

Next morning, as usual Belinda went to hang out washing. Cameron came out of the back door with an armful of inflatable bananas.

'What have you there?' she asked, deserting the clothes basket for closer inspection.

'Have a banana!' He handed her one, fumbling with the others, which quickly floated from his clasp. The wind blew them across the drive and she spent the next few minutes helping him round them up.

'They're going in the car,' he said, stuffing them through the sunroof of a bright yellow Citroen 2CV he had commandeered from the car mart. 'Perhaps I shouldn't have blown them up first?'

Miranda suddenly appeared, carrying a large box, Ollie trailing behind.

'What have you got there?' asked Belinda.

'More bananas, damned things, they're all over the place.' She began passing them to Cameron.

'Hey, remember I'm in here!' a muffled voice cried.

'Oh, don't mind Jay. He's used to it - he's from down under!' wailed Cameron.

'Daddy, *please* can I have a banana?' Ollie badgered.

'Mummy said "no" but here, there's one tied with string. Belinda, you keep one for Freddie and Carla. I can't squeeze any more of these things in!'

Spotting the spectacle, Tom appeared grinning broadly, with Freddie and Carla trotting alongside. 'Forgive me for asking, but what exactly are you all up to?'

'Well, Jay has this brilliant idea for a promotion - you could say its "the dog's bananas". At work we've just acquired an ex-fleet of yellow Fiestas and clever clogs

251

suggested we could hang up flying bananas round the forecourt to attract customers.'

'You'd better tie them up well, or they'll bc all round the village!' warned Miranda.

'Yeah, yeah, course we will my sweetness. I've got the banana expert on it - can't go wrong! In fact, it's such a bright idea I think we could be looking at Hospitality Hall's new sales manager - if you can see him under all those bananas!'

As the Citroen slipped away, Cameron and James barely visible in a sea of yellow plastic, Belinda went off to finish hanging the washing. Task completed, she decided to stroll a circuit round the house before returning. She needed some space after yesterday's momentous events. Her head was reeling from James' shock disclosure, but she had decided to keep it to herself. There were more pressing matters on her mind. She again asked herself, were the mad Maclaren's leading them on again? Did she really want her and Tom to stay on and help run a corporate hospitality venue?' But leaving the house they had all come to love would be such a wrench and the upheaval of down-sizing again was unthinkable. She started thinking about the roof door, which apparently resulted in Milton's demise and the saying suddenly came to her: "As one door shuts, another opens". There was the answer.

Pausing at Billie's grave, she thought she heard giggling. It was the same high-pitched sound she had heard that day long ago in Roderick's old room. She looked around. She was completely alone. Had she imagined it? Deep down she knew it was Billie, finally free of torment. Now the ghosts had been laid to rest, Haggleby Hall was at peace at last - or was it?

The End

If you have enjoyed reading this book please would you kindly review it? You can do this by going to Customer Reviews next to the book on Amazon Books, or
Share it on Facebook:JulieAnneRuddAuthor, or
Tweet it at: Twitter:@JulieAnneRudd

Printed in Poland
by Amazon Fulfillment
Poland Sp. z o.o., Wrocław